ALLEN STEELE

This special
signed edition
is limited to
1000 copies.

THE LAST
SCIENCE FICTION
WRITER

THE LAST
SCIENCE FICTION
WRITER

Allen Steele

SUBTERRANEAN PRESS 2008

First Edition

ISBN
978-1-59606-152-1

Subterranean Press
PO Box 190106
Burton, MI 48519

www.subterraneanpress.com

CONTENTS

INTRODUCTION:
A SPACE CADET TURNS FIFTY

This is my fifth collection of short fiction, but its title shouldn't be taken literally: I don't consider myself to be the last science fiction writer. Not only would that be narcissistic to the extreme, but untrue as well. Dozens of new authors have entered the field in the last several years, and no doubt that they will be followed by even more. So it'll be a long time before the last science fiction writer appears on the scene...if ever.

On the other hand, I've come to realize that I'm no longer the new kid on the block. It doesn't seem so long ago that my first story was published, but the fact remains that nearly two decades have passed since "Live From The Mars Hotel" appeared in the mid-December 1988 issue of *Isaac Asimov's Science Fiction Magazine*. Considering that we're close to the end of the first decade of the 21st century, this means most of my work (so far, at least) was published in the last century.

Meanwhile, the author himself is getting long in the tooth. I didn't have much trouble turning forty; fifty, though, is another matter entirely. It's one thing to find the first grey hairs in one's scalp, or get invitations from the AARP in the mail. With human longevity on the rise, it's lately been said that fifty is the new forty. However, I've had two writers, both in their 30's, recently tell me that they were reading my stuff when they were in college. This came as a shock—have I really been around so long that I'm on the verge of becoming a senior citizen in the field?

Now that I've turning fifty, I find that I'm writing less short fiction than I used to. One reason is that my work has become longer and more complex. The Coyote series, originally conceived to a single book, has become a trilogy that, in turn, has spawned two spin-off novels; a sixth volume in the cycle is a distinct possibility, and other novels beg to be written as well. That doesn't leave much time for short fiction, however much I enjoy writing it.

So this collection may be my last, at least for some time to come. However, while it consists of stories I wrote during a relatively short period of time, in some ways it also represents a cross-section of my career thus far. "Moreau^2" and "High Roller" are later entries in the Near-Space series not included in *Sex and Violence in Zero-G*; "The War of Dogs and Boids is a stand-alone episode of the Coyote cycle. "Take Me Back To Old Tennessee" and "Hail to the Chief" are related to one another; "An Incident of the Luncheon of the Boating Party" shares the same background as an earlier story, "'...Where Angels

Fear to Tread'" (along with its novel-length expansion, *Chronospace*). "World Without End, Amen" is the latest in a loosely-linked series that includes "Agape Among The Robots" and "Jake and the Enemy" (both in my previous collection, *American Beauty*) while continuing the same thematic concerns of my novel *The Jericho Iteration*.

Other stories stand on their own. "Escape From Earth" was originally intended to be a young-adult novel until Jack Dann and Gardner Dozois invited me to contribute a novella to an anthology of YA science fiction. "The Teb Hunter" is straight-out satire, a comment on hunters and hunting; "The Last Science Fiction Writer" is much the same, although this time the target is science fiction itself, in particular some of its beloved and well-worn tropes.

This is also the twentieth book I've published since 1988 (not counting two novellas published as hardcover chapbooks). Twenty books in twenty years: not a bad track record for an aging space cadet. And while I'm not planning to retire any time soon, nonetheless it represents a milestone of sorts. To my long-time readers, my thanks for sticking around for so long. I hope you enjoy the show.

—Whately, Massachusetts;
June, 2007

ESCAPE FROM EARTH

always wanted to be an astronaut.

I don't remember when the space bug first bit me. Maybe it was when I was six years ago, and my dad took me to my first science fiction movie. It was the latest Star Trek flick, and maybe not one of the best—Steve, my older brother, fell asleep halfway through it—but when you're a little kid, it's the coolest thing in the world to sit in the Bellingham Theatre, scarfing down popcorn and Milk Duds while watching the *Enterprise* gang take on the Borg. It's also one of my favorite memories of my father, so that may have something to do with it.

Or perhaps it was when Mr. Morton moved away. Mr. Morton wasn't well-liked in our neighborhood; he drank a lot, which was why his wife left him, and once he called the cops on Steve and me when he caught us skate-boarding in his driveway. So when the Narragansett Point nuclear power plant shut down and he—along with a few hundred other people who'd worked there—was forced to look elsewhere for a job, no one was sad to see him go. Mr. Morton packed as much as he could into a U-Haul trailer, and the rest was left on the street for Goodwill to pick up. His tail-lights had barely vanished when everyone on the block came over to see what they could scavenge.

Amid the battered Wal-Mart furniture and crusty cookware, I found a cardboard box of books, and among all those dog-eared paperbacks I discovered two that interested me: *A Man on the Moon: The Voyages of the Apollo Astronauts*, by Andrew Chaikin, and *Rocket Boys: A Memoir*, by Homer H. Hickam, Jr. I took them home, and read and re-read them so many times that the pages began to fall out. I was twelve years ago old by then, and those two books whetted my appetite for space. Mr. Morton may have been a nasty old coot, but he inadvertently did one good deed before he split town.

But what really put the lock on things was the first time I saw the space station. My eighth-grade science teacher at Ethan Allen Middle School, Mr. Ciccotelli, was trying to get the class interested in space, so shortly after the first components of the International Space Station were assembled in Earth orbit, he checked the NASA web site and found when the ISS could be seen from southern Vermont. He told us when and where it would appear in the evening sky, then as a homework assignment told us to watch for it, and come to class tomorrow ready to discuss what we'd seen.

So my best friend, Ted Markey, and I got together in my back yard after dinner. The night was cold, with the first snow of the year already on the ground. We huddled within our parkas and stamped our feet to keep warm; through the kitchen window I could see Mom making some hot chocolate for us. We used my Boy Scout compass to get our bearings, and Ted's father had loaned him a pair of binoculars, but for a long time we didn't see anything. I was almost ready to give up when, just as Mr. Ciccotelli predicted, a bright spot of light rose from the northwest.

At first, we thought it was just an A-10 Thunderbolt from Barnes Air National Guard Base down in Massachusetts, perhaps on a night training mission. Dad was in the National Guard, so I'd been to Barnes a couple of times, and we were used to seeing their Warthog squadron over Bellingham. Yet as the light came over the bare branches of the willow tree at the edge of our property, I noticed that it didn't make the dull drone the way Warthogs usually do. It sailed directly above us, moving too fast for Ted to get a fix on it with his binoculars, yet for a brief instant it looked like a tiny *t* moving across the starry sky.

I suddenly realized that there were men aboard that thing, and at that very same moment they were probably looking down at *us*. In that instant, I wanted to be there. Out in space, floating weightless within a space station, gazing upon Earth from hundreds of miles. I didn't say that to Ted or Mr. Ciccotelli, and especially not to Steve, who had all the imagination of a cucumber, because I thought it would have sounded stupid, but that was when I knew what I was going to do when I grew up.

Some kids want to be pro athletes. They idolize the Red Sox or the Patriots or the Bruins, and spend their afternoons playing baseball or football or ice hockey. In my town, there's a lot of farm kids who follow the family trade, so they join 4H and bring the roosters, pigs, and calves they've raised to the state fair in hopes of taking home a blue ribbon. Ted read a lot of comic books; he drew pictures of Spider-Man and the Teen Titans in his school notebooks, and dreamed of the day when he'd move to New York and go to work for Marvel or DC. And, of course, there's guys like Steve, who never really figure out what they want to do, and so end up doing nothing.

That night, I decided that I was going to be an astronaut.

But sometimes you get what you want out of life, and sometimes you don't. Maybe it was impossible for Eric Cosby from Bellingham, Vermont, to be an astronaut. A couple of years later, I was beginning to think so. By then my father had been killed in Iraq, my mother was working two jobs, my brother had become a poster child for DARE, and the night I stood out in my backyard and watched the space station fly over had become a fading memory.

That was before I met the weird kids. After that, nothing would ever be the same again.

It happened early one evening in late October. Just before sundown, that time of day when the sun is fading and the street lights are beginning to come on. I was hanging in front of Fat Boy's Music Store on the corner of

Main and Birch, wondering what I was going to do that Friday night.

Fat Boy's was a block from the Bellingham Youth Club, where I'd become accustomed to spending my free time until federal cutbacks for after-school programs caused them to shut their doors. One more thing I owe Uncle Sam, along with sending my dad to some hellhole called Falluja. The corner of Main and Birch wasn't so bad, though. It was in the middle of downtown Bellingham, with the Bellingham Theatre just a half-block away. I missed the foosball and pool tables of the BYC, but Fat Boy's had speakers above the door, and if you stood outside you could listen to new CDs. The guys who ran the store didn't mind so long as you didn't make a public nuisance of yourself, and that constituted blocking the door, leaving empty soda cans on the sidewalk, or doing anything that might attract the cops.

Which amounted to doing anything above and beyond breathing, and that was why hanging out at Main and Birch wasn't such a good idea. The leaf-peepers from New York and Connecticut had come up for the fall foliage, and the local constables didn't want ruffians like me loitering on the streets of Ye Olde New England Towne. Once already a cop car had cruised by, with Officer Beauchamp—aka "Bo," as he was not-so-fondly known—giving me the eye. If he'd stopped to ask what I was doing here, I would've told him I was waiting for Mom to pick me up.

Mom was still at the factory, though, and after that she'd only have an hour or so before she started serving drinks at Buster's Pub. Dinner was in the freezer: another microwave entrée', a choice between beef-this or chicken-that. I'd see her late tonight, if I stayed up long enough. And if I stayed up even later, I might catch the reappearance of Smokin' Steve, Bellingham's favorite convenience store clerk and part-time dope dealer.

So ask me why I was propping up a wall on the street corner, watching what passed for rush hour in my town. I'm not sure I knew, either. I told myself that I was waiting for Ted to show up, and after that we'd grab a bite to eat and maybe catch whatever was showing at the theater—it looked like another horror flick about evil children with butcher knives—but the fact of the matter was that I was trying to avoid going home. The house seemed to have become empty now that Dad was gone, and every minute I spent there only reminded me how much I missed him.

But it wasn't just that. I was sixteen years old, and lately it had occurred to me that I might be stuck in Bellingham for rest of my life. Only a year ago, my dream had been to follow my heroes—Alan Shepard and John Glenn, Armstrong, Aldrin, and Collins, John Young—and become the first man to set foot on Mars. Heck, I would've settled for a seat on a shuttle flight to deliver a satellite to orbit. But the only person who'd ever encouraged my ambitions was now six feet under, and no matter how many times I'd bicycled out to the cemetery to have a talk with him, he never answered back.

Damn. If only Dad hadn't re-upped with the National Guard. If he was still around, he'd...

"Pardon me. Could you give us some directions?"

Wrapped up in my thoughts, I jumped when a voice spoke beside me. Startled, I looked around, saw a guy…

No. Not a quite a guy. Another teenager, about my own age, give or take a year or two. Average height, dark brown hair, sharp eyes. I'd never seen him before, but that didn't mean anything. Like I said, a lot of tourists came through Bellingham in the fall.

Nor was he alone. To his right was another kid… or at least I assumed he was a kid, because his face was young. But only once before I'd met a kid as big as he was, and although Josh Donnigen was the quarterback for the Bellingham Pilgrims, this dude would've smeared Josh all over the scrimmage line.

Yet it was neither the kid who'd spoken nor the giant on his right who attracted my attention, but the girl between them. There were two or three gals at school who interested me; the best of the bunch was Pauline Coullete, who I'd known since the fifth grade, and whom I'd lately been trying to muster enough courage to ask out for a date. Yet this girl—petite and slender, with light brown hair and the most beautiful eyes I'd ever seen—made Pauline look like she'd just finished shoveling out the barn.

"Yeah, sure," I said. "Where do you want to go?"

"Umm…" The kid hesitated. "It's difficult to explain, but could you tell us…?"

"We require guidance to the Narragansett Point Nuclear Power Station." This from the big guy, in a voice was that surprisingly mild. "Topographical directions will suffice, but linear coordinates would also…"

"Be quiet, Alex." The girl cast him a stern look, and Alex immediately shut up. Which I thought was strange. If Pauline had spoken to me the same way, I would've been embarrassed, yet this guy showed no trace of emotion. Didn't even blink. Just continued to stare at me, like...

"We're trying to find the nuclear...I mean..." The first kid stammered as if English was a foreign language, even though his accent was American. "The Narragansett Point..."

"You mean the nuke?" I asked.

"The nuke, yes." He exchanged a glance with the girl. "That's what we...I mean, I...that is, we..." He squared his shoulders. "Can you tell us how to get there?"

That's when I noticed the way they were dressed... and I almost laughed out loud.

Go to a flea market, or maybe a vintage clothing store. Select what you're going to wear at random, relying on dumb luck to get the right size. That's what they looked like they'd done. The kid who couldn't speak plain English wore plaid bell-bottoms with a purple disco shirt under a Yankees field jacket. His pal sported a patchwork sweater with camouflage trousers that rose an inch too high above his ankles, revealing a pair of pointed-toe cowboy boots. The girl had the best sense of style, but even then, I've never met anyone who'd matched a tie-dyed Grateful Dead T-shirt with red pants and a faux-fur overcoat.

Their outfits may have been appropriate for a Halloween party, or maybe a rave club in Boston, yet they were as out of place in a small town in Vermont as a clown costume in church. Maybe this was some sort of post-punk, post-grunge, post-whatever fashion statement, yet I had a distinct feeling that they were trying to dress like American teenagers, but couldn't quite get it right.

And I wasn't the only one who noticed. An all-too-familiar police cruiser came to a stop at the traffic light, and I glanced over to see Officer Beauchamp checking us out. He saw me and I saw him, yet for once he was less interested in what I was doing than in my companions. The two guys didn't notice him, but the girl did; she hastily looked away, yet I could tell that Bo made her nervous.

She wasn't alone. We weren't doing anything illegal, but this bunch was awful conspicuous, and less attention I got from the law, the better. Although my record was clean, nonetheless I was Steve Cosby's kid brother. So far as Bo was concerned, that alone made me a possible accomplice to every sleazy thing my brother did. Time to get rid of these guys, fast.

"Sure." I pointed down Main Street, away from the center of town. "Go that way two blocks to Adams, then hang a right. Follow it five more blocks to Route 10, then cut a left and follow it out of town. Plant's about ten miles that way. Can't miss it."

"Thank you." The girl gave me a smile that would have melted the ice on the school hockey rink. "You've been most kind." She hesitated, then added, "I'm Michaela. My friends call me Mickey."

"Michaela." I savored the name on my tongue. "I'm Eric. Are you from...? I mean, I know you're not from here, but..."

"Pleased to meet you, Eric." The big guy extended his hand. "I'm Alex. His name is Tyler. We're..."

"Alex, be quiet." Tyler swatted his hand away from mine, and once again Alex went silent. What was it with them? Didn't they want Alex to talk to me?

The light changed. Bo cast one more glance in our direction, then his car slowly glided forward, heading in the direction of the theatre. I knew that he'd just swing around the block and come back for another pass. It would probably be a good idea to be gone by then.

"We must go." Tyler apparently realized this, too, for he took Mickey's arm. "Thank you for the directions..."

"Bye, Eric." Again, Mickey turned on her smile. "Nice to meet you."

I was still trying to unstick my tongue from the roof of my mouth when Tyler led her and Alex across the street. He was in so much of a hurry that he didn't notice that they were walking against the light. As it happened, a Ford Explorer was approaching the intersection from Birch. The SUV blared its horn, startling Mickey and Tyler; Alex, though, calmly stepped in front of his friends, raising his hands as if to protect them.

For a second, I thought Alex would bounce off the Explorer's hood. Or maybe—just for an instant—exactly vice-versa; Alex was utterly complacent, even the SUV bore down upon him. Yet as the Explorer skidded to a halt, Tyler grabbed Mickey and yanked her across the street, while Alex lowered his arms and sauntered behind them, ignoring the obscenities yelled at him by the driver.

They continued down Main, heading in the direction I'd given them. Just before they passed Rumke's Department Store, though, Mickey glanced back over her shoulder. I thought she smiled at me, but Tyler dragged her away before I could wave goodbye.

I was still watching them go when Ted showed up. "Let me guess," he said. "You've just met the perfect girl, and now she's gone."

Again, I jumped. It was the second time that evening someone had snuck up on me. Even if it was only Ted, that was one time too many.

"Forget it. They were just asking directions." I looked up Birch; sure enough, I could see Bo's cop car coming our way. "C'mon, let's get out of here. Bo's on my case tonight. Pizza at Louie's?"

"Sure. Why not?" Ted didn't need to ask why Officer Beauchamp might take an interest in me; he knew my recent family history. When the light changed again, we crossed the street, then cut up Birch to an alley that would take us behind the block of buildings along Main, a short-cut to Louie's Pizzeria. "So who were they? And who was the babe?"

"I dunno." I darted a glance behind us as we entered the alley. No sign of Bo. Good. "Just some guys asking how to get to Narragansett."

"Oh, yeah. Right." Ted snickered as he gave me a sidelong look. "The way you were talking to her, I thought maybe you and she…"

"Never saw her before in my life." I caught the look in his eye. "She was just asking directions, okay?"

Ted was my best and oldest friend, so I forgave him for a lot of things, not the least of which was being a total geek. We'd both recently discovered girls, and were trying to figure out how to deal with them, yet Ted's interest in the other half of the human race was misinformed by comic books and TV shows. He didn't want a date that ended with a kiss at the door, but a hot night with Lana Lang. He was no Clark Kent, though, glasses aside, and until he learned how to degeekify himself, he had as much of a chance of getting a steady girl as Brainiac.

"Sure, yeah." But now his expression had become pensive. "But why would they want to go out there?"

"I dunno." We'd come out of the alley, and were walking across a parking lot. "Maybe they were part of a school group taking a tour."

"On a Friday night?" Again, he looked at me askance. "And since when did the plant let anyone inside?"

He had something there. At one time, New England Energy allowed local schools to take field trips to the plant. But after 9/11 they closed the plant to the public, and it wasn't long after that when Narragansett Point was decommissioned. The reactor may have gone out of service, though, but everyone knew that the spent fuel rods were still being stored on-site until they could be shipped to the Yucca Mountain nuclear waste facility in Nevada. So there was no way a school group would be allowed on the premises.

"Maybe they were looking for a spot to go parking." Even as I said that, it sounded wrong. Sure, the old visitors parking lot had once been a favorite make-out spot, but security patrols around the plant had put an end to that before I had a chance to borrow Steve's car for my fantasized date with Pauline.

Besides, how would some out-of-town kids know about the Point? And come to think of it, how where they going to get out there in the first place? The plant was ten miles from town, and I didn't see them get in a car.

"It doesn't make sense," Ted said. "Unless they're…"

"You mean they're not interested in the World's Biggest Rocking Chair? Or the Farm Museum?" Despite my own misgivings, I grinned at him. "Where's your civic pride? Aren't you a proud citizen of Bellingham, Vermont, the greatest town in…?"

I stopped myself. By then we'd come upon another alley, this one leading from behind the Main Street shops to Winchester Street, where the pizza place was located. A Chevy van was blocking our way, though, so we had to go around it. As we started to walk past, I saw that its side doors were open; within the light cast by its ceiling dome, someone was fiddling with something on a fold-down work bench.

A girl just a little older than Ted and me stood in the open back door of the one of shops. She saw us coming, and raised a hand. "Hey, Eric. How'ya doing?"

Sharon Ogilvy, who'd graduated from Bellingham High just last spring. I knew her because she'd gone out with Steve for a short while. Like a lot of my brother's ex-girlfriends, she'd broken up with him because…well, because he was Smokin' Steve, and there were better dates you could have than guys who'd make you walk home alone in the rain because you weren't cool enough for him and his crew. But she and I had remained friends, although she never dropped by our house any more. Not that I blamed her; I often wished I lived somewhere else, too.

"Hey, Sharon." I strolled over to her, stepping around the front of the van. The workman barely glanced up at me; now that I was closer, I saw that he was a locksmith, using a portable lathe to make a set of keys. "Just getting some pizza. What are you doing?"

"Working here now." She frowned. "Or at least I hope I'll still have a job tomorrow, after what happened today."

"Break-in?" Ted had noticed the locksmith, too.

"Yeah. Found the door open when I came in this morning. Someone busted the lock…"

"Busted, hell." The locksmith didn't look up at us. "Whatever they did to it, they didn't use a crowbar." Before I could ask what he meant, he reached forward to pick up the knob he'd just replaced. "Damnedest thing I ever saw," he went on, handing it to Ted. "Like someone put an acetylene torch to it."

I took a look at it. As he said, the knob itself hadn't been damaged…but the bolt looked as if it had been melted. "Whoever did this had a fine touch," the locksmith continued. "No scorch-marks on the back-plate or the door frame. You'd wonder why they even bothered." An apologetic look at Sharon. "No offense."

"Well, if they thought they'd find enough money…" Ted began.

"You kiddin'?" Sharon laughed. "What do you think this is, a jewelry store? We barely make enough to pay the rent."

"What do you…?" I shook my head. "Sorry, but I must be missing something. What is this place?"

"S'okay. You can't tell with the door open like this." Sharon stepped aside to half-shut the door. Now we could see the sign on its outside:

SALVATION ARMY THRIFT SHOP

Deliveries Only—No Dumping

Please Take All Donations To Front Door

"Why'd anyone take the trouble to break into this place…" She shrugged. "I mean, we make maybe forty, fifty dollars a day, and it gets deposited at the bank after we close up. If you want to steal something, why bother? Most everything here would cost you less than a Happy Meal at McDonald's…"

"So what was stolen?" I asked, feeling a sudden chill.

"Just a few clothes, so far as I can tell. Found the hangers on the floor." She glared at the locksmith. "You could've gotten here earlier, y'know."

"Sorry. Been a long day." He finished with the keys, test-fitted them into the new lock. "Had another break-in just like this at Auto Plaza. Wonder who stole the welding equipment…?"

I was no longer paying much attention. "Gotta go," I said. "Take it easy." Then I nudged Ted and continued heading down the alley.

"You've got something on your mind," Ted said quietly, once we were out of Sharon's earshot. "Want to talk about it?"

"Maybe. I dunno." Clothes stolen from a thrift shop. The same sort of clothes I'd seen some guys wearing only a few minutes earlier. The same guys who'd asked me the way to the local nuclear power plant. "Let's talk about it later. I think better when I've got some food in me."

Louie's didn't have the best pizza in town—that distinction was held by Le Roma, out near the interstate—but it was the cheapest, if you didn't mind a bit of grease. Ted and I ordered our usual Friday night poison—a large pizza with Italian sausage, mushrooms, and green peppers—and a pitcher of Pepsi, and threw a couple of quarters in the pinball machine while we waited. We'd tucked away about half of the pizza before either of us brought up the guys I'd met an hour ago.

"What if they're terrorists?" Ted suddenly asked.

I'd just taken a drink from my soda when he said that; it almost came out through my nose. "Aw, man..." I forced myself to swallow, then pulled a paper napkin from the dispenser and wiped my mouth. "You gotta be jokin'. Terrorists?"

"Seriously. What if they're scoping out the plant?" Ted stared at me from across the table. "Look at the set-up. It's perfect. Closed-down nuke only about a hundred miles from Boston…"

"A hundred and ten miles from Boston. Northwest and upwind…"

"Whatever. It's still a sitting duck. You break in, set a bomb near the reactor, blow the thing…"

Ted my have been my best friend, but there were times when his imagination got the better of him. I glanced around to make sure no one was overhearing us; we were in a corner booth near the front window, and the waitress was on the other side of the room. Still, I wasn't taking any chances.

"Keep your voice down, willya?" I murmured. "Dude, the containment is steel-reinforced concrete, twenty feet thick. It's built to withstand meltdowns, earthquakes, airplane crashes…"

"Yeah, but what if…?"

"Just listen to me, okay?" I peeled off another slice of pizza. "Even if you had a bomb big enough to crack the dome, how would you get it in there? You've seen what kind of security they've got around that place. Chain-link fences, vehicle barriers, checkpoints, TV cameras, motion detectors, vault doors with keycard locks…not to mention a lot of guys with guns." I smiled. "I pity da fool who try to break inta dat joint."

As always, Ted grinned at my Mr. T impersonation; we'd grown watching *A-Team* reruns on cable. "Yeah, but still…"

"Besides, there isn't any uranium in the reactor." I took a bite, talked around a mouthful of food. "Don't you read the paper? They started removing the fuel rods last spring, storing them in casks outside the building... and don't get me started on how big those things are. Not only that, but..."

I stopped myself. Until now, I was feeling rather smug, being able to rattle off stuff about the plant that I remembered from the tour we'd taken back in the sixth grade. What I'd been about to say, though, was so dumb that I swallowed it along with the cheese and sausage.

"But what?" Ted asked.

"I dunno." I shrugged. "They just didn't seem like terrorists."

"They didn't *seem* like terrorists?" He laughed out loud. "What do you think they do, wear little stick-on name badges? 'Hello, my name is Osama...'"

"You know what I mean." Even as I said this, though, I couldn't help but remember the way Mickey reacted when she spotted Bo. Sure, cops tend to make guys my age a little nervous, even when we've done nothing wrong. If someone was murdered, and the police were to round up five suspects—Al Capone, Charles Manson, Saddam Hussein, Jack the Ripper, and me—and put us all in a lineup, guess which one the eyewitnesses would probably finger?

Still, Mickey had been awful skittish. So was Tyler. And Alex...Alex was weird as a three-dollar bill.

Nonetheless, I shook my head. "Look, whatever they are, they're not terrorists. Probably just some guys from out of town who want to see the plant..."

"On a Friday night? C'mon...this town ain't *that* dead." Ted started pulling bits of sausage off the pizza. I hated it when he did that. "You saw the way they were dressed..."

"Yeah, right." I rescued another slice before he could dissect it. "This from the guy who wears a Fantastic Four T-shirt to gym class."

He glared at me. "Eric, no one dresses like that... not even me. And don't tell me it's just a coincidence that the Salvation Army store gets broken into, with nothing taken except some clothes." I started to object, but then he pointed out the window. "Remember what that guy said? About a break-in just like it at Auto Plaza?"

I remembered, all right. What the locksmith had told us sounded odd even then, but I'd pushed it to the back of my mind. Auto Plaza was the biggest car dealership in town; they sold mostly new Fords and GM trucks, but also had a lot full of used cars that they'd acquired as trade-ins. *All makes, all models, best selection in southern Vermont!* the radio ads went. *We've got hot coffee for Mom and Dad, and free balloons for the kiddies!* If you were passing through Bellingham and, just for the hell of it, decided to steal a car, this was the place to go. They even advertised.

"Look..." I reached for the pitcher, refilled my glass. "Let's put this together. I run into three guys about our age..."

"Whom you or I have never seen before."

"Who dress funny..."

"The same day a thrift shop has been broken into."

"And they ask directions to Narragansett Point..."

"Uh-huh." Crossing his arms, Ted regarded me with the patience of a priest. "Go on. And they're not quite right, are they?"

I paused. No, they weren't quite right. The way Tyler had spoken, as if English was a foreign language. Mickey getting twitchy when Bo cruised by. Both of them trying to prevent Alex from talking to me. Alex stepping in front of the Explorer that was about to run them down.

"Yeah," I admitted, "they were acting pretty strange..."

"And how do they think they intended to get to the plant?" Ted raised an eyebrow. "Walk? Or maybe use a car...a stolen car...that they'd parked behind a house or in an alley just a few blocks away?"

"Yeah, but..." I let out my breath. "C'mon, man... terrorists?"

Ted said nothing for a moment. Clasping his hands together, he idly gazed out the window. Night had fallen on downtown Bellingham, all five blocks of it; the stores had closed, and there were only a few cars on the street. Right now, Mom was serving drinks at the local watering hole. At least she behaved like a responsible adult; Ted's parents were probably whooping it up at the same place. With any luck, they'd get home without one of them having to take a roadside test. Neither of us came from happy, wholesome families.

"Yeah. Terrorists." He said this as if it was a matter of fact, not conjecture.

"Get real..."

"Okay, then let's get real. Let's head down to the plant, see if they show up."

"Be serious..."

"I *am* serious. If I'm wrong, then I'm wrong. But if I'm right..."

"If you're so sure, then call the cops." I fished a quarter out of my pocket, slapped it down on the table. "Pay phone's over there. Go do it."

Neither of us had cell phones. Those are for rich kids. Ted gazed at the quarter, a little less certain than he'd been a moment ago. He knew as well as I did how the rest of this would go down. *Hello, Bellingham Police? Yeah, I'm calling to report a terrorist plot to blow up the nuclear power plant. How do I know this? Well, my best friend and I met just some guys who asked directions how to get there. Oh, and they dress funny, too. Who am I? My name's Ted Markey and my friend's name is Eric Cosby, and we're calling from Louie's Pizzeria, and...*Five minutes later, Bo shows up to give us a free ride in a police car. Mom would just love that. I'm sure Ted's folks would be similarly amused.

"Yeah, well..." He pushed the quarter back across the table. "So what do you want to do tonight? Catch a movie? Or go down to the nuke and see if these guys appear?" He shrugged. "Up to you, man. Whatever you want, I'm game."

Crap. He was throwing this in my lap again. Yet, I had to admit to myself, he had a point. This was a mystery, and a pretty good one at that. And there *had* to be better things to do on a Friday night than doze through another stupid horror movie...

"Maybe. But how do we get down there?" I wasn't looking forward to hopping on my ten-speed and peddling all the way out to Narragansett Point. Not at night, and not for ten miles.

"You've got your learner's permit, right?" Ted asked, and I nodded. "Well, then, all we need are the wheels."

It took a second for me to realize what he was implying. "Oh, no," I said. "Not on your life…"

But it wasn't his life that he was willing to put on the line. Just mine.

Steve was already home by the time Ted and I got back to my house. I wasn't surprised; my brother called in sick so often, his boss at Speed-E-Mart probably thought he had tuberculosis. Steve's second-hand '92 Mustang was in the driveway; a couple of his buddies had come over, but they'd remembered to leave their cars on the street so Mom would have a place to park. Which was fortunate, because it made what I was about to do that much easier.

Ted and I came in through the kitchen door, careful not to slam it behind us. Not that Steve would have heard the door shut; from the basement, I could hear the sullen back-beat of my brother's stereo thudding against the lino-leum. There was a half-finished TV dinner on the kitchen table and Budweiser cans in the garbage; Steve was still underage, but that didn't stop him from swiping a six-pack or two from work. He might get rid of them before Mom came home, or maybe not. Ever since he'd moved into the basement, Steve had come to treat the house where we'd grown up more like a hangout than a home.

Once again, I wondered why Mom hadn't told him to find his own place. Perhaps she was still hoping that he'd eventually clean up his act; more likely, she loved her older son too much to throw him out. Not for the first time, though, I found myself wishing that she would.

Ted said nothing. He'd been over to my house enough times to know that my family had gone seriously downhill since Dad died. And with two overage party animals for parents, his own home life wasn't that much better. So he quietly waited while I looked around. Sure enough, Steve had tossed his black leather jacket on the living room couch. I checked the pockets. Just as I figured, there were his car keys. All I had to do was take them, and...

No. I couldn't do that. My brother was a deadbeat, but he was still my brother. Leaving the keys where I found them, I told Ted to wait outside, then I went down to the basement.

The stereo was deafening: Guns 'n Roses, with Axel Rose screaming at the top of his lungs. Steve had a thing for '90s headbanger stuff: music by the dumb, for the dumb, so that the dumb wouldn't perish from the face of the earth. The cellar door was shut, but I could smell the pot smoke even before I was halfway down the stairs. Why these idiots couldn't open a window and put a towel against the bottom of the door was beyond me. I knocked twice, waited a second, then let myself in.

Steve sat cross-legged on the mattress he'd hauled down from what used to be his bedroom, a plastic tray he'd swiped from a shopping mall food court in his lap. His two cronies were slumped in the busted-out chairs he'd taken from the junk heap Mr. Morton had left behind; they were watching him clean the seeds and stems from the pound of marijuana he'd just acquired from his supplier, perhaps hoping to snag a joint or two before Steve divided the motherlode into half-ounce Baggies that he'd sell on the street. The old Sony TV my brother had "found" somewhere was on, a rerun of *Jeopardy* ignored by high-school dropouts who couldn't have supplied the question to American History for $200 ("He wrote the Declaration of Independence") if a gun was pointed to their heads. The nude girlfriends of millionaire rock stars glowered at me from posters taped to the cement walls, as beautiful as the distant galaxies and just as untouchable.

Everyone made a nervous jerk when I opened the door, and relaxed when they saw that it was only me. "Oh, it's you," Steve muttered. "What d'ya want?"

"Can I borrow your car?" My voice came as a dry croak; I was trying hard not to inhale. Anything that made Steve the way he was, I didn't want to have in my system.

"No. Get outta here, you little twerp." His friends snickered and passed the bong they'd momentarily hidden from sight.

"Okay." I backed out of the room and shut the door behind me. Then I went back upstairs and took the keys from his jacket.

I felt guilty about doing this...but let's be honest, not *too* guilty. Besides, judging from the looks of things, I guessed that he'd be in the basement for two or three more hours. Enough time for Ted and me to make a quick run to Narragansett Point and scope out the situation. With luck, I'd be home before Smokin' Steve and his smokin' crew pried themselves from their hole.

Sometimes it helped that my brother was a loser. I consoled myself with that idea as I backed the 'stang out of the driveway, being careful not to switch on the headlights until I hit the street. But I would've liked it a lot better if he didn't call me a twerp whenever he saw me.

Narragansett Point was located at the east side of town, on a broad spur of land next to the Connecticut River. Built in 1962, it was one of the country's first commercial nuclear power plants, and was thus smaller than the ones that followed it. All the same, the plant once represented the pinnacle of technology, and at one time had supplied Vermont with most of its electricity.

But that was when most Vermonters still said "a-yuh" and Phish was something you pulled out of the river with a 20-test line and a handmade lure. The accident at Three Mile Island scared the beeswax out of a good many people, and it wasn't long before a local anti-nuke group began protesting in front of the main gate. Despite the plant's good safety record, they believed that Narragansett Point was a meltdown waiting to happen, and it helped their cause when NRC inspectors discovered hairline fractures in the reactor's secondary cooling lines.

The plant was shut down for awhile and the pipes were replaced, yet that was the first indication that the plant was getting old. Nukes are difficult to run; once billed as being able to supply energy "too cheap to meter," few people truly appreciated how much effort went into maintaining such a complex machine. Shutdowns became more frequent, and after another decade or so the repair work slipped the cost-benefit ratio over to the red end of the scale.

By then, New England Energy realized that it stood to make more money by purchasing power from Canadian hydroelectric plants than from keeping Narragansett Point on the grid. Facing pressure from various environmental and public interest groups, and having failed to find a buyer for the aging plant, the company decided to close it down for good.

Truth to be told, I'd never felt one way or another about having a nuclear power plant in my backyard. It was just there, making no more or less difference in my daily life than the occasional nor'easter or the Pats going to the Superbowl again. Dad used to tell me that he'd taken Mom to a protest rally on their first date, but I think it was mostly because Bonnie Raitt was doing a free concert. And like every other guy who got his drivers license before I did, Steve took girls to the visitors parking lot because it was once the best make-out spot in town.

But that was before 9/11 caused New England Energy to hire more cops to guard the plant, and in the interest of national security they chased away the teenagers and low-riders. I kept that in mind as I got off the state highway and drove down the narrow two-lane blacktop leading to the Point. It wasn't long before I saw signs advising me that trespassing was strictly prohibited, and that possession of firearms, knives, explosive materials, two-way radios, alcoholic beverages, drugs, pets, and just about everything else was punishable under federal law by major prison time and fines that I wouldn't be able to pay off even if I mowed lawns until I was 70.

Not cool. Not cool at all. I was all too aware of the lingering stench of marijuana in Steve's car, and we'd already found empty beer cans rattling around on the floor of the back seat. No telling what surprises may lie in the ashtray or in the glove compartment. I was half-inclined to do a U-turn and head back, but I didn't want to wuss out in front of my best friend, so I ignored the sign and kept going.

By now we could see the plant: a collection of low buildings illuminated by floodlights, the containment dome that housed its 640-megawatt pressurized water reactor looming over them like an immense pimple. Narragansett Point didn't have one of those big hourglass-shaped cooling towers that typified nukes built later, but instead a long structure from which steam used to rise on cold days when the plant was still in operation. Those days were long gone, though, and now the nuke lay still and silent, like some elaborate toy a giant kid had once played with, then abandoned, but had forgotten to turn off.

It wasn't until we reached the visitor's parking lot that we noticed anything peculiar.

"Look sharp," Ted murmured. "Cop car ahead."

I'd already spotted it: a Jeep Grand Cherokee, painted white and blue, with disco lights mounted on its roof.

It was parked near the outer security fence, blue lights flashing against the darkness; beside it was another car, a red Ford Escort, its front left door open. No one in sight; I figured that a security officer had pulled over the driver and was now checking his license and registration.

With any luck, maybe the cop would be too busy to give us more than a passing glance. The way the parking humps were arranged, though, meant that I'd have to make a swing through the lot before I could turn around. I downshifted to third and tried to drive as casually as possible. *No problem here, officer. Just a couple of bored teenagers out for a Friday night cruise to the ol' nuclear power plant...*

As we drew closer, though, I saw that the Escort was empty; no one was seated behind the wheel nor in the back seat. I caught a glimpse of the chrome dealer stamp on the trunk above the rear bumper: AUTO PLAZA, BELLINGHAM, VERMONT. The Jeep's driver's side door was open, too, but I couldn't see anyone behind the wheel...

"Hey!" Ted pointed at the front of the Jeep. "Look at that!"

I hit the brakes. Caught within the Jeep's headlights was a figure laying face-down on the asphalt, his arms spread out before him. A guy in a dark blue uniform, his ball cap on the ground beside him.

"Holy...!" Without thinking twice, I grabbed the parking brake and yanked it up, then opened the door and jumped out.

Ted was right behind me as I rushed over to the fallen security guard. At first I thought he was dead; that caused me to skitter to a halt, but when I looked closer, I didn't see any blood on his uniform or on the pavement. So I kneeled beside him and gently touched the side of his neck. His skin was warm, and I felt a slow pulse beneath my fingertips.

"He's alive," I said. "Just unconscious."

"Oh, man…" Ted stood a few yards away, reluctant to come any closer. "Oh man oh man oh man…"

"Shut up. Let me think."

The night was cold, with a stiff breeze coming off the Connecticut; I pulled up the hood of my sweatshirt and looked around. Now I saw things I hadn't noticed before. A Glock .45 automatic, only a few inches from the guard. A hand-mike also lay nearby, attached to his belt radio by a spiral cord. The situation became a little more clear; the guard had pulled over the Escort, asked the driver to get out, then seen or heard something that had given him reason to draw his gun while grabbing his mike to call for back-up.

Then he was knocked out. Exactly how, I hadn't the foggiest, but nonetheless it happened so fast that he hadn't a chance to sound an alert. Otherwise, where were the other security cops? Why wasn't there…?

"Dude, we gotta get out of here." Ted was inching toward Steve's car. "This is too much. We gotta…"

"Yeah. Sure." My own first instinct was to run away. This wasn't our problem. It something best left to the authorities…

Then I took another look at the fallen security guard, and noticed that he was a young guy, no older than forty. About my dad's age when he'd bought a piece of Falluja. His buddies hadn't abandoned him, though; two of his squad-mates had taken bullets hauling his body to the nearest Humvee. The soldier's code: leave no man behind.

How could I do the same? Like it or not, this was my responsibility.

"Go on," I said. "Get outta here."

"What?" Ted stared at me in disbelief. "What are you...?"

"I'm staying." I nodded toward Steve's car. "The keys are in it. Motor's running. Run back to town, find the cops..." I stopped myself. Bo knew my brother's car, from all the times he'd pulled Steve over. No telling what'd he'd do if he saw Ted driving my brother's Mustang. "No, scratch that. Find the state troopers instead. Tell 'em what we found."

"But..."

"Go on! Get out of here!"

That woke Ted up. He almost tripped over himself as he backpedaled toward the Mustang. He hadn't yet earned his learner's permit, but he'd spent enough time in driver's ed to know how to handle five on the floor. Barely. He slipped the clutch and left some rubber on the asphalt, but in seconds the 'stang's tail-lights were disappearing up the road.

I watched him go, then I started jogging toward the front gate. There wasn't much I could for the guard. What I needed to do now was make sure that plant security knew what had just happened here.

Oh, they knew, all right. They found out, just seconds before the same thing happened to them.

+ + +

The front gate was wide open.

The concrete anti-vehicle barriers were still in place, the tire slashers raised from their recessed slots beneath the roadway, yet sprawled all around the gatehouse were unconscious security guards, some with handguns laying nearby. My nose caught the lingering stench of something that smelled like skunk musk mixed with red pepper; someone had lobbed a tear gas grenade. Even though the wind was carrying it away, there was still enough in the air to make my eyes water. But someone had walked through this as if it wasn't there.

I stepped around the fallen sentries, cautiously made my way down the driveway. About twenty yards from the gate, I found a Humvee. Its engine was still running, its doors were open, and on either side of it lay two more security officers. These guys wore military body armor and gas masks; I spotted an Ingram Mac-10 assault rifle resting nearby. There were even a pair of Doberman Pinschers, looking for all the world as if they'd suddenly decided to lie down and take a nap.

And above all this, an eerie silence. No sirens, no klaxons, no warning lights. Just a cold autumn breeze, carrying with it the mixed scent of tear gas and fallen leaves.

By now I was really and truly freaked out. Whatever happened here, the guys at the front gate had just enough time to call for back-up. Even so, at least a dozen men, along with two attack dogs, had been taken down...and yet there was no blood, no gunshot wounds.

Who could do something like this?

Calm down, man, I said to myself. *Get a grip. This is no time to panic...*

Just ahead lay the employee parking lot. A handful of cars, with no one in sight. Beyond it lay the administration building: lights within a ground-floor windows, but no one moving inside. Another ten-foot chain-link fence, this one topped with coils of razor-wire; its gate was still shut. Past that were the turbine building, the control center, and the containment dome. So far as I could tell, though, everything looked peaceful, quiet...

No. Not so quiet.

From somewhere to the left, I heard voices.

I couldn't make out what was being said, but nonetheless someone was over there, on the other side of the a row of house trailers being used by the decommissioning crew.

For a moment, I considered picking up one of the guns dropped by the guards. They hadn't helped these guys, though, so what good would they do me? Besides, it was only a matter of time before Ted fetched the authorities and led them back here. Did I really want to be caught with a Mac-10 in my hands when a posse of Vermont state troopers stormed the place, along with the National Guard and, for all I knew, the Army, the Air Force, and the Marines?

No, I thought. *You're just a kid, not Bruce Willis. Get a little closer, see what you need to see. Then high-tail it back to the Jeep and wait for Ted to bring the cavalry.*

(I didn't know it then, but Ted had problems of his own. By then, Smokin' Steve and his buddies had decided to go cruising for burgers. When he'd discovered that his precious Mustang was missing, it'd taken all of five minutes—swift thinking, Sherlock—for him to deduce who'd done the deed. So he and his pals piled into another car and went looking for us, with murder on their minds.

(As bad luck would have it, they spotted Ted just a couple of miles before he reached the local state police outpost. They whipped their car in the right lane and blocked the Mustang, forcing it into a ditch. Ted knew an ass-kicking when he saw it coming; he abandoned the 'stang and lit out across a pumpkin field. He managed to get away...but about the same time I'd was trying to decide whether to pick up a gun, my friend was making his getaway through next week's Halloween jack-o'-lanterns, praying that he'd survive the night with all his teeth intact. So much for counting on Ted...)

Following the sound of the voices, I made my way among the trailers, careful to remain in the shadows. Another ring of floodlights was just ahead; peering from behind the foreman's shack, I saw that they surrounded a fenced-in enclosure. Within it was a broad concrete pad, slightly elevated above the ground, and upon it were rows of concrete casks.

I'd been paying attention in Mr. Hamm's physics class, so I knew what I was looking at: the temporary repository for the plant's fuel rods. Sixteen casks, each thirteen feet tall and holding thirty-six rods, a half-inch wide and twelve feet long, which in turn contained the uranium-235 pellets that once gave Narragansett Point its oomph. After being used in the reactor, the spent rods—which now contained mainly post-fission U-237, along with trace amounts of plutonium waste and unfissioned U-235—were stored in a pool, twenty feet deep and filled with distilled water, inside the containment dome.

The decommissioning process began when the rods were removed from the pool, one at a time, by robotic cranes, and placed within carbon-steel drums three and half inches thick. Those in turn were transported by truck to the storage yard, where other cranes lowered them into the casks, which themselves were insulated with twenty-one inches of steel-reinforced concrete. Each cask weighed 110 tons and, as the *Bellingham Times* had said, they were "heavily guarded at all times."

No doubt the last part was true. All the same, a half-dozen or so guys lay on the ground near the storage yard. And standing on top of one of the casks was Alex.

From the distance, it was hard to tell what he was doing. All I could see was that he was bent over, and a white-hot beam of energy coming from something within his hands. It lanced straight down into the cask, causing it to spit pieces of concrete, with molten steel drooling down the sides. He should have been wearing welder's goggles and gloves, yet it appeared that he was both bare-handed and bare-faced.

Once again, I found myself wondering what kind of guy he was. The Terminator when he was a teenager, with breaking into nuclear power plants as his idea of a high-school prank. And I thought picking up the basketball coach's '69 Volkswagen and carrying into the gym was a hoot...

Tyler and Mickey stood at the base of the cask. Tyler was watching Alex; he seemed nervous, because he restlessly paced back and forth. Mickey was a little more calm, but she had something in her hands that looked like an oversize calculator. She kept it pointed away from the cask, though, toward the plant instead.

A motion detector? I didn't know, but when she moved it in my direction, I held my breath and froze, not daring to twitch a muscle. She paused for a moment, then continued to scan the vicinity.

Okay. Perhaps they weren't your average Islamist terrorists. But neither were they the sort of guys I liked to find at my neighborhood nuclear power plant. Either way, I'd seen enough. I took a couple of steps back...

Wrong move. I was still within range of whatever Mickey was using to sweep the area. Shouting something that sounded only vaguely like English, she pointed in my direction. Tyler whipped around, drew something that looked like a weapon...

To this day, I don't know why I did what I did. Maybe it was because I didn't want to be more guy found unconscious at Narragansett Point. Maybe I was too stupid to be a hero and too brave to be a coward. Or maybe I just didn't know what I was doing.

At any rate, instead of running, I stepped out from behind cover.

"Hold on, guys!" I yelled, throwing up my hands. "It's me!"

Tyler stopped, his gun half-raised. Mickey stared at me is disbelief. Alex paused in whatever he was doing and peered in my direction. For a moment, I don't think they recognized me. Then Mickey said something to Tyler, and he took a step closer to the fence.

"Is that you, Eric?" he called back, using plain English this time.

"Yeah, it's me." I kept my hands in the air. "Don't shoot, okay? I'm harmless. Look...no gun, see?"

Tyler didn't seem quite convinced, but since he wasn't aiming his weapon at me, I supposed that I was getting through to him. "What are you doing here?" he demanded. "Did you follow us?"

How to answer that? The truth was too hard to explain, but a lie would have been obvious. So I settled for something in-between. "Just wondered why you guys wanted to come out here," I said, thinking as fast as I could. "Thought...y'know, maybe there was a party going on."

Tyler said nothing, but I heard Mickey stifle a laugh. Whoever these guys were, whatever they were up to, they were still teenagers all the same...and every teen who's ever lived knows the attraction of a party. "Look, I'm coming up," I added. "Just don't shoot, all right? I've got nothing."

"You shouldn't be here," Tyler said. "Go away."

I hesitated for a second, then decided to ignore him. His weapon looked like something I could have bought at Toys 'R Us, but he'd managed to use it against a well-armed security force. If he was going to use it me, too,

then fine, so be it. Maybe I'd wake up with a bad head-
ache, but I knew already that its effects weren't fatal. And
I was damned if I was going to simply scamper home.
Maybe they weren't terrorists—and judging from what
I'd seen so far, Ted's theory that they were working for
al-Qaeda or Islamic Jihad was highly unlikely—but
nobody breaks into a nuclear power plant in my town
and gets away with it.

"Eric…" Mickey watched as I approached the fence,
stepping around the unconscious guards in my way.
"Tyler's right. The less you know what we're doing, the
better off you'll be."

"Yeah, well, maybe. But…" The gate was half-open,
and it looked if something had melted the lock. Now I
knew what. I pushed it open, stepped through. "Y'know,
you didn't leave me your phone number, so how else am I
going to ask you for a date?"

This from a guy who would've *never* used that line
on Pauline Coullete. Yet fear makes men accomplish
impossible things. Mickey's face broke into that incred-
ible smile of hers, and I felt like James Bond sinking
Ms. Moneypenny with the best wisecrack of all time.

"You're brave," she said quietly. "I like that."

Tyler scowled at me. For a moment I thought I'd
pushed my luck too far. Perhaps I did, because he glanced
down at his pistol, as if remembering that he had it.
Before he could do anything, Alex called down from
the cask.

"I've penetrated the seal, Lieutenant. Shall I remove
the outer cover?"

Tyler forgot about me for a moment. "Go ahead and open it, Alex." Glancing my way, he suddenly became self-conscious. "Resume prior communications protocols," he added. "Use period dialect from now on. "

Alex responded in the language I'd heard them use before, something that sounded like a polyglot of English, French, and Spanish. What made me more curious, though, was the formal way Alex had addressed him. Lieutenant? Lieutenant in which service? Whatever it was, it probably wasn't the Coast Guard...

"You must leave." Mickey's voice was quiet. "Now, Eric. Please."

"Uh-uh." I folded my arms together. "Not until I..."

Whatever I was about to say, I didn't get a chance finish it. I was too busy watching Alex bend down and grasp the steel handles on either side of the cask cover. It probably weighed two tons, at least; there was the grinding sound of concrete surfaces rasping across each other, then he hoisted the cover with little more effort than me picking up a armchair, and tossed it over the side of the cask.

It hit the ground with a solid thump. Alex stood erect, looked down at me, and smiled. I gulped. Whatever high school football team he belonged to, I prayed that I'd never meet them on the fifty-yard line.

Mickey was speaking into her pad, saying something urgent in whatever tongue she and her friends used. By then, I was having second-thoughts about being here. This was far too weird for me. When the cops showed up, maybe I could pretend to be unconscious. Play possum, claim that I hadn't seen anything...

I begun to back away, inching my way toward the gate, when there was a howl from somewhere above us. Wincing, I doubled over, gritting my teeth as I clasped my hands against my ears.

Then I looked up, and saw a spaceship coming down from the sky.

The spacecraft was a little larger than a commuter jet, or about half the size of a NASA shuttle. Sleek and streamlined, its broad delta-shaped wings tapered downward at their tips, while twin vertical stabilizers rose from either side of a hump at its aft section that I took to be a drive of some sort; there were no rocket engines so far as I could see. The bow canted slightly forward at the end of a short neck, and wraparound viewports above a beak-like prow lent the ship a vaguely avian appearance, like a giant sea gull.

I didn't know whether to laugh, faint, or wet my pants. I did none of the above; instead, I stared at it with open-mouthed wonder, and hoped that I didn't look like some hillbilly who'd never seen technology more advanced than Grandpa's moonshine still.

The ship slowly descended until it hovered twenty feet above the cask on which Alex was standing. A broad hatch on its underside slid open; standing within it was a lone figure, wearing what I took to be a spacesuit. Alex waved his right arm, motioning for the craft to move further to the left. The pilot complied, inching the craft a few degrees port until the hatch was directly above Alex and the cask.

"Seen enough?" Tyler asked. "Good. Time for you to take a nap."

I looked down, saw that he'd raised his weapon again. There was nothing I could do; I stood still, and hoped that being zapped wouldn't hurt...

"Stop!" Mickey suddenly put herself between him and me. "You can't do this!"

Tyler quickly pointed the gun toward the ground. "What are you...?"

"You're right...he's seen enough. Too much, in fact." Still shielding me from Tyler, she pointed up at the hovering spacecraft. "He's the only witness. If you stun him now..."

Tyler muttered something I couldn't understand, but that I figured was obscene. "But what else can we do if we don't...?"

"Take me with you," I blurted out.

Tyler's eyes widened, and Mickey glanced back at me in astonishment. "Look," I went on, talking as fast as I could, "maybe this is none of my business, but...hey, if you just showed me what this is all about, then maybe we can...I dunno, work something out."

"Nice try." Tyler raised his weapon again. "Stand down, McGyver. That's an order."

"Don't try pulling me rank on me, Tyler." Mickey glared at him. "Remember, Captain Van Owen put *me* in charge of..."

She was interrupted by another hatch opening within the spacecraft, this one on the port side. A teenage girl about our age stood within the hatch, her arms braced along its sides; she made an impatient gesture—*c'mon, hurry up!*—and Mickey lifted a hand to her right ear and ducked her head slightly, as if listening to something hidden by her hair. A moment passed, then she looked at me again.

"Do you know anything about local air defense network?" she asked.

"A little." Which was the truth. I knew what everyone else who lived around here knew, plus whatever else Dad had told me. "Why, what do you...?"

Mickey muttered something in her own language, waited a moment, then looked at Tyler. "Hsing says bring him aboard. We'll let the skipper sort it out later."

"But..."

"We're running out of time. Shut up and help Alex, or the captain's going to get this in my report. Understood?"

Tyler nodded reluctantly, then put away his gun and turned toward the cask. From the cargo hatch, two thick cables with hooks at their ends were being lowered; Alex reached up, preparing to grab them once they came within reach. It was obvious what they intended to do, but why...?

"You *do* know what you say you know?" There was apprehension in Mickey's eyes as she turned to look at me. "You're not...um, putting us on...are you, Eric?"

"I'm no expert, but..." I shrugged. "I'll do what I can do."

"Very well. Let's go." She hesitated, then quietly added, "I just hope neither of us regrets this."

Again, she reached beneath her hair to touch something at her ear, and murmured something in her language. A few seconds later, the girl standing in the side hatch tossed something overboard: a rope ladder, uncoiling as it fell. It snapped taut as its weighted end hit the ground; Mickey grasped its rungs and began to climb upward. I waited until she was nearly halfway up, then followed her.

The girl at the top of the ladder was no older than Mickey or me. Perhaps even younger; the baby-blue jump-suit she wore looked a little too big for someone who would've been a freshman at my local middle school. The compartment was barely large enough for the three of us; while Mickey had a short conversation with her, I got a chance to look around. Recessed storage lockers, a couple of control panels here and there. Obviously an airlock; an interior hatch on one side of the compartment lay open, apparently leading forward to the cockpit, and on the opposite side of the airlock was another hatch. This one was shut, but it had a small window. Figuring that it led to the cargo bay, I was about to peer through the window when something caught my eye.

Hanging within one of the lockers was a spacesuit, although like none I'd ever seen before. Resembling a scuba diver's wet-suit, it was made of some fabric that seemed impossibly thin, with a neck-ring around its collar and sockets along its sides. A helmet with an angular face-plate rested on a shelf above the suit, and a small backpack was clamped to the inside of the door.

But that wasn't what got my attention. Above the locker was a small sign; the language was indecipherable, but I know Roman alphabet when I see it. Perhaps that alone should have been a shock—*wow, it's not Klingon!*—yet then I saw the mission patch embroidered on the suit's left shoulder, and I felt my heart skip a beat.

At the center of the patch was a emblem that looked much like a classic diagram of an atom—a nucleus surrounded by electrons—until I realized that it was actually a tiny sun surrounded by eight planets. And wrapped around above the emblem was:

SOLAR CONFEDERATION FLEET

S.C.S. VINCENNES

My knees went weak, and I grabbed for something for support. As it happened, it was the girl who'd helped us aboard. She wrapped an arm around my shoulder to keep me on my feet, then said something to Mickey. Following my gaze, she saw what I'd seen. Giving me a sympathetic smile, Mickey pried me from loose from her friend.

"There's a lot that needs to be explained," she murmured. "But not now. We have a job to do."

The cockpit was larger on the inside than it appeared from the outside; seats for the pilot and co-pilot up front, with six passenger couches arranged behind it. The pilot was about Steve's age; looking away from his console as we came in, he frowned when he saw me, and said something I couldn't understand yet obviously wasn't warm and friendly. Mickey gave him a curt reply, and he returned his attention to the controls.

His hands were gripped tight around a T-shaped control bar, and he was visibly making an effort to hold the craft in position. No wonder; the wind was causing the deck was pitch back and forth, and we had to hold tight to the seatbacks just to stay on our feet.

"Just a second." Mickey reached up to an overhead storage bin and slid it open. The bin was stuffed with equipment I didn't recognize; pulling out a small box, Mickey opened it to produce something that looked like a hearing aid, except that it had a tiny prong that curved to one side and a miniature wand that went in the other direction.

"Put it in your right ear," she explained. "Like this, see?" Pulling back her hair, I saw that she wore an identical unit. When I fumbled with it, she patiently helped me insert the thing, with the prong fitting around my upper lobe and the wand nestled against my throat. Once it was in place, she touched a tiny button.

A double-beep, then nothing. "I don't get it," I said. "What's this supposed to do?"

"Oh, for the love of..." The pilot glanced at me in irritation. "Where'd you find this idiot, Mickey?"

My left ear heard the same weird language he'd been speaking before; my right ear heard plain English. "She found me on the street corner," I replied. "What's it to you?"

He glared at me, and Mickey hid her smile behind her hand. An auto-translation device of some sort; now we could understand each other. "It's a long story, Hsing," she said. "His name's Eric. He says he can help us. Give him a chance."

Hsing hesitated. "Okay, kid. Come here and tell me what I'm looking at."

Not really believing I was doing this, I stumbled forward until I was just behind his seat. His controls looked like nothing I'd ever seen before: row upon row of fluorescent touch screens arrayed along a wraparound console, with recessed holograms displaying information I couldn't even begin to comprehend. I'd been inside cockpits before during air shows at Westfield, but this one made the most advanced Air Force jet look like something the Wright brothers had cobbled together from birch wood and piano wire.

"What do you want to know?" I asked. As if I had anything to offer. *Me know spaceship, uh-huh. Me want to help...*

"This." Hsing tapped a small holographic display midway between him and the co-pilot's seat. It expanded, revealing a wire-frame hemisphere with a topographic map at its base. "That's SLIR..." he pronounced it as *sleer* "...side-looking infrared radar. It works on the principal of..."

"I know radar. Go on."

Hsing glanced first at me, then at Mickey. "Got a mouth on him, doesn't he?" he said to her, then he pointed again at the display. "See those? They're coming at us from the south-southwest. Now tell me what they are, smart guy."

I looked closer. Three small red blips, near the outer edge of the hemisphere and one-quarter of the way to its apex, rapidly approaching a blue blip hovering close to the ground at the center of the map. "How far away are they?"

"Sixty-two kilometers and closing. Altitude 6,300 meters, speed..."

"Warthogs." I felt something cold at the pit of my stomach,

Hsing looked at me again. "Repeat?"

"A-10 Thunderbolts...Warthogs, if you want to call then that. Coming in from Westfield." I pointed to the lowermost right part of the holo, beneath the blips. "They belong to the 104th Fighter Wing, Barnes Air National Guard Base. They probably scrambled as soon as NORAD picked you up on the air-defense grid." I gave him a sidelong look. "Guess they picked you up when you entered the atmosphere. Right?"

Hsing didn't reply, but his face went pale. "Do they pose a threat to us?" Mickey quietly asked.

"Oh, yeah. You definitely have something to worry about." I took a deep breath. "They're built for low-level runs against tanks, anti-aircraft missile launchers, that sort of thing. Gatling guns, air-to-ground missiles..."

"Can they operate at night?" Hsing asked, and I threw him a glance he couldn't help but understand. "Oh, boy..." he murmured, then he glanced over his shoulder. "Libbie, we have a situation!"

"We've got the canister!" the girl yelled from the airlock. "Alex and Deke are securing it now!"

"Then seal the cargo hatch and get back here!" Hsing tapped his headset wand. "Tyler, get aboard. We're ready for liftoff."

"Make a hole!" Libbie charged in from the airlock, unapologetically shoving me out of the way. She jumped into the right-hand seat and yanked down a padded harness bar. "Cargo hatch sealed," she snapped, her hands racing across her side of the console. "Initiating main engine sequence…"

"Let's get you strapped down." Mickey pushed me into a couch behind Libbie. "We're going to be pulling a few G's until the inertial dampeners kick in, so be prepared for some rough flying."

I had no idea what she meant by inertial dampeners, but I knew all about g's. The harness was much like those on a ride at Six Flags; it came down over my head and shoulders and clicked into place across my chest. I gave Mickey a thumbs up; she acknowledged it with a brief nod as she secured herself into a seat across the aisle from me.

"MEI green for go." Hsing's voice was tight as a wire. "APU powered up. Main hatch…hey, why isn't the hatch secure? Tyler, where are you?" Clasping his right hand over his headset. "What's that? Repeat, please…"

I peered over his shoulder at the SLIR. The three red blips were very close to the center of the holo; they couldn't be more than twenty miles away. If we were going to make a clean getaway, the ship would have to launch *now*…

"Aw, hell!" Hsing yelled. "Tyler's down!"

"What?" Libbie stared at him. "How did he…?"

"I don't know He's fallen off the ladder, says his knee's twisted." The pilot glanced at the SLIR again, swore under his breath. "We don't have time for this. Libbie, prepare for liftoff."

"You can do that!" Mickey grabbed the back of Hsing's seat. "He's...!"

"Those jets are almost on top of us." Hsing jabbed a finger at the holo. "We don't have a choice. We're going to have to leave him..."

Leave no man behind...

"Hold the bus!" Before I knew what I was doing, I shoved the harness upward. Mickey stared at me as I leaped from of my seat; she raised a hand to stop me, but I was already halfway to the airlock. "Gimme a minute! I'll get him back!"

"No way!" Hsing shouted. "I can't risk...!"

"They won't attack! Trust me!" I didn't have time to explain; I could only hope that the pilot would take my word.

The side hatch was open, the ladder still lowered. Through the cargo bay window, I caught a glimpse of Alex and the other crewman, holding tight to bulkhead straps on either side of the fuel-rod canister. They stared at me in mute surprise as I turned around, kneeled down, and carefully put my legs through the airlock hatch. My feet found the top rungs; I grasped the ladder with both hands and began to climb down.

Tyler lay on the concrete pad below me, clutching at his left knee. He shouted something I couldn't understand, so I chose to ignore him. The ladder swayed back and forth; the spacecraft was in motion, and for an instant I thought Hsing was about to lift off. Then I saw that the distance between me and Tyler was getting shorter, and realized the pilot was carefully maneuvering his ship closer to the ground.

I jumped the last five feet, bending my hips and knees to let my legs take the impact. Tyler saw what I intended to do; he struggled to his right knee, wincing as he put weight on his left leg. "Hang on!" I yelled, wrapping my left arm around him. 'We're gonna get you out of here!"

"You're out of your…!"

He didn't get a chance to finish before the rest was lost in the roar of three Warthogs making a low-level pass over Narragansett Point. Looking up, I saw the amber glow of their jets as they hurtled less than a thousand feet above us. The A-10s howled past us, then peeled apart from one another as they made a steep climb above the Connecticut River.

"C'mon, move!" I hauled Tyler to his feet, carried him to the dangling ladder. "Get your ass up there!"

Tyler didn't argue. He grasped the rungs and began to climb, favoring his left leg but nonetheless using it to balance himself. He didn't have far to travel; Hsing had brought the craft within fifteen feet of the ground, its starboard wingtip nearly grazing the top of the nearest waste cask. Looking up, I saw Mickey crouched within the hatch, reaching down to help Tyler climb aboard.

I didn't wait to make sure he was safe. I grabbed the ladder, scrambled up it like a monkey on a coconut tree. The A-10s were gone, but they'd back as soon as the hog drivers reported what they'd seen. I had little doubt that whoever was in charge at Barnes would give them permission to open fire upon the strange craft they'd spotted hovering above the local nuclear power plant. Nonetheless, I knew that they wouldn't attack immediately, but instead obey the chain of command. Thank heavens I'd grown up as a soldier's boy. Otherwise I might not have known this.

Yet the clock was ticking, but seriously...

Reaching up, I planted my hand against Tyler's butt, gave him a mighty shove. Mickey already had him by the shoulders; she dragged him the rest of the way through the hatch. I scampered up the ladder, then helped Mickey haul it up behind us.

"Clear!" Mickey slammed the hatch shut and twisted a lockwheel. "Main hatch sealed!"

"Copy that!" Libbie called back. "Hang on!"

Tyler had already limped to the nearest seat. Mickey shoved me into another couch, then planted herself in the one across the aisle. We barely had time to pull down our harnesses before the spacecraft's prow tilted upward.

"Go for launch!" Hsing shouted.

"Punch it!" I yelled. Mickey's hand grabbed mine, and then we fell into the sky.

Countless times, I've imagined what it might be like to be aboard a rocket during liftoff. Although the closest I'd ever been to a real spacecraft were the ones at the National Air & Space Museum, where my father had taken Steve and me during a family vacation to Washington D.C., my fantasies had been fueled by film clips of shuttle launches, movies like *Apollo 13*, and dozens of science fiction novels. So I thought I was ready for the real thing.

I wasn't.

We went up *fast*. As the craft violently shook around me, an invisible hand pressed my body back into the couch. Blood pounded in my ears as I gulped air and fought to keep down the pizza I'd had for dinner.

"They're after us, Hsing." Libbie's voice was tight. "Range three-fifty meters and closing."

I glanced at the SLIR. Three blips following a blue dot straight up the center of the hemisphere, getting closer every second. On a small screen on Libbie's side of the console, I caught a brief glimpse of three small, angular objects, fuzzy and green-tinted, a phosphorescent glow coming from their aft sections. The Warthogs were right on our tail. If they managed to lock on...

"Hang tight, everyone!" Hsing snapped. "I'm going evasive!"

Terrified, I instinctively turned my head away. Bad idea; the same invisible hand caused my neck to twist painfully. Not only that, but it was at this same moment that Hsing rolled the craft 180 degrees. Through a side-window, I caught a brief glimpse of my home town, as seen at night from about 10,000 feet. A small constellation of house lights and street lamps, very pretty...except that it was upside-down, and rapidly disappearing behind us.

"Easy. Easy." Mickey clutched my hand. "Look straight ahead, take deep, short breaths."

I managed to pull my face forward, concentrated on breathing. For a moment, I saw clouds, backlit by the lights of town. Then we ripped through them, and suddenly there were only stars. Pretty, but I was in no mood to admire them; the invisible hand had become a fat guy who'd just come away from an all-you-can-eat buffet, and decided that my chest was a fine place to sit down.

"They're falling back." Libbie's voice was taut, but no longer alarmed. "Range 400 meters...600...800..."

"We should be near the limits of their operational ceiling." Hsing held tight to his yoke. "We're almost in the clear, guys."

My guts were beginning to settle down, and it getting a little easier to breathe; the fat guy got up and went to check out the dessert bar. By now I could see the stars more clearly; they didn't glimmer and twinkle, as I'd seen them while standing on the ground, but instead shined steadily...and all of a sudden, I realized that there were far more than I'd ever seen in my life.

Carefully turning my head, I looked over a Mickey. She met my gaze, saw that I was doing okay, and gave me a wry smile. I was about to do the same when dawn broke.

As sunlight streamed through the starboard windows, I raised a hand against the sudden glare...and then stopped myself when I realized what I was seeing. No, not sunrise...*sunset*, my second one of the day. Or at least it would early if I was still in Bellingham, Vermont.

Yet I was no longer there, was I? What I was witnessing was the sun going down somewhere west of the Rockies. Out in California, some guy my age would be strolling the beaches of Monterey, watching the sun paint the waves of the Pacific. And meanwhile, I was witnessing the same thing, although from a considerably higher perspective.

It was then—my body floating upward against the seat harness, watching sunlight turn a vast curved horizon into a crimson-hued scimitar, feeling my ears pop as I swallowed—that I realized that I was no longer on Earth.

"Holy..." I swallowed again. "I'm in space."

Sure, it sounded moronic. It probably was. All the same, I couldn't get over what I was seeing. It wasn't a movie or a TV show, it wasn't something I'd read in a science fiction novel, it wasn't even a particularly vivid dream. This was *real*...

Damn. I *was* in space.

"Really? No kidding?" From behind us, Tyler snickered. "Wow, what a revelation. And here I was, thinking we were..."

"Shut up." Mickey looked at him in disgust, then her expression softened. "How's your leg? Want me to break out the med kit?"

"I'll manage." Tyler reached down to gently massage his swollen knee. "It'll wait until we're back aboard ship. The doc will take care of it." He regarded me for a moment, then slowly let out his breath. "Thanks," he added, albeit reluctantly. "You didn't have to do that."

"No problem." I was having trouble staying focused. "You'd have done the same for me if..."

My voice trailed off. No, he would not have, and we both knew it. Yet Tyler wasn't about to let me have the last word. "I was thinking about dropping you off somewhere in China," he muttered, "but I guess we can't do that now, can we?"

My face must have gone red, because Mickey grasped my hand again. "You might try to be a little more grateful," she said, then she turned her attention forward. "How are we doing?"

"Fine. On course for rendezvous and pick-up." Hsing didn't look back at us as his hands roamed across the console. "Sorry about the ride. We had to execute some high-g maneuvers to get away from those planes."

"S'okay. Think nothing of it." I was no longer queasy; astonishment had taken care of that problem. Besides, I couldn't help but feel sorry for the A-10 pilots we'd left behind; they were probably on their way back to Westfield, going *hummanahummanahummanna* and trying to figure out how to explain *this* one to the CO.

Yeah, okay. Maybe the Massachusetts Air National Guard had a mystery on their hands, and so did the Narragansett Point security team. Yet I was only slightly less clueless than they were...

I looked at Mickey again. "Look, I know it's a lot to ask, but...would you mind telling me what's going on here?"

She said nothing for a moment. Libbie gazed back over her shoulder at her. "It's not too late to consider China," she murmured. "Maybe some remote village near the Tibetan border...?"

"No." Mickey's voice was cold. "Set coarse for rendezvous with the *Vincennes*. And re-engage the I-drive... I want us there in two and a half standard hours, max."

Libbie and Hsing shared a glance. "On your orders, chief," the pilot said, then he pressed his fingers against his console. "IDE in five...four...three...two..."

"Hold on," Mickey said quietly to me. "This may be…"

"One…zero."

Weight returned, as abruptly as if I was aboard an elevator that had been plummeting down a bottomless shaft, only to have its brakes abruptly kick in. All of a sudden, I went from zero-gee to one-gee…and even if the rest of my body was ready for change, my brain wasn't, and neither was my stomach.

Particularly not my stomach. A Friday night special from Louie's tastes great going down. Coming back up again, it's not so wonderful.

"Aw, for the love of…someone get a bag under him!" Tyler snapped, while Mickey held my shoulders and let me heave all over the deck.

Libbie tossed back a folded paper bag from a compartment beneath her seat, but by then the damage was done. "Sorry 'bout that," I apologized to no one in particular, sitting up straight and wiping my mouth with the back of my hand. "If you'll show me where you keep the paper towels, I'll…"

I stopped, staring down at where I'd thrown up. The pool of puke was disappearing, as if the deck itself had become a sponge and was rapidly absorbing it. Looking closer, I saw what looked like thousands of tiny maggots eating away at the edges of the vomit. Gross…

"Decontamination nanites," Mickey explained. "They automatically activate when a foreign biological substance touches an interior surface and convert it into inert matter. Keeps the shuttle clean." She touched my arm and stood up. "Come with me...I've got something to show you."

I followed her only too gladly; the nanites creeped me out. Still feeling a bit rocky, I followed her back to the airlock. Tyler watched us go, and I could feel his eyes at my back. Perhaps I'd saved his bacon, but he still wasn't ready to accept me as anything but a nuisance. Or maybe it was more than that...?

Mickey stopped at the cargo bay hatch. She glanced through the window, then stood aside to let me look inside. The fuel-rod canister was snug within a pair of padded braces; Deke, the third crew member, wore a thick outfit that I took to be anti-radiation armor of some sort, yet Alex was still wearing only the patch-work sweater, cammie trousers, and cowboy boots he'd swiped from the thrift shop. They stood on either side of the can-ister, patiently waiting for us to get to wherever we were going. Spotting me looking in on him, Alex smiled, then raised his hand to give me a happy, carefree wave.

"Aren't you worried about him?" I asked. "I mean, no telling how many REMs he's taking in there."

"You don't need to worry about him. Alex isn't..."

She stopped herself. "He's not human, is he?" I asked.

"No." She shook her head. "Alex isn't human. I sup-pose you could say that he's an android, although that's an antiquated term. His name is an acronym for Artificial Lifeform Experimental..."

"Right. Alex. I get it." It explained a lot about him, but I wasn't about to let her off the hook so easily. "Look, Mickey," I went on, dropping my voice so that the others couldn't hear us, "or whatever your name is, or what it stands for…"

"Mickey's my real name." Her face colored a little. "Alex is the only artificial person aboard."

"Great. You had me worried there for a second." I paused. "You might as well tell me the rest. I'm here, right? Either that, or dump me in China or Tibet or wherever. And if you do that, you ought to just hurry up and kill me, because all I have are the clothes on my back, five bucks, my student I.D., and a Blockbuster Video card."

"We're not going to do that." She glanced back at the cockpit. "Don't mind Tyler. He's just sore because…"

"Sure. Whatever. Just tell me one thing…are you guys from the future?"

Her face went pale, and she stepped back from me. Before she could say anything, though, I went on. "Don't tell me you're from another planet…"

"But we are."

"Oh, yeah? Which one?"

"Mars."

"Sure." I tapped the sign above the suit locker I'd spotted earlier. "And I suppose that's Martian, and what you're speaking is…"

"Martian." She hesitated. "Or at least the Martian dialect of what you know as English. That's why we need the autotranslators. In my time…"

Once more, she stopped herself. "There it is again," I said. "'My time'…like that's different from 'your time.' C'mon, I'm not stupid. Tell me the rest."

She looked down, said nothing. From the corner of my eye, I could see that we were no longer alone. Tyler stood in the hatchway leading to the cockpit, and behind him was Libbie. I had no idea how much they'd overheard, but neither of them looked any more happy with me than Mickey.

Mickey must have noticed them, too. Although she tried not to acknowledge their presence, she was visibly uncomfortable. "I just wanted...I just wanted to show you that the fuel-rod canister was intact, and assure you that it wouldn't be used to make an atomic weapon. Since that's your major concern, that is..."

"Thanks." She was stating the obvious; the real explanation was still unsaid, but I was in no position to press the issue. "I appreciate it."

She nodded, then silently left the airlock, squeezing between Tyler and Libbie. I let her go, then turned to look at her two companions. "Okay, then," I said, squaring my shoulders, "which one of you Martians wants to tell me where we're going?"

I was trying to be funny, but neither of them were the type to take a joke. Libbie turned to follow Mickey, while Tyler gave me a cold look. "You want the truth?" he asked, and I nodded. "Lunar stationary orbit, on the far side of the Moon. We'll be there in about two hours, twenty minutes, standard."

"Aw, c'mon. That's..."

"That's the truth. Take it or leave it..." Tyler started to turn away, then stopped. "Thanks for rescuing me," he added. "I appreciate it. So here's my payback...2337."

"Huh?" I shook my head. "What does that...?"

"2337," Tyler repeated. "That's the year we left Mars."

✦ ✦ ✦

A little less than two hours later, we reached the Moon.

Stop and think about that for a moment. The Moon is approximately 240,000 miles from Earth. The first men to go there were Frank Borman, James Lovell, and William Anders; in 1968, it took three days for them to make the journey—from December 21, 7:51 a.m., when Apollo 8 lifted off from Merritt Island, to December 24, 7:30 a.m., when they transmitted the first close-up TV pictures of the lunar surface—and during that time they established a new world speed record of 24,200 MPH.

I didn't have a watch, so I don't know what exactly time it was when we made our getaway from Narragansett Point, with three A-10s in hot pursuit. All I know is that, when I woke up from a brief nap, I gazed out the window to behold the same awesome sight that Borman, Lovell, and Anders had first seen nearly forty years ago. I didn't ask anyone what time it was, so I have to assume that Hsing had obeyed Mickey's order to get us there in two hours.

How fast had we traveled? Do the math, if you want; I didn't. I was too busy staring out the window beside my seat, watching the barren grey landscape as it rushed past only a few hundred miles below us. Down there were mountains, hills, and craters that only twenty-seven men had ever seen before with their own eyes. A brief glimpse of Mare Tranquillitatis, where Armstrong and Aldrin planted the flag back in '69, then we slingshot around the limb of the Moon and were hurtling toward deep space beyond the lunar farside.

I didn't realize Mickey was standing beside me until she said something "Beautiful, isn't it?" she asked, keeping her voice low as she gazed past me.

"Yeah," I replied, feeling something pinch my throat. "It's...it's awesome."

"Uh-huh." Only then did I notice that her hand lay lightly upon my arm. "This means something to you." she murmured. "Not just seeing the Moon...it's personal, isn't it?"

"Yeah, I..." I stopped myself. I didn't want to lay my life story on her; this wasn't the time or place. "I've always wanted to do this," I said. "Y'know, be an astronaut. But I never thought I...I mean, I didn't think I...."

I halted, looked away. "Never thought what?" Mickey asked. "That you could?"

"Yeah." Then I shook my head. "I mean, no...naw, I mean..." Tongue-tied, I let out my breath, struggled to articulate myself. "Look, it's something that...y'know, I once thought I could do, but..."

"You gave up?"

I didn't answer that because I couldn't. Whoever these guys were—Mickey, Tyler, Hsing, Libbie, Deke, even Alex—they'd come from a time and place where the impossible had become easy. You don't tell a girl who just stolen a few tons of spent fuel rods from a heavily-guarded nuclear power plant that you quit believing that you could become an astronaut just because your father's dead, your mother works two lousy jobs, and your brother's a pothead.

Mickey waited a moment for me to answer. When I didn't, her hand left my arm. ""Better strap in," she said, returning to her own seat. "We're coming in for rendezvous with the *Vincennes*."

"Rendezvous with the...?" I was about to ask what she meant when I looked forward, and saw something that made the Moon seem like a minor attraction.

Fifty-five thousand miles beyond the far side of the Moon, parked in lunar stationary orbit and concealed from all the telescopes and radar systems of Earth, was a starship.

Nearly four hundred feet long, illuminated by red and green formation lights on either side of its sleek grey hull, the SCS *Vincennes* was a leviathan in space. Streamlined from the slender cone of its bow to the stunted wings of its stern, it retained the same basic design of its shuttlecraft, including the vertical stabilizers that rose on either side of aft-section bulge. Yet there were significant differences: open-end nacelles, vaguely resembling intakes of enormous jet engines, lay on either side of the hull just forward of the wings, while a superstructure that looked somewhat like a submarine conning tower was elevated above the cylindrical mid-section leading to the bow.

An enormous hatch yawned open within the upper side of the vessel's aft section; I didn't need anyone to tell me that this was the shuttle bay. Yet as we glided closer, I noticed that most of the portholes along the ship's slender forward section were dark; only a few were lit, along with those on the forward tower. The *Vincennes* had gone dark; somehow, it looked less like a starship than a derelict in space.

"Oh, boy," Tyler murmured from behind us. "They've gone to low-power mode."

"Roger that." Hsing gently coaxed the shuttle closer, swinging it in a broad arc above the darkened vessel. "Command reports all major systems except life-support and station-keeping have been shut down. Docking will be manual."

"Copy that." Libbie's hands moved across her console. "Coming in on manual. All hands, stand-by."

"Does that mean we're in trouble?" I asked Mickey.

"Don't worry," She grasped the bars of her harness. "Just means that *Vincennes* won't be guiding us in on autopilot. Hsing's a good pilot, though. He'll get us down safely."

She knew what she was talking about, of course, but nonetheless I gripped the armrests of my seat. As the shuttle glided into position above the hangar, I looked down to see a broad circle blinking red upon the deck. A moment later, Libbie cut the inertial dampeners; I felt my guts lurch a bit as we became weightless once more. There was a thump beneath our feet, signifying that the landing gear had been lowered, then the shuttle began to slowly descend into the mothership.

However, we didn't touch down. Since the *Vincennes'* own dampeners had been shut down as well, the shuttle was unable to land in a conventional sense. Instead, Hsing guided the craft until it was just a couple of meters above the deck, then held position. Several crewmembers, wearing the same type of skin-tight spacesuits I'd seen earlier, floated toward us, using backpack maneuvering units to haul mooring lines into place. Once the shuttle had been secured, the hangar doors began to close. From my window, I watched while an enclosed gangway telescoped out from the hangar walk. There was a hollow thump against the hull as a crewman mated it with the shuttle's side hatch.

"All right, we're down." Hsing let out his breath; he reached up to push buttons along the overhead console. "Give us a second to match pressure, then we'll pop the hatch. Remember, we're on emergency discipline, so you know what that means."

"What *does* that mean?" I whispered to Mickey.

"Zero-g," she said softly, raising her seat bar, her hair floating around her. "Just follow me, and try not to bump into anything."

"Mickey, Tyler…" Hsing gazed back at us. "Skipper wants to see you both on the bridge, soon as possible." He paused, listening to his headset, then glanced at me. "And bring your guest, too. The old man wants to meet him."

"I bet he does." Tyler had already pushed himself out of his seat. Grasping a rail running along the ceiling, he pulled himself toward the hatch, his feet dangling in midair. "Sorry, but I'm not taking the heat for this."

"I don't expect you to." Mickey's voice was cool, and for a second they shared a look of mutual animosity.

Then Tyler twisted the hatch's lockwheel and pulled it open.

Cold air flooded the shuttle, and I felt my ears pop. Mickey waited patiently while I pushed my seat bar upward; still, I found myself reluctant to leave the safety of my seat. "Come on," she said, extending a hand to me while holding onto the ceiling rail with the other. "It's not that hard. You might even like it."

"Sure. Whatever you say." But it wasn't weightlessness that bothered me. It was meeting the captain.

Mickey was right: zero-gee is *wicked* cool.

I'll admit, I floundered around for the first few minutes, feeling like a little kid in swim class who'd been taken out of the baby pool and tossed into the deep end for the first time. The difference is that you're operating in air, not water, and there's nothing like zero-g to teach you some respect for Newton's third law.

Every action produces an equal and opposite reaction. That means, when you bump into a bulkhead to your left, you bounce to the right, and when you grab a railing above your head, if you're not careful with your feet, they might swing around and kick the guy in front of you.

To make matters worse, the *Vincennes'* passageways were narrow. Even when there was internal gravity, there was barely enough room to two people to pass one another without sucking in your gut; in microgravity, it was like being inside a pinball machine. So I bruised my shoulders and elbows a couple of times, and also put a lump on my head and put my foot against Mickey's behind before I finally got the hang of it.

But I can't lie; it was fun. At some point, words like *up*, *down*, *left*, and *right* lost their meaning; once I got used to that, then everything else was a hoot. Crewmen who passed us in the corridors stared in bafflement at the guy in blue jeans and hooded sweatshirt who was laughing out loud as he performed somersaults that would have put him in the hospital back home. Mickey finally had to grab my shoulders and get me under control; several yards ahead, Tyler regarded at me with disgust, as if I was a country bumpkin who'd just used toilet paper for the first time.

Once I got over that, though, I noticed a couple of things.

First, the lighting within the passageways was dim. Much dimmer that it should have been; ceiling panels were dark, leaving only recessed amber lamps here and there to guide our way. Not only that, but as we passed hatches leading various compartments, I saw through their slot windows that they were without light. Not only that, but the entire ship felt cold; it couldn't have been more than sixty-five degrees. I was born and raised in New England, where temperatures like that mean it's time to put away to put away the snow-shoes and start wearing T-shirts and shorts, but everyone I saw wore jackets above their jumpsuits, and some were wearing light gloves. If these guys were from Mars, then Mars in the 24th century must have the climate of Daytona Beach.

And that brings me to the second point: they were young.

By young, I mean that almost no one I saw was older than twenty-one, with the median age somewhere between fifteen and seventeen. I passed one or two crewmen in their mid-thirties, and spotted one geezer with a few threads of white in his mustache and crows-feet around his eyes. Otherwise, though, the guys looked as if they just learned how to shave, and the girls...well, not to be too specific, but most of them weren't exactly women yet.

A starship full of teenagers. Martian teenagers, at that.

"What's so funny? Mickey saw the expression on my face.

"I dunno. I think I just fell into a Sci-Fi Channel movie." She gave me a puzzled look, not getting the joke. "Never mind," I added. "What I'm trying to say is...um, is everyone aboard a kid?"

"No. The captain and senior officers are all adults." She paused to let another crewman slide past us; he couldn't have been than fifteen, yet was as serious as someone twice his age. "But, yes, most of the crew are between fourteen and twenty. By Earth reckoning, that is...about half that if you use the Martian calendar." She smiled. "That makes me eight years old, where I come from."

"Eight. Right..." I was having trouble dealing with this. "Look, where *I* come from, you can't even drive a car until you're sixteen...eighteen, in some states. So you're telling me..."

By now we'd come to a ladder leading up a narrow shaft. Without looking back at us, Tyler was already ascending it, barely touching the rungs as he floated upward. "It's a long story," Mickey said quietly. "I'll tell you the rest later...if the captain lets me."

"But..."

"Eric..." Mickey paused at the bottom of the ladder. "Do me a favor and keep your mouth shut. Don't speak unless the captain speaks to you first...and be careful what you say. Understand?"

I made a zipping motion with finger across my lips. Mickey nodded, then led me up the shaft. We ascended about thirty feet, passing a closed hatch leading to another deck, and emerged through an open manhole. And that's when I found myself on the bridge of the *Vincennes*.

In many ways, it resembled pictures I'd seen of the control rooms of nuclear submarines: a long, narrow compartment, with officers seated at consoles on either side of a central aisle. What appeared to be a plotting table rested in the middle of the compartment, except this one displayed a holographic wire-frame image of the Earth-Moon system, with a tiny replica of the *Vincennes* positioned beyond the lunar farside. On the far side of the compartment, wrapped in a 180-degree arc, were five large portholes; the center one looked out over the ship's bow, and it was in front of this window that I saw the commanding officer of SCS *Vincennes*.

If I was expecting someone more heroic—James T. Kirk, maybe, or even Jean-Luc Picard—then I was disappointed. Captain Van Owen looked no more intimidating than my high school geometry teacher; short and narrow-shouldered, with barely enough brown hair to keep his head from getting cold. He would have looked better if he had glasses and maybe a mustache. One look at his eyes, though, and I knew that this one guy you didn't throw a spit wad at while his back was turned to you.

"Mr. Ionesco, Ms. McGyver…" His voice was low, yet demanding respect. He was standing upright, and it took me a second to realize that the toes of his shoes were tucked into stirrups on the deck. "Welcome back. I see that your mission has been a success…for the most part, at least."

"Yes, sir." Tyler grasped the handrail surrounding the plotting table; Mickey and I had to settle for rungs here and there along the low ceiling. "We've retrieved a cache of uranium fuel rods from the objective, and have transported them to…"

"Yes, I know. I can see that." The captain gestured to a flatscreen above a console to our left. Looking at it, I saw an image of the hangar deck. Several spacesuited figures were guiding the stolen fuel rod canister from the shuttle, allowing its weightless condition to do most of the heavy-lifting for them. At the aft end of the hangar, another crewman hovered near an open hatch, apparently waiting for them to pass through. "Well done. But…"

He paused, then looked past Tyler at both Mickey and me. "Apparently there were some unforeseen difficulties."

"Yes, sir, there were." Mickey moved a little closer. "Captain, we had problems almost as soon as we entered the vicinity." She glanced back at me. "However, if it hadn't been for…"

"Sir, I must protest." Tyler interrupted her. "*Midshipman* McGyver overstates the situation…"

"She does, does she?" Van Owen raised an eyebrow; he hadn't missed the way Tyler have emphasized her rank. "She hasn't even told me what that is…and as I recall, she was in charge of the retrieval phase, not you."

"Yes, but…" Tyler's face colored. "Sir, she allowed an indigenous native to observe the operation." The way he said *native* made it sound as if I wore a loin cloth and had a bone in my nose. "She then brought him aboard, despite my objections…"

"Sir, with all due respect, the *native* observed the operation on his own initiative." Mickey spoke as if I wasn't beside her. "There was nothing we could do to prevent his intervention…"

"No, sir, that's not true." Tyler jabbed a finger at me. "When I had an opportunity to stun him, she deliberately intervened, and when I insisted that he be left behind…"

"Tell him what happened when we almost had to leave *you* behind." Letting go of the ceiling rail, she pushed herself closer to Tyler. "Tell him what he did after you fell off the ladder."

"That's enough, both of you." Although Van Owen's voice remained low, both Mickey and Tyler clammed up. "Lt. Ionesco, I'll remind you that it my order, relayed to Lt. Wu, that this person be brought aboard. Ms. McGyver was simply following my instructions."

That settled Tyler's hash. "Yes, sir," he murmured. "I didn't understand that, sir."

"Now you do." Ignoring both him and Mickey for a moment, the captain looked straight at me. "What's your name, son?"

· "Eric...Eric Cosby, sir." My mouth felt dry. "Captain, sir, I didn't mean to...I mean, I wasn't trying to..."

"Easy, boy. You were just caught up in something you don't understand." He paused, studying all three of us. "Nonetheless, this is a serious situation...and Tyler, you've made some serious charges. I'll speak to you alone."

Tyler nodded, not looking back at Mickey and me. The captain gestured toward the hatch behind us. "Ms. McGyver, please escort Mr. Cosby to the observation lounge. Remain there and keep him company until I summon you."

"Yes, sir."

The captain hesitated. "And while you're at it, tell him whatever he needs to know." A wry smile appeared on his face. "He's come this far...might as well let him learn the rest."

The observation lounge was located on the deck below the bridge. Barely wide enough for three people to stand abreast, it had two circular portholes, each six feet in diameter, on either side of the compartment, with chairs anchored to the floor in front of them. Like the rest of the ship, the lounge was almost totally dark, save for a red emergency glowing above the hatch.

"This is my favorite place on the ship." Grasping a ceiling rail, Mickey led me to the two chairs facing the starboard viewport. "I don't get a chance to come here very often, though...usually too busy. Would you like to sit, or...?"

"Uh-uh. I'd just as soon...um, float, if it's okay with you." I couldn't take my eyes from the starboard window. Once my eyes became accustomed to the darkness, I saw billions of stars—planets, suns, nebulae, distant galaxies—spread out before us in a broad swath, with the Moon an oval patch of darkness, sunlight forming a slender crescent around its western terminator.

"So would I." Mickey grasped a handrail encircling the porthole, anchoring herself next to the window; I took hold of the rail on the other side. "This is a treat, believe me. No gravity...and the place all to ourselves."

Better than the drive-in, that's for sure. But that wasn't what was on my mind. "Mickey...what's going on here? Why are you...I mean, why did you...?"

"Of course. Questions." She took a deep breath, then released the handrail and folded her legs together in a position that I would've called "sitting" if she wasn't three feet above the floor. "It's like this..."

By the year 2337 (she explained), the human race had not only colonized most of Earth's solar system—the Moon, Mars, the asteroid belt and the major satellites of Jupiter and Saturn, along with space stations as close as Venus and as distant as the Kuiper belt—but it had also ventured out to the nearby star systems: Alpha Centauri B, Wolf 359, Epsilon Eridani, and Bernard's Star, among others. The development of nuclear engines had opened the solar system as a frontier during the 21st century; the subsequent invention of hyperspace travel during the 23rd century had carried humankind to the stars.

During this time, Earth's nearby colonies decided to form the Solar System Confederation, a democratic alliance that sought to maintain trade and diplomatic ties among both the near-Earth colonies and the extrasolar settlements. This wasn't an easy task; the colonies often quarreled, and more than once war had threatened to tear the union apart. So in order to keep the peace, as well as facilitate further colonization, the Solar Confederation Fleet was established.

The *Vincennes* was one of three heavy cruisers belonging to Mars, which—next only to Earth itself—was the most populated and politically powerful of the SSC worlds, particularly after it had been terraformed during the 22nd century. The *Vincennes* took its name from the flagship of the United States Exploratory Expedition of 1838, and was the oldest of its class; constructed at the Deimos shipyards in 2278, it remained in service until 2329, when it was retired from active duty and turned over to the Mars campus of the Confederation Fleet Academy as a training vessel.

"Whoa, Wait a minute…" Hearing this, I held up a hand. "You mean this…?" I looked around myself, at everything I'd seen so far. "You mean this is…this is just a training ship?"

"Sort of a let-down, isn't it?" There was a sad look in her eyes as Mickey glanced up at the ceiling. "Maybe she doesn't look it, but she's obsolete. Range limited to only fifty light-years. Nothing like the…"

"Okay, I get it." I shook my head. *Only* fifty light years... "So I guess that, compared to whatever else you guys have, it's beat to crap..."

"Hey, that's my ship you're talking about." Mickey scowled at me, and suddenly I realized that I'd just crossed the line. "Maybe you think this is funny, but here in this century, your people still thought liquid-fuel rockets were..."

"Easy. Easy." I held up my hands. "Bad joke, okay? No offense."

Mickey relaxed. Uncurling her legs, she grasped the rail again. "Of course. I forget that irony was a preferred form of humor in your...never mind. Let's go on."

When it departed from Phobos Station on Aquarius 47, 2337. the *Vincennes'* crew included sixty-five cadets, ranging from ensigns to junior-grade lieutenants, along ten senior officers who acted as their instructors. Not to mention Alex, whose full name was Alex Elevendee and who was just as much a part of the *Vincennes* as its lifeboats and life-extinguishing equipment: another piece of hardware, albeit a little more conversational than, say, the toaster. This particular mission was the third one for the Class of '38, and was supposed to be relatively simple: a quick jaunt through hyperspace from Mars to the Moon, a couple of orbits around Earth to test the cadets' knowledge of planetary rendezvous procedures, then another jaunt back through hyperspace to Mars. No one had brought more than the clothes on their backs and their datapads; they'd fully expected to be home by evening mess.

"But it didn't work out that way, did it?" I asked.

"No, it didn't." Mickey shook her head. "The jaygee at the navigation station laid in the wrong jump coordinates. He accidentally transposed the elements for the *c*-factor for the *t*-factor, which in turn caused..." She caught the look on my face. "You haven't had quantum mechanics, have you?"

I snapped my fingers, glanced up at the ceiling. "Gee, y'know, they offered it this year, but I went for trig instead because I heard it was a crip coarse."

"Never mind." From her expression, I could see that she couldn't tell whether I was putting her on again or not. "Look, plotting a hyperspace jaunt is a very precise business. You've got to get everything right the first time, or..."

"Uh-huh. And I take it this guy screwed up."

She nodded. "In a major way, yes. Oh, he got us to the Moon, all right...but through a curved timelike loop that opened a wormhole through the space-time continuum. So instead of arriving here in our own year..."

"You arrived here in *my* year. Let me guess the rest... you can't get back, right?"

"Oh, no. Returning to our time isn't the problem. Once we realized what had happened, all we had to do was sort through the onboard log, detect where the mistake had been made, and figure out how to correct it. If everything had worked out as it should have, we could have been home in less than an hour."

"So what went wrong?" I corrected myself. "I mean, what *else* went wrong?"

"Because the main computer detected a flaw in the flight profile, it automatically tripped the master alarm as soon as we came out of hyperspace. I was on the bridge when it happened, and it was really scary. All the lights went red, and then the horns went off all at once, and then..."

Mickey suddenly stopped. Looking away from me, she gazed out the porthole at the far side of the Moon. "It...it was my fault," she said quietly. "I was minding the power control station. I was confused, just as they'd warned us might happen when we came out of hyperspace, when I saw the red-alert light on my console, I..."

Now I saw a strange thing. Tiny bubbles, like miniature spheres of water, departing from the corners of her eyes, gently float upward. Tears in the moonlight. A girl crying in zero-g.

"Mickey..." I leaned forward, touched her arm. "C'mon..."

"I'm sorry. I'm still..." She reached up to her face, dried her eyes. "I dumped the reactor," she murmured. "The alarm confused me, and I...I mean, we didn't know what had happened. All I knew was...that is, I thought the main reactor was about to meltdown, so I jettisoned the rods. Which is what they tell us to do in an emergency."

"You use a nuclear reactor?" As soon as I said this, I knew it sounded dumb. What was I expecting, dilithium crystals? Perhaps nuclear fission hadn't worked out so well in my time, but that didn't mean it couldn't be used three hundred years later. "Sorry. Go on...so you dumped the reactor, and that meant..."

She didn't say anything, only looked at me, and that was when everything came together. Sure, the crew of the *Vincennes* knew how to get home...but without fuel for their reactor, there was no way they'd be able to make another jump through space-time. So they did what they had to do: parked the ship in lunar stationary orbit on the far side of the Moon, where it couldn't be seen from Earth, and sent down a team to steal some nuclear fuel rods.

"So how did you...?" I paused. "I mean, how did you know about Narragansett Point?"

"The ship's library system has complete historical records." Mickey snuffled back her tears. "Meant for download into colony computers for educational purposes. Someone did a little research and discovered that, in this time, your nuclear power plant was being decommissioned." She shrugged. "That seemed to be the least dangerous means of getting what we needed. Minimal security...or at least nothing that our stun guns and Alex couldn't take down..."

"I was wondering about that. All those guards, and the guys inside the plant..."

"We used a sleeper. Sort of like a grenade, only that it emits an electromagnetic pulse that temporarily disrupts higher brain functions. We hid in the vehicle we'd stolen while Alex penetrated the front gate, then detonated the sleeper to knock out the sentries."

"Right. Got it." But that still left much unexplained. "But if you guys knew about our nuke, then why come into town? Why ask me for directions?"

"We knew there was a plant near Bellingham, but we didn't know exactly where it was located. Also, we needed to take out the security and find the spent fuel before we could bring in the shuttle to take it away. That was my part of the operation. So very early this morning, Hsing dropped us just outside town, then landed the shuttle out in the hills and waited for us to send him a signal. We hiked in, stole an automobile and hid it in an alley, then broke into a shop to steal some clothes..."

"I know about that." I tried not to grin as I glanced at her Dead T-shirt and faux-fur overcoat. "Someone should've told you how we dress in my century. You guys stuck out."

"We did?" She looked down at herself, and laughed at herself "Well, what do I know? Besides, we would've looked even stranger in our academy uniforms." Mickey sighed. "But I think our biggest mistake was asking you for directions."

"Thanks a lot..."

"No!" Her eyes widened. "I didn't mean it that way. It's just that our orders were to avoid contact with the inhabitants as much as possible." She frowned. "But Tyler was in charge of that part of the operation, and he became frustrated when we couldn't find a map that would show us exactly where the plant was located. So when he saw you..."

"Let me guess. Since I'm your age, he figured that asking me for directions wouldn't be as risky as talking to an adult. Right?"

"Something like that." She gave me a grim smile. "It wasn't the first mistake Tyler made. The first was setting the wrong coordinates for the hyperspace jump."

"He...?" Now it was my turn to be surprised. "I don't get it. If you two were the guys responsible for this mess, why did the captain pick you to...?"

"Because we *were* responsible." She let out her breath. "One of the first things they teach us in the academy is that, if you make a critical error, you're the one who has to make it right."

"You break it, you bought it." She gave me a quizzical look, and I smiled. "Something we say in my time."

"'You break it, you bought it.'" Mickey smiled as she repeated my words. "I like that. Anyway, once we knew how to find the plant, we went out there, and...well, you know the rest."

"Yeah, okay." Then I thought about it for a moment. "No, I don't. What good would nuclear waste do you? I mean, what you stole were spent fuel rods. How could you...?"

"Only about three-quarters of the U-235 contained within nuclear fuel rods is actually consumed during fission. The rest gets thrown away along with the U-237 and plutonium waste...or at least by standards by which 20th century nuclear power plants normally operated. But our ships are designed to reprocess spent fuel rods from other ships in the event of an emergency." She nodded in the general direction of the stern. "Right now, nanites are disassembling those uranium-dioxide pellets, molecule by molecule, and recombining the usable U-235 as fuel for our reactor. Believe me, it's a very fast process. We should be back to full power any minute now."

"Oh, I believe you." I remembered how quickly nanites in the floor of the shuttle had cleaned up my vomit. Maybe it wasn't the most savory example of the wonders of the 24th century, but nonetheless it was the one that came to mind. "Then..."

Then? Then nothing. She'd told me everything I needed to know, just as the captain had told her to do. Once again, I gazed out the window. Here I was, aboard a starship lurking above the dark side of the Moon, farther from Earth than anyone had ever been before. I should have been awestruck, or delirious with wonder, or...something, I don't know what. Yet instead, I only felt hollow. Something was missing, but I didn't know what it was...

"Eric?"

"Yeah?" I didn't look at her. "What?"

For a moment, Mickey said nothing. Then I felt her come closer to me, and as I turned around, she took my face within her hands, looked me straight in the eye, and kissed me.

Exactly three times before, a girl had given me a kiss. I won't go into details about the earlier ones, but take my word for it: this was the best one yet.

And, by the way, did I forget to mention that zero-g is really cool?

It might have lasted longer, but then a shrill alarm came over a ceiling speaker. Hearing this, Mickey reluctantly pulled herself away from me. "Inertial damp-eners are coming back online," she murmured. "We're going to get gravity again in about ten seconds." She reached up to grasp the ceiling rail. "Brace yourself."

I had just enough time to grab the rail myself be-fore we went from microgravity to one-g. This time, I was ready for it; no puking in front of my new girlfriend, or at least not for the second time tonight. We waited until the alarms shut off, then dropped to the floor.

"Thanks." I took a deep breath, then took a step closer to her. "So, where were we...?"

Mickey blushed, but she didn't back away as I took her hands. "I think I was thanking you for..."

The hatch clicked, and we had a chance to retreat from each other before it swung open. Then the ceiling lights came open; squinting against the abrupt glare, I looked around to see Tyler standing in the hatchway.

He stared at us for a moment, then looked at Mickey. "Skipper wants to talk to you now," he said, with plenty of frost in his voice. Mickey's face went pale, but she said nothing to me. Instead, she silently nodded, and marched out of the observation lounge, taking care not to brush against Tyler on the way to the ladder.

Tyler and I silently regarded one another. For a sec-ond, I was afraid that he'd join me in the lounge—there would be no hugging and kissing between the two of us—but instead he turned toward the corridor. I was relieved that he was going to leave me alone, but then a smug grin crept across his face, and he wagged a finger at me.

"See you in China," he said.

"Sure thing, bud," I replied. "Right after you learn quantum math."

His face went red, and then he slammed the hatch shut.

I was alone in the observation lounge for only ten or fifteen minutes. Then an ensign barely old enough to try out for the junior varsity basketball team came to fetch me. Yet I was escorted not to the bridge, as I expected, but to another compartment on the same deck.

The captain's quarters were little larger than the janitor's closet at my high school; just enough room for a small desk, a chair, a locker, a fold-down bunk, and a door leading to what I assumed was a private john. Captain Van Owen was seated at his desk when the ensign led me in; he accepted the kid's salute with a cursory nod, then waited until he shut the hatch behind me.

"Mr. Cosby...or may I call you Eric?" I swallowed and nodded, and he gave me a brief smile. "Eric, then... please be seated."

There was no where else to sit except his bunk. "Thank you, sir," I said, and sat down on the very edge, trying to disturb its drum-tight covers as little as possible.

"You're welcome..." His eyes never left mine. "I believe that Midshipman McGyver has fully debriefed you of our situation. Correct?"

"Yes, sir. She's told me everything." And a bit more, although the last thing he'd ever learn from me was the exact nature of our debriefing.

"Very well." Sitting back in his chair, the captain crossed his arms. "First, let me express my appreciation for the assistance you've given my team. Judging from what both Ms. McGyver and Mr. Ionesco has told me, your performance has been outstanding...particularly in regards to the lieutenant's rescue."

"Yes, sir. Thank you, sir." Perhaps I wasn't a member of the crew, but nonetheless I found myself addressing him as if he was my commanding officer. "I did what I had to..."

"Of course. And if you were one of my cadets, I'd expect no less." Van Owen hesitated. "Which leads us to our predicament, because you don't belong to the *Vincennes*, and I'm at a loss to know what to do with you."

Pushing back his chair, he stood up, walked over to the porthole. "As you now know, this was supposed to be a covert mission. No one on Earth was ever supposed to be aware of our presence. Of course, there'll be an investigation of how spent uranium was stolen from a secure nuclear facility, but I'm gambling that it will be done quietly, with no one in public ever learning what happened tonight."

"Even with Air National Guard jets chasing your shuttle?"

"Yes, even despite that." Van Owen gazed through the porthole, his hands clasped behind his back. "In fact, I'm willing to bet that those pilots have already been thoroughly interrogated by military intelligence. Even if their story is believed...and how many unconfirmed UFO sightings were there during your time?...chances are that they'll be sworn to silence about what they saw, or thought they saw."

"I..."

"Eric, the last thing anyone will suspect is the truth. Think about it for a moment. All eyewitnesses on the ground were rendered unconscious by unknown forces. A single cask of nuclear waste was lifted from the site by an unidentified aircraft that bore no markings and managed to evade military jets. The only clue left behind was a stolen vehicle, and the fingerprints won't match any in law enforcement databases. Now, put yourself in their place. Would you conclude that this was done by men from outer space...or by a well-equipped terrorist organization?"

He had a point. Ever since 9/11, the news media had come up with scenarios for future terrorist actions that sounded as if they'd come straight from a bad movie. If you believed everything you read in the magazines or saw on TV, al-Qaeda wasn't a gang of Islamist fanatics led by geek named Osama bin Laden, but SPECTRE itself, with Blofelt in charge. A group of teenage space cadets—from the future, no less—making off with nuclear material to refuel a stranded starship? How absurd could you possibly get?

"I think I see what you mean," I said. "Sir."

"Of course you do." Van Owen gave me a sly wink as he turned back around. "I wouldn't have risked this if I thought otherwise." Then he frowned. "But we still have one loose end..."

"That's me, isn't it?"

The captain slowly nodded. "You're the one thing we never expected...a witness to valuable to simply knock out and leave behind. You helped my people escape from Earth, and now we have to decide what to do with you."

Leaning against his desk, he raised his fingers one at a time. "First option...we kill you." Seeing my expression, he quickly shook his head. "Don't worry, that's out of the question. We're not barbarians." He raised a second finger. "Second option...we take you back to Earth, but drop you off in an area so remote that it's unlikely that you'll ever make your way back to civilization."

I had no doubt who'd suggested this one. Before I could object, though, the captain shook his head. 'That's also out of the question, for that's almost as bad as the first option...and I'm making it a point to officially reprimand the cadet who made it. He's in enough hot water with me already, so this won't look good on his service record."

Oh, boy. Tyler was in a lot of trouble once he got home. I tried not to smile. "The third option," Van Owen continued, "is that we take you back to where we found you, drop you off, and trust that you'll never, ever breathe a word to anyone about what you've seen. Not now, not tomorrow, not in ten or twenty or fifty years, not ever." He stared at me. "Do you know what I'm asking, Eric? Complete and utter secrecy, for as long as you live."

I swallowed when I heard that. Sure, I can keep a secret...but about something like this? It's one thing not to let anyone know that your brother sells dope, or that your best friend wears boxer shorts printed with the Superman logo. It's another to promise that you'll never reveal that you've been to the Moon, or seen the inside of starship from the 24th century...

Yet who'd ever believe me? At best, they'd simply think I was making it up, and then I'd be a liar, and a bad one at that. At worst, they'd assume I was delusional; then I'd be sent to a state mental hospital, and spend the next few years playing checkers with all the other guys who'd spent quality time with space aliens.

"I don't have a problem with that," I said.

"All right." Van Owen nodded. "I think I can trust you to keep your word...but you still haven't heard the fourth option."

"There's one?"

"Yes, there is," he said, and this time he didn't bother to raise a finger. "You can come with us."

I didn't say anything. I just stared at him, and waited for my heart to start beating again.

"As I said," he went on, "if you were a member of my crew, your conduct would be considered outstanding. You have a quick mind, you're quick to adapt to a crisis situation...and most of all, you've displayed true heroism, under circumstances that would've caused ninety-nine out of a hundred men to run for their lives."

The captain paused, then folded his arms together. "Son, you've got what it takes to be a spacer. I don't say that lightly, and neither does Midshipman McGyver. Come with us, and I'll personally recommend you to the academy...and I'd be proud to have you aboard the *Vincennes* once you pass basic training."

Not knowing what to say, I didn't say anything. Instead, I walked over to the porthole and looked out at the stars.

I was tempted. Damn, but I was tempted. Everything I'd ever wanted in my life, within reach of my fingertips. I wouldn't even have to worry about graduating high school; trigonometry would be a thing of the past, because I'd be studying quantum mechanics instead. And not long after that, a berth aboard this very ship, and a chance to see things no one in my time had ever dreamed of seeing...

And meanwhile, my mother would be left wondering what had happened to her son, who'd disappeared one October night without a trace. She'd already lost my father; now she'd lose me as well. That would kill her. And did I really want to be the kid brother whose picture Steve would see printed on the side of milk cartons he restocked at Speed-E-Mart? Smokin' Steve was a jerk, but I didn't want to leave her and Mom alone together, trying to put together the pieces after I was gone.

Sometimes, the galaxy can wait. If only just a little while longer...

"Thank you, sir." My voice was a dry rasp. "I appreciate the offer, but..."

"You'll go for the third option." Captain Van Owen nodded, and smiled. "Somehow, I thought you would."

"You did?"

"Yes, I did." Then he offered his hand. "Because you're that sort of person...sir."

+✦+

I returned to Earth that same night, arriving shortly before dawn. The sun was still below the horizon when the shuttle descended upon a cow pasture about three miles from town. Mickey dropped the ladder overboard; we shared a brief moment in the airlock, then I hastily climbed down the ladder. My feet barely touched ground before she pulled the ladder up behind me. A last wave, then she closed the hatch.

I watched the shuttle as it sprinted into the starlit sky. This time, there were no Warthogs in hot pursuit; I guess the Massachusetts Air National Guard had enough UFO-chasing for one night. In any case, the shuttle vanished within seconds, and then I began the long walk home.

I'd hoped to slip in through the kitchen door without waking anyone, but my luck wasn't with me; Mom had stayed up all night, watching TV in the living room while she waited for me to come home. I couldn't tell whether she was mad or relieved: both, probably. She sniffed my breath, looked closely at my eyes to see if they were bloodshot, then demanded where I'd been.

I was too tired to come up with a decent lie, so I told her that I'd been abducted by men from Mars. She stared at me for a long moment, then apparently decided that, since I obviously hadn't been drinking or smoking dope, she'd let me have my little secrets. Maybe she figured that I'd been out with a girl. And that wasn't too far from the truth either...

Anyway, she had worse things to think about. As if turned out, Steve had been busted earlier that night. Officer Beauchamp spotted his Mustang tearing down the highway a few miles from Narragansett Point, so he pulled my brother over, and when Steve cranked down his window, Bo caught a strong whiff of reefer smoke. Bo called for backup, and when the cops searched Steve's car, they found all the stuff that had made me so nervous. Mom got the call from the police shortly after she got home from work, but before she went downtown to spring him from jail, she first went downstairs to visit his room.

And that's how my brother lost his car, a pound of marijuana, and his status as Smokin' Steve, all in the same evening. The pot was flushed down the pot, the 'stang was sold to repay Mom for the bail she had to post for him, and Steve spent his free time for the next twelve months picking up roadside trash on behalf of the Honor Court. He didn't call me a twerp after that, either; Mom let him know that he was on probation so far as she was concerned, too, and that if he didn't treat us both with a little more respect, he'd find just how far his Speed-E-Mart paycheck went toward paying for rent, utilities and groceries.

Not that I got off scott-free. Mom grounded me for a month, which meant that I didn't spend much time that fall hanging out in front of Fat Boy's Music. I didn't mind, though, because now I had a new interest in life.

Just as Captain Van Owen predicted, no one ever learned the truth what really happened at Narragansett Point that night. There was nothing about it in the news media, although a couple of days later Homeland Security escalated the Terror Alert to Code Orange, and Fox News made a squawk about civilian nuclear power plants being put under increased vigilance. As always, no one paid much attention to all this—you've heard one duette-tape alert, you've heard 'em all—although I couldn't help but wonder if my friends hadn't done us a favor, albeit unintentionally.

When I saw Ted at school the next Monday, he didn't want to talk about what he'd seen. In fact, he even denied that we'd done anything after we had pizza at Louie's. It took me a few days to get his part of the story out of him, and then only in hushed tones, under the seats of the football field bleachers during gym class. Once he'd escaped from my brother and his friends, Ted beat it to the nearest gas station, where he used the pay phone to call the state police. But what he didn't get were Vermont smokies, but instead two guys from the FBI field office in Burlington. They put him on the griddle for a couple of hours, then told him that if he ever breathed a word about what he'd seen, he'd find that his ambition to become a comic book writer would be limited to doing funnies for a federal prison newspaper. So, as far as he was concerned, our little adventure together was something that never happened.

I didn't object. Ted was right. Nothing significant happened that night, except that my brother got his comeuppance, my best friend became a little more cautious, and my mother stopped spending so much time away from the house.

And me...?

I hit the books as hard as I could. Every minute I had left in the day, I spent doing my homework, trying to jack up my grades so that I could qualify for a scholarship. The Air Force Academy was my first choice; if not that, then Annapolis. And if those options failed, then MIT, or Stanford, or CalTech. Any school that might lead me, in the long run, to NASA astronaut training, and—if I was lucky—a seat aboard the first ship to Mars.

I'd rediscovered my dreams, sure. I'd also learned that I didn't have to live in Bellingham for the rest of my life. High school is just something you get through, and the corner of Main and Birch is just a temporary resting place along the way. But that's not all. The perfect girl is out there, waiting for me. And when we shared our last kiss aboard the shuttle just before she dropped me off, she told me how to find her again.

I won't tell you how this is going to be done, only to say that we worked it out on the way back from far side of the Moon. Time isn't an obstacle; it's just an inconvenience. Besides, you wouldn't give out your girlfriend's phone number, would you?

And, like I said, I always wanted to be an astronaut.

THE WAR OF DOGS AND BOIDS

This is the story of how the dogs of Coyote chased the boids from Liberty, and thereby saved the lives of their human companions. It is a tale of bravery and sacrifice, of courage and vigilance...and no human will ever know it, for only the dogs are aware of all the facts, and they speak in ways that transcend human awareness.

Dogs have their own society. From since the time before the beginning of recorded history, when wolf cubs who lurked around the refuse pits of human encampments overcame their primal instincts to allow themselves to be approached by the nomads who'd entered their domain, canines have roamed together as pack animals, forming their own hierarchies, their own mores and social codes. They have communicated with one another through growls and yips, barks and howls, yet their means of expression has never been limited to mere language. A certain gleam in the eye is all that separates friend from foe, just as a squirt of urine upon a tree trunk is a more effective means of asserting territory than a hundred-page treaty. Humans spend vast amounts of time and energy trying to determine sexual availability; for dogs, a quick sniff of the hindquarters is all that it takes for one to decide if the other is of the opposite gender and whether they're receptive for mating. The rules of the pack are simple. The old and weak are protected by the young and healthy. Offspring are protected at all costs. Loyalty is lifelong; treachery is unforgiven.

Little has changed after the long-forgotten day, countless millennia ago, when the first orphaned wolf cub, wary yet famished, allowed himself to lured into camp by a two-legger intelligent enough to see the potential benefit in befriending a wild animal. Over the course of time, descendents of that lonesome cub were domesticated, crossbred, trained, and beloved by their two-legged patrons; in exchange, they received food, warmth, shelter, and companionship. And yet, even then, the dogs have been a breed apart. In ways seldom understood by their human companions, they've continued their ancient ways, obeying primal instincts that have confounded the best efforts of scientific observers. The rules of the pack.

So dogs traveled across oceans and continents, bearing silent witness as their mentors explored and settled the distant frontiers of the planet they shared. And when humankind went to the stars, they brought dogs with them.

Which is how Star came to Coyote. A medium-size mutt—part Rhodesian ridgeback, part pit bull—he'd never known life on Earth, save as an fetus removed from his mother's womb during her last month of pregnancy, to be placed in hibernation for the long journey to 47 Ursae Majoris aboard the URSS *Alabama*. Star wasn't the only dog to be selected for humankind's first interstellar voyage, nor were dogs the only animals to make the trip; also placed within biostasis were fetal-stage sheep and goats, along with dozens of embryonic chicken eggs. Mission planners determined that cats were much too dependent to be useful to a fledgling colony, just as cattle consumed too much grazing land for such relatively little return. But dogs...oh, yes, dogs had long-since earned their right to settle a new world.

So Star left Earth as little more than an unborn pup, suspended within a milky fluid inside the aluminum tube that bore his original name: ST7456-R. It took the *Alabama* 230 years to make the journey to the fourth moon of the third planet of the 47 Ursae Majoris, and nearly a year after that before the commanding officer, R.E. Lee, determined that the colony was stable enough to support livestock. Yet the day eventually became when the small cell containing ST7456-R was loaded into the machine that decanted his tiny form, combined it with biosynthesizers, and eventually produced a small, squealing puppy. Someone noted the tiny white splotch at the tip of his tail and the comet-like streak at the end of his nose, and so he was given his name.

But Star was just a word by which two-leggers chose to address him. He eventually learned to answer to it, yet among the six other dogs who also survived the long voyage to Coyote—three didn't—he was known as something else. His true name, his dog-name, was impossible to translate into any human language, for it was communicated not by sound or written alphabet, but rather by odor: a complex chain of organic acids and proteins, relayed by sweat, piss and anal odor, that was as unique among his kind as fingerprints were among humans. In human language, other dogs might have called him Short-Fur-Barks-Loud-Runs-Fast, but even that was only an approximation. For lack of better elucidation, his name was Star; he liked the sound of it, even if he had no idea what it meant.

For the first eight weeks of his life, Star lived in a pen with the other puppies, none of whom looked like one another, yet who regarded themselves as litter-mates. The humans who fed them with squeeze-bottles of reconstituted milk during their infancy had given them names; there was Geronimo, a German shepherd, and Trixie, a white lab, and Dexter, a border collie, and Sally, an English terrier, and Barney, a golden retriever-collie mix, and Rayn, a beautiful Irish setter who was the favorite among the humans. Among the dogs, of course, they had their own names, and as usual within a pack, there was some initial feuds and fights until they sorted out who was the leader. To no one's surprise, that turned out to be Geronimo, mainly because he was the largest and most aggressive of the males. However, Sharp-Teeth-Howls-At-Night wasn't a bully; once he marked his territory by peeing in the corner of the pen that caught the most sunlight during the day, he was willing to make friends with the others. Star and Geronimo became close pals, and spent their free time playing dog games: chasing each other around the colony's log cabins, splashing through the creek that lay near the settlement, having contests to see who could bark the loudest.

Yet their lives were not carefree forever. Coyote was an Earth-like world, yet it wasn't Earth. Although the colony of Liberty had become self-sustaining by the time Captain Lee allowed the dogs to be decanted, food was still scarce; more often than not, the dogs survived on a gruel of corn mash, nutritious but not the carnivorous fare their bodies instinctively desired. And as soon as they were old enough, the dogs began to be trained for their principal task, protecting the farm fields from the native creatures that emerged from the surrounding savannah to feed upon the crops.

The last wasn't so much a job as it was a game. Swampers were easy; little more than large rodents, they were defenseless against dogs that could sniff out their whereabouts from fifty feet away and kill them with a single bite to the back of the neck. And they were good to eat, too; Rayn was the best hunter, and she quickly became plump from all the ones she knocked off (which only added to her desirability, for among male dogs nothing is more sexually attractive than a fat bitch in heat). Swoops were more difficult; large, broad-winged birds, they'd long-since preyed upon swampers, and more than once tried to do the same with the puppies until they grew too large for them to carry away. None of the pack ever managed to kill a swoop, yet they learned how to scare them away by barking and baring their teeth while they circled above the fields. The hardest opponents were creek cats; even after the dogs grew to full size, they were still only slightly larger than the felines, who'd back down only if they were circled by two or three dogs. The humans didn't like creek cats any more than the dogs did, though, and after awhile the dogs learned that all they had to do was use their snouts to point out where a cat was lurking in the high grass until a human could dispatch it with a rifle.

Yet, by far, the most menacing animals on Coyote were the boids.

Few humans ever saw a boid and lived to tell the tale, or at least until automatic guns equipped with motion-detectors and infrared heat-seekers were established around the colony perimeter. Yet the dogs knew all about them; late at night, as they curled up together for warmth, they'd hear high-pitched cries from across the grasslands. Sally, Barney, and Dexter would whimper and huddle closer to the others for comfort, while Geronimo, Trixie, and Rayn would bark in response, warning the unseen menace to keep its distance or face the wrath of the pack.

Star remained silent, obeying the wisdom of the pack leaders. He didn't want to challenge what he couldn't see, and it'd become clear to him that even the humans, despite their guns and godlike omniscience, were just as fearful of these creatures as he was.

Yet more than once, in the early hours of the morning, when Bear hung above the colony, its rings casting a wan silver glow upon the savannah, he'd be awakened by a strange avian scent. Raising his head, he'd look around to see, not far away, a pair of cold eyes reflecting the planetlight, regarding him from the tall grass just beyond range of the perimeter guns.

The boids were out there. Waiting for him to venture into their territory.

+ + +

Late spring slowly bloomed into early summer, and the day finally came that the pack was separated from one another. The dogs had become full-grown by then, and the pen they'd shared since puppyhood was no longer large to hold them comfortably. Besides, Rayn was pregnant with Geronimo's offspring, and Sally had been recently humped by Dexter; it was time for everyone to go their separate ways.

One by one, colonists came over to the pen and picked out the dogs they wished to adopt. Or at least that was what they thought they were doing, for the fact of the matter is that dogs adopt humans as well. A human looks into a pen mobbed with mutts happily barking and climbing on top of each other, and believes they're all vying for attention, and in some ways that's true; a dog isn't happy until he has a two-legger for company. But the dog has a choice in the matter, too, and it's not until they look deep into the eyes of a human, and perceives a glimmer of the soul within, that he or she decides whether they've found the person they want to love and protect for all the rest of their days. This is one of the most binding moments in all creation; a human may simply take a dog, of course, but unless the dog has found the right companion, they will never be close friends.

In Star's case, he found Carlos Montero.

It was a good match, because Carlos himself was also an orphan. His parents, Jorge and Rita, were killed by a boid on the third day after the colonists arrived on Coyote. Carlos and his younger sister Marie were temporarily adopted by another couple, Jim and Sissy Levin, yet as soon as he passed his sixteenth birthday, Carlos moved out of the Levin home, taking his sister to live with him in a log cabin built for them by the other colonists. Even for one so young, Carlos was always independent; the Levins already had two sons, Chris and David, and he didn't want to continue to be a burden upon them.

So Carlos became Star's human, although Carlos certainly believed, as humans tend to do, that it was the other way around. Star slept beside Carlos's bed, often sneaking up in the middle of the night to curl up at his feet, and in the morning he patiently waited for his friend to make him a kibble of corn mash for breakfast, on occasion mixing in some chicken giblets. Then they would go out to the fields, where each of them had their tasks; while Carlos plowed and weeded and spread seeds, Star would remain vigilant for swampers, swoops, and creek cats. And just as Carlos had friends his own age—Chris and David Levin, Barry Dreyfus, and Wendy Gunther, with whom Carlos was becoming increasingly close—Star also saw the rest of the members of his pack, who'd also adopted Carlos's friends as their companions.

In the afternoon, once the chores were done and everyone had lunch, the teenagers would go to Dr. Johnson's house, where they spend the rest of the day in school; although the colony was still struggling to survive, it'd been decided that the kids would complete their education. This left the pack on their own, at least for a few hours. Some would find a sunny place to take a nap, while others would aimlessly roam Liberty looking for something to do. And some would go hunting.

Like Geronimo and Rayn, Star had developed a taste for swampers. He'd learned how to stalk them through the marshes that surrounded the settlement, catching their scent and following it until his ears picked the faint sound of them moving through the sourgrass. Geronimo and Rayn made good hunting buddies; for hours on end, they'd prowl the edge of Liberty, sometimes catching and killing as many as a half-dozen swampers a day. Star once tried brought one home to Carlos as a gift—after all, if they were good enough for him to eat, why shouldn't his human miss out on a good meal?—but Carlos didn't seem to appreciate the gesture, even though Star had thoughtfully decapitated the carcass on his behalf. Well, so much the better: just more for Star to eat.

One afternoon, their tracks took them further into the savannah than they'd gone before, beyond the tripod-mounted guns established in a broad oval surrounding Liberty. The perimeter guns were programmed not to open fire upon anything more than fifty-four inches in height, so the dogs were safe from them, yet they neglected the danger of what the guns had been set up to protect the colony against. And that was their undoing.

It was only luck that Star didn't catch the swamper-scent; he was investigating a grasshoarder nest, even though the tiny birds had already flown away. Yet Geronimo and Rayn had been searching the high grass only a few dozen yards away, their noses pressed close to the ground. When Rayn caught the smell of a swamper who'd just recently passed by, she bounded off in search of an easy catch, with Geronimo close behind. Star didn't know they'd left him behind until it was too late.

When he heard Rayn barking, he lifted his head, his ears perking up at the sound. From the timber of her voice, he knew that she'd just found something. An instant later, Star heard Geronimo bark as well...only this time, it was his battle-cry, something he'd seldom heard before. Star's ears flattened against his head. For a moment he hesitated, then he dashed into the grass, heading in the direction of his friends' voices.

By then Rayn's bark changed as well, becoming more louder, high-pitched. She was afraid. And Geronimo sounded less brave; gone was his fearlessness, to be re-placed by something more urgent. Even as Star heard it, he knew that Geronimo was calling for him.

He was almost within sight of his pack-mates when he heard a sharp, canine scream—Rayn's voice, raised in agony—that abruptly came to an end. Geronimo was still barking, more loudly than before, but now Star's nose caught a new scent: something darker, more threatening.

Star continued to barrel headlong through the tall grass. From the far distance, he caught the sound of human voices. For an instant, he thought he heard Carlos calling his name. He pushed this to the back of his mind, though, as he raced to his friends, even as clingberry bush caught at his fur and shards of grass filled his mouth.

Then, suddenly, he came upon Rayn and Geronimo. And the boid.

Six feet tall, the boid loomed over the two dogs At first, Star thought it was nothing more than a giant chicken—dun-colored feathers, small vestigial wings, backward-jointed legs—but its enormous, parrot-like beak, dripping with blood, was enough to bring him to a sudden halt. This was a creature he'd never seen before, indescribably terrifying, its scent hitting him like an awful wave.

Rayn lay at the creature's feet, her life-blood splattered across the trampled grass. It took a moment for Star to realize that her head had nearly been torn from her body. Geronimo stood his ground only a few feet away; his fur was raised, his eyes narrowed and his teeth bared, yet his tail tucked between his legs. Lunging forward, then retreating a few steps to bark again, Geronimo was gathering his courage to attack the creature towering before him, while the boid rocked back and forth on its spindly legs, its beady eyes studying the large furry thing that dared to challenge it.

Growling in fury, Star broke from the high grass. Startled, the boid turned its massive head and snapped at him. Star dodged to one side, avoiding its massive beak;

seeing that the boid was distracted, Geronimo hurled himself at the creature. His jaws sank into the side of the bid's neck; the giant avian screeched, and for a moment it seemed as if it was about to topple backward. But then it regained its balance; violently twisting its neck, it shook off Geronimo, sending him sprawling to the ground.

Then, before Star could do anything, the boid turned around, raised its right foot and, in one quick movement, slashed its talons across Geronimo's exposed belly. Geronimo howled as blood jetted from his chest and stomach; he trashed upon the ground, trying to escape even though he was already dying.

Star leaped at the boid. He managed to nip the back of the monster's leg; foul-tasting blood and feathers filled his mouth, and the boid screamed in rage. Turning back toward him, the boid snapped at him once more, yet Star was too quick; he raced away, his four legs propelling him into the high grass.

He stopped, turned around. Geronimo was still back there; he had to protect him. But then he heard the boid screech again, and an instant later it hurtled through the grass, coming straight at him.

Star turned and ran for his life, with the boid in hot pursuit. Any thoughts of fighting this thing vanished; escape was his only chance for survival. Yet the boid was just as fast as he was; the tall grass would hide him for a few seconds. So Star ran as fast as he could, heading in the general direction of the settlement.

Blades of grass whipped past his face, blinding him; he tasted dirt on his tongue, felt humid air burning his throat. From somewhere nearby, he heard Carlos's voice, calling his name. Despite his terror, though, Star didn't dare lead the boid to his companion. So instead he veered away from Carlos, cutting through the marshland even as he heard the boid thrashing through the sourgrass only a few feet behind him.

Star didn't know it, but his flight brought him within range of one of the perimeter guns. He heard a whirr and a click, then suddenly an angry mechanical chatter filled the air. Another screech from the boid, only this time in pain.

Star stopped, looked around just in time to see the monster stagger upon its long legs as bullets ripped through its body. Tawny feathers and pink blood spewed in all directions. The boid cried out once more, then it fell backward, disappearing within the grass.

Panting hard, Star cautiously went back to where it had fallen. He stared at the dead boid for a long time, waiting for it to stop twitching. Once again, he heard Carlos's voice. His companion was trying to find him. Star moved away from the boid and drudged through the grasslands toward his friend. He needed someone to take him in his arms and ruffle his fur, stroke his ears and tell him that everything would be all right, that he was safe.

But the boid's blood was still upon his tongue, warm and salty. He had the taste of the creature in his mouth, and its scent was fresh within his nostrils.

And somewhere behind him, Geronimo and Rayn lay dead.

✦✦✦

For the next several days, Star mourned the death of his friends.

So did the humans. Geronimo's and Rayn's companions retrieved their bodies from the grasslands and laid them to rest near the creek where they'd once frolicked. Yet as much as the two-leggers were upset by the savage demise of two favorite pets, their grief was nothing compared to that of the other dogs. Geronimo, after all, had been the pack leader; since their days in the puppy-pen, he'd been the alpha-male, the one to whom all the others deferred. And Rayn's death was even more tragic; only a few weeks away to giving birth to a new litter, her death signified the loss of a blood-line.

Dogs can't shed tears, or at least not as humans do, yet they can weep all the same. Instinctively, the remaining members of the pack closed together; although they continued to spend their nights in the homes of their companions, during the day they clung to one another, and were seldom apart for very long. No longer did they play tag or chase their tails, and when they followed their companions into the fields, it was only with great reluctance, their steps slow and their heads lowered.

Star was most disconsolate of all. For two days, he refused to leave Carlos's cabin, and even then only briefly, with his companion at his side. He ate only when he needed to, and without much appetite. Marie tried to interest him in playing fetch, yet he simply lay on his side, barely giving her a distracted thump of his tail when she'd toss a stick for him. When he slept, it was only fitfully;

nightmares, unremembered when he awoke, caused him to growl in his sleep and his paws to twitch.

With Geronimo gone, the role of pack leader fell to him, if only by default. When he finally came out of hiding, he found the others waiting for him. They looked him in the eye and sniff his anus, and their tails, half-lowered yet nonetheless erect, would swish back and forth; they were waiting for him to do something. And although his dreams were still haunted by the awful memories of his narrow escape, a new emotion gradually replaced fear.

Rage.

Early in the morning, when the rest of Liberty was still asleep, Star would wake up to hear the boids. The one that had killed Geronimo and Rayn was dead, and yet he could still hear the awful cries of his brethren, coming to him from across the grasslands. Carlos never awoke to see his companion, sitting upright on the end of his bed, staring through the open window at savannah bathed by the ghostly light of the ringed planet hovering high above, nor did he ever hear the low growl coming the dog's throat as he searched the night for eyes that he instinctively knew were also searching for him.

All the same, something changed within his dog. Carlos didn't know it, but he was no longer the happy-go-lucky mutt he'd adopted only a few months earlier. Deep within his small heart, there now lurked the soul of an avenger.

A war had begun.

✦✦✦

Early one morning, while Carlos was still getting ready for the day ahead, Star slipped out of the cabin. Most of the colonists were still having breakfast, so few people observed him, and those who did paid little attention to the small brown dog trotting down the dirt road leading through the center of town. At one point, Star heard Carlos and Marie calling for him; pausing for a moment, he glanced back in the direction of the cabin, wondering if he should be a *good dog* and go *home* (two human phrases which, with repetition, he'd come to understand). Yet he had a duty to perform, as dangerous as it may be, so instead he continued on his way, his head lowered and his tailing hanging low.

His steps brought him to the farm fields, and beyond its furrows of just-planted crops, the trackless grasslands into which he'd last ventured only a couple of weeks ago. Once again, he hesitated; for a moment, he remembered the fate he'd narrowly escaped, and with came an instant of fear. But he knew what needed to be done, so he quietly padded into the tall sourgrass, and began to hunt for the boids.

For hours he roamed the savannah, randomly moving back and forth through the high grass, his nose pressed close to the ground. It wasn't long before he passed the safe zone guarded by the perimeter guns; the weapons didn't even register his presence. The sun rose higher in the sky and the day became warmer; he slacked his thirst by drinking from puddles of tepid water he found here and there, then continued his quest.

Star was almost about to give up when his nose caught a now-familiar scent; rank and ugly to his senses, it could only be a boid. It grew faint as he followed it to the east, closer to Liberty; as he'd come to suspect, the boids approached the settlement at night, when there was no one to see them, but stayed just beyond sensor range of the perimeter guns. But when he followed the scent to the west, away from the camp, it became stronger.

So that was the direction from which they'd come. Moving carefully, much as if he was stalking a swamper, Star began to track the boid away from Liberty. Now and then he'd stop, sniffing the air as he raised his ears, peering into the grass for any unusual movements. He knew that the boids could be lurking anywhere, and that they could see him before he spotted them. He had to be careful now; his life depended on his skills as a hunter.

The scent took him deeper into the grasslands, past clusters of ball plants and sprawling stands of blackwood trees. Swampers scurried away from him, and he had to resist temptation to chase them. But the boid-scent continued to grow stronger with every step he took, until it was almost overpowering; he came upon a small pile of turds, dark brown and ropy. A quick inspection told him that it had been left by his prey. He was close now, very close.

The trail led him to a dense clump of clingberry bushes; it was hard to see past them, yet it seemed as if the grass didn't grow as tall past the bushes. Crouching low to the ground, Star slowly crept closer, until he was able to peer through the thicket. And there, within a small clearing where the grass had been trampled close to the ground, was a boid.

The creature rested upon a thick mound of grass and cloverweed, its long legs folded beneath itself; its head was lowered to its chest, and its enormous beak tucked halfway beneath one of its wings. Star studied it for several moments before he was realized that it was asleep; his mouth opened and his tongue lolled in satisfaction, but even that small movement was enough to cause the boid to stir. It sleepily raised its head and looked around, and Star froze, closing his mouth and remaining as still as possible. Satisfied, the boid went back to sleep.

Although he had the instinctive urge to attack the creature while its guard was down, Star knew that this would be unwise; the boid would become alert to his presence within seconds, and would kill him as soon as he got close. So he remained where he was, lying down upon his stomach while he continued to spy on his enemy.

After awhile, obeying instincts of its own, the boid woke up. Its head rose upon its long neck, and its beak opened to emit a high-pitched squeak that could only have been a yawn, then it slowly clambered to its feet. Turning around, it lowered its head again to peer closely at its nest. Then, apparently satisfied by what it saw, it marched off into the high grass, shoving through the clingberry bushes that hid its nest as if it was no more than a minor obstacle.

Star stayed where he was until he was sure that the boid was gone, then he raised himself from his belly and, ever so cautiously, eased himself through a break in the thicket.

Within the nest lay a half-dozen eggs, pale yellow and spotted with small reddish blotches, each nearly the size and shape of a football. Star had seen eggs before, in the coops where the chickens were raised; he'd also seen what came out when those eggs hatched, and once when he was a puppy he'd made the mistake of killing a few chicks, and had been spanked for it. But these eggs were different; they were not forbidden to him.

Carefully stepping into the nest, Star sniffed at the boid eggs for a moment, feeling their warmth with the tip of his nose. He prodded one with his right foreleg, and watched as it rolled over on its side. Then he opened his mouth, grasped it in his jaws, and clamped down hard. The shell resisted for only a moment before it shattered; he tasted yolk, oily and sour, and found something soft at its center. He tried to swallow the embryo, but it made him ill, so he vomited it and proceeded to the next egg.

It didn't take but a minute for him to destroy everything he found. A soft growl escaped his throat as he thrashed his way through the nest, crushing some of the eggs with his forepaws, biting others with his mouth. When he was done, Star raised his left leg and urinated long and hard upon the broken shells.

Then he leaped from the nest and dashed off into the tall grass, running as fast as he could for the safety of the settlement.

He'd just reached the safety of the nearest perimeter gun when, from the distance behind him, he heard an outraged shriek. Star stopped, gazed back in the direction in the direction from which he just come. He raised his hind leg again and pissed on the gun's tripod. Then, having marked his territory, he sauntered past the gun.

Revenge had never been more sweet.

Carlos was angry at Star for having disappeared all day, and scolded him when he finally returned home, yet the other members of the pack were impressed. One by one, they sniffed his fur with curiosity, catching the boid scent that lingered on his body; Star allowed Barney and Trixie to lick some of the yolk that had dried on his muzzle. These nonverbal clues revealed more than mere words could have possibly conveyed: Star had found a way to kill the boids.

And so, two days later, when Star once again stole away from the settlement, Barney, Trixie and Dexter went with him. Sally wanted to come along, too, but after much growling and many hard-eyed looks, she reluctantly stayed behind; as pregnant as she was, she was much too heavy to run fast.

The dogs went into the grasslands, and once again they picked up the scent of a boid and tracked it to a nest. This time, there was no adult guarding it; Star showed Barney, Trixie, and Dexter how to destroy the five eggs they found, then they fled back the way they came. But before they returned to camp, Dexter's nose picked up another boid-scent, and when they followed it, they came upon yet another nest. This one they demolished as well, and once again their work was undiscovered until after they reached the safety of the perimeter guns.

The dogs didn't know this—and neither did their humans, at least at the time—but they'd unwittingly timed their raids to coincide with the boids' annual spawning season, which occurred during the first month of Coyote's long summer. If they'd waited any longer, then the nests would have been filled with newborn hatchlings that would have also been guarded more closely by their parents. Yet since boids often left the unhatched eggs alone during the day in order to go hunting, they became easy targets for the dogs...and the boids hadn't yet adapted to the intrusion of four-legged aliens who could locate their nests through sense of smell and who, unlike swampers and creek-cats, hadn't learned to give them a wide berth.

Day after day, over the course of the next two weeks, the dogs sneaked away from Liberty during the early morning. It became easier to find the boid nests, but it was never less dangerous; more than a few times, a boid would spot them, and then they'd have to flee for their lives. But they presently learned how to detect the presence of the avians before the boids saw them; taking cover beneath clingberry bushes, they'd lay low until the creatures stalked past. They hunted as a pack, and never allowed themselves to be separated from one another.

As wars went, it was a silent one, conducted with secrecy and stealth. All the two-leggers knew of it was that the dogs would mysteriously disappear for hours upon end, only to come home late in the afternoon, their fur matted with clingberries. Star was often spanked by Carlos; he accepted his punishment with scarcely a whimper, frustrated that his human didn't understand what he was doing, yet satisfied by the quiet knowledge that he was protecting his companion.

And then, early one morning before the sun had risen, Star awoke to hear...nothing.

Climbing up on Carlos's bed, he gazed through the open window, listening intently to the cool breeze as it gently drifted across the savannah. For the first time in his life, he didn't hear the mating cries of boids, and although he stared long and hard at the grasslands, he didn't see hostile eyes reflecting the light of the ringed planet far above.

When Carlos awoke a few hours later, he found his dog curled up at his feet, sound asleep. Giving Star a fond scratch behind the ears, Carlos told him that he was a good boy; Star yawned and stretched, then fell asleep again.

The colonists were puzzled for awhile as to why the boids that once haunted the grasslands around Liberty were suddenly no more to be seen or heard. Believing that the creatures had learned to avoid the perimeter guns, they congratulated themselves for their technological ingenuity. Never once did any of them seriously suspect that the dogs had anything to do with it.

And the dogs, of course, kept their own secrets.

AN INCIDENT AT THE LUNCHEON
OF THE BOATING PARTY

I swear to you, it was an accident. I never intended to interfere with the past; indeed, I had been trained to avoid doing anything that might alter the timeline. It was just a fluke, a minor mistake. And it wasn't as if I changed history. Not much, at least.

Let me explain...

The night before, the *Miranda* dropped me on the outskirts of Chatou, a village on the Seine about fifteen kilometers southwest of Paris. The timeship was in chameleon mode when it made its brief touchdown; no one observed my arrival. After making my way into town, I took a room at a small inn, one which the advance team had already selected as appropriate for a young lady traveling on her own. My cover story, if anyone asked, was that I was from Orleans and on my way to Paris to visit my brother. No one at the inn was curious, however, and I spent the night unnoticed.

The following morning, I made a point of asking the innkeeper to recommend a place where I might have lunch. He told me about several cafes in town, but I pretended to be uninterested until he happened to mention the Restaurant Fournaise, located on a small island in the Seine near Chatou. Oh, but that's perfect! How may I get there? The innkeeper, being a proper host—who says the French are rude?—immediately sent a boy down to the waterfront to hire a boat for me.

It was a warm Saturday in late August, 1880; the first colors of autumn were upon the trees, and although the air was humid, nonetheless there was a breeze upon the river. As the oarsman paddled his rowboat toward the island, I caught sight of the restaurant: a three-story chateau, built of red brick and white limestone, rising above a small wooden pier where several sailboats and canoes had been tied up. A second-floor balcony overlooked the Seine, and I could make out several figures standing beneath its orange-striped awning.

I tried not to stare, even though I felt a rush of anticipation. Here was the place where one of the great masterpieces of European art had been—that is, would be—created. Yet I wasn't greatly concerned. After all, this was only a Class-3 mission: very low-risk, with minimal danger and little chance of affecting the timeline. Not at all like other historical surveys undertaken by the Chronospace Research Centre, such as the Class-1 expeditions to the Battle of Little Big Horn or the sinking of the *Titanic*. Indeed, it was only because Chief Commissioner Sanchez had a personal fondness for the 19th century Impressionist movement that I was allowed to undertake this sortie in the first place. Perhaps it wasn't as important as, say, witnessing the Kennedy Assassination, but nonetheless history would be served by whatever I managed to discover.

Reaching up to my hat as if to keep it from being snatched away by the breeze, I surreptitiously activated the recorders concealed within its band. From here on, everything that I saw and heard would be stored in memory. The oarsman helped me out of the boat, and I walked down the pier to the ground floor entrance.

The maitre'd met me at the door, inquired if I needed a table. Oh, no, I'm here to meet a friend for lunch. I believe I may be early, but we're supposed to rendezvous on the balcony. Raising an eyebrow, he smiled knowingly. *Oui*, of course. This way, please. And then he led me inside, escorting me up a flight of stairs and through the dining room, until we reached an open door leading to the balcony.

A long row of small, square tables, each covered with white linen, with wooden chairs arranged around each one. The maitre'd seated me at the end of the balcony, asked if I'd like some wine while I waited. Of course, *merci*. A short bow, then he vanished, leaving me alone.

Pretending to be a young mademoiselle waiting for the arrival of a gentleman friend, I gazed down the row of tables. Here and there, people were having lunch; they were casually dressed in the fashions of the period, the women wearing long dresses, the men in light cotton jackets. Upper middle-class Parisians, out for a weekend in the country: a morning spent rowing upon the Seine, followed by a leisurely lunch at the Fournaise. Chatting amongst themselves, they paid little attention to me.

At the far end of the balcony, an artist's easel had been set up. It held a large canvas, nearly two meters long by a meter-and-a-half wide; behind it were two tables, both set with plates, glasses, platters of grapes, and several bottles of wine, yet oddly vacant, as if a large party had recently been seated there, then suddenly vanished. Only two men were present: both in sleeveless white undershirts, each sporting a yellow straw hat. They were carrying on a conversation, one leaning against the railing with his back to the river, the other sitting on a wooden chair turned backward to the nearer of the two tables.

I knew who they were, of course, from my prior research. The man at the railing, the one with the beard: Alphonse Fournaise, the son of the restaurant's owner. And the younger man sitting nearby—that would be Gustave Caillebotte, an excellent painter in his own right, not to mention a wealthy patron of the arts who'd helped support many of his friends by buying their works, even when no one else would. Yet the artist himself was nowhere to be seen; he'd disappeared, leaving behind only a palette and a clay jar holding several damp brushes.

Here was my chance. Rising from my seat, I casually strolled down the balcony, my hands clasped behind my back, pretending to be idly curious. Neither man took notice of me as I drew closer.

The painting was still incomplete, but nonetheless it was immediately recognizable. More than a hundred years later, conservators at the Phillips Collection would submit the finished work to X-ray examination, and discover a charcoal undersketch beneath the surface, much like the first draft of a novel that had not been entirely erased during subsequent revisions. That was what I saw now: black-and-white drawings of figures, lacking definition, seated at the tables or standing in the background, like the ghostly afterimages of men and women who'd long since left the scene.

Yet the artist had begun to use his oils to fill in the details. At the right side of the painting, two men spoke to a woman in a black dress who cupped her ears with gloved hands, as if hearing an indecent comment she didn't appreciate. In the foreground to the left, a pretty girl played with an English terrier she'd put upon the table. Behind her, Alphonse leaned against the balcony, gazing in the direction of the woman with her hands against her ears; Alphonse struck that same pose even now, and it was then that I realized that the artist had been at work on his portraiture just before he'd left the easel.

The rest of the scene, however, still existed only as a rough sketch. There were charcoal smears here and there upon the canvas, where the artist had carefully adjusted postures, making one man in the far background a little shorter than the other, turning another woman's face toward the camera instead of away. And, yes, just as art historians suspected, the awning was missing; it would be added later, perhaps in the last stage of composition, to add a subtle balance to the painting. Seeing this, I couldn't help but smile. There was another sailboat on the Seine that would never be seen...

"Pardon, madam?" Alphonse had finally noticed me. "You find something amusing?"

"No, no...not at all." I hastily stepped back from the canvas. "I was...I was simply admiring, that's all."

He scowled at me, but Gustave grinned. "You like this?" he asked, half-turning in his chair to gaze at me. "It pleases you?" When I nodded, he looked back at his companion. "See? Just as I told you. The hell with the Solon. Art is meant for the people..."

"Explain that to Zola." Alphonse folded his arms across his chest. Until now, I hadn't realized just how muscular he was. He may not have been very handsome but, I had to admit, he had a nice body. "Claims that you and colleagues haven't produced any great work. Did you read what that idiot wrote about Claude's last show...?"

"Hush. Don't let Pierre-Auguste hear that." Gustave glanced at me again. "Don't mind us. We're just here to sit for a friend. He's gone off to answer the call of nature..."

"And I wish he'd hurry." Alphonse rolled his eyes in disgust. "How long does it take him to piss, anyway?"

I'm sure I blushed, but it wasn't because of the indelicacy of his remark. One by one, Pierre-Auguste's friends had come to this balcony, to pose for hours on end while he added their likenesses to his painting. The scene itself might have been imaginary, but the people in it were real. Even looking at the rough sketch, I could name them all. The actress Ellen Andree. The Baron Raoul Barbier. Charles Ephrussi, the editor of the *Gazette des beaux-arts*. Models and writers, journalists and politicians. Even his fiancée, Aline Charigot, who'd brought along her small dog.

He hadn't painted this scene all at once, though, but had brought them in for individual sittings, one or two at a time. It had taken weeks, perhaps months to get this far. And when he was away from the canvas, what they'd said behind his back...

Suddenly, a door opened behind me, "Alphonse, where's your damned sister? She was supposed to be here by now."

Looking around, I saw a young man walk out onto the balcony. Slender, of average height, he had deep-set eyes and a trim goatee that was beginning to grow bushy at the chin. His white smock was that flecked with daubs of paint, and his face was almost as red as the pigments on his fingernails.

"I have no idea." Alphonse removed his hat to wipe sweat from his forehead. "I told her that today was her turn, that she wasn't to be late..."

"Oh, for God's sake." Striding past me with scarcely a glance in my direction, Pierre-August walked to the railing, held a hand up against the sun as he gazed up at the sky. "I'm losing the light. What does she expect me to do, finish this in the studio?"

"Well, you could..." Catching the irate expression on his friend's face, Gustave wisely stopped himself. "I'm here. Go ahead and paint me. I've got nothing else to..."

"No. I'm sorry, but not yet. I..." Turning away from the railing, Pierre-Auguste clenched his fists in frustration. "I can't work that way," he said, patiently trying to articulate his thoughts. "There's a certain form, a certain process. Left to right, understand? I've already had to compromise once with Paul, Jeanne, and Eugene…I don't want to have to do it again."

Alphonse shrugged. "Well, look, the table's all set up." He gestured to the wine bottles, glasses and plates on the table between him and Gustave. "That's easy enough. You're finished with me. Now you could…"

"No! I wanted Alphonsine to be here today! I told her to be here, and now…"

"Well, then, damn it," Gustave said, "if you can't get Alphonsine, then use her instead."

And then he pointed to me.

I promise, I swear, I totally insist…if I could have cut and run, I would have done so. All I had to do was back away, claim that I had another engagement, find some sort of excuse…

But I didn't. To this day, I don't know why. Maybe I was caught up in the moment. Perhaps it was only vanity. It might have even been because this was the way history intended it to be. I don't necessarily believe in predestination, yet nonetheless you have to take it into consideration. It may have been that I was simply meant to be there.

In any case, I didn't refuse. Pierre-Auguste was peeved that his chosen model didn't show up when she was supposed to, so he turned to the nearest woman he could find. I went to the railing and struck the pose that he'd intended for Alphonsine in his charcoal sketch: leaning forward, with my right hand cupping my face and my left arm draped across the railing, my eyes turned toward the empty chair where the Baron would be seated. Alphonse stood nearby, glaring at me because I'd taken his sister's place in the composition. Gustave drank wine and told raunchy stories about various members of Parisian high society that made it difficult for me to maintain the coy smile that Pierre-Auguste wanted.

The session lasted most of the afternoon. When it was over, the artist offered to pay me a fee for my services. I demurred, however, and beat it out of there before anyone thought to ask my name. The maitre'd was a little surprised that I left before my lunch companion arrived, but I suppose that it wasn't the first time he'd seen a girl stood up by a date.

And that's how I came to be in *The Luncheon of the Boating Party*, considered today to be one of the great works of the Impressionist period. Some art books state that the young lady in the middle-background is Alphonsine Fournaise, while others say that she's an "unidentified woman." Commissioner Sanchez was furious with me when I returned to the 24th century, and after the Review Board completed its investigation, I was no longer allowed to participate in historical missions for the CRC.

To be honest, though, it matters little to me. It's a magnificent piece, and I like to think that I was a better model than Alphonsine. And now I know what it was like to pose for a painting during a summer afternoon in a restaurant near Chatou and, for just a little while, to gaze into the eyes of Renoir.

—for Elizabeth Steele

THE TEB HUNTER

"The trick," Jimmy Ray says, "is not to look 'em in the eye."

The truck hits a pothole just then, jouncing on its worn-out shocks and causing stuff to skitter across the dashboard: shotgun shells, empty chewing tobacco cans, wadded-up parking tickets ignored since last May. A little plastic bear swings back and forth beneath the mirror; Jimmy Ray reaches up to steady it, then glances back to make sure nothing has come loose in the rear bed. Satisfied, he takes a swig from the box of Mountain Dew clasped between his thighs.

"That's why I don't take kids," he continues. "I mean, it's just too much for 'em. My boy's too young for this anyway...next season, maybe, after he gets a gun for Christmas...but a couple'a years ago, I tried taking my nephew. Now Brock's a good kid, and...hang on..."

Jimmy Ray twists the wheel hard to the left, swerving to avoid another pothole. A can of Red Man falls off the dashboard into my lap. "Gimme that, willya?" I hand it to him; he pops the lid off with his thumb, gives the contents a quick sniff, then tucks it in his hunting vest. "Like I was saying, Brock's bagged a couple'a deer with no regrets, but I got him out here and he took one look at 'em, and that was all she wrote. Just wouldn't shoot, no matter what. Fifteen years old, and here he is, bawlin' like a baby." He shakes his head in disgust. "So no kids. This is man's work, if you know what I mean."

The woods are thick along either side of the dirt road, red maples shedding their leaves, tall pines dropping cones across the forest floor. We slow down to pass over a small bridge; the creek below is fogged with early morning mist, its clear waters rushing across smooth granite boulders. Jimmy Ray slurps the last of his Mountain Dew, then tosses the empty box out the window. "God, what a beautiful morning," he says, glancing up through the sunroof. "Great day to be alive." Then he winks at me. "Less'n you're a teb, of course."

Another quarter-mile down the road, he pulls over to the side. "'Kay, here we is." The door rasps on its hinges as Jimmy Ray shoves it open; he grunts softly as he pries his massive belly from behind the wheel and climbs down from the cab. Another few moments to unrack his rifle from the rear window—a Savage .30-.06 bolt-action equipped with a scope—before sauntering over back to the back of the truck. The canopy window sports stickers for the NRA and a country-rock band; he throws open the hatch, then pulls a couple of bright orange hunting vests and the six-pack of Budweiser .

"Here. You can carry this." Jimmy Ray hands me the beer. He reaches into his jacket pocket, produces a laminated hunting license on an aluminum chain; briefly removing his dirty cap to reveal the bald spot in the midst of his thick black hair, he pulls the chain around his neck, letting the license dangle across his chest. He removes the chewing tobacco from of his pocket and uncaps it, then pulls out a thick wad away and shoves it into the left side of his face between the cheek and his teeth. He tosses the can into truck, slams the hatch shut "Hokay," he says, his inflection garbled by the chaw in his mouth, "les' go huntin.'"

About fifteen feet into woods, we come upon a narrow trail, leading east toward a hill a couple of miles away. "Got my blind set up that way," he says quietly. "We may come up on one'a them 'fore that, but it won' matter much. This is real easy, once y'know how to do it. All y'need is the right bait."

We continue down the trail. We're a long way from the nearest house, but Jimmy Ray is confident that we'll find tebs out here. "People git sick of havin' 'em 'round, so they drive out here, set 'em loose in the woods." He turns his head, hocks brown juice into the undergrowth. "They figger they'll get by, forage for berries and roots, that sort of thing. Or maybe they think they'll just up and die once winter kicks in. But they 'dapt to jus' 'bout any place you put 'em, and they breed like crazy."

Another spit. "So 'fore you know it, they're eatin' up everythin' they can find, which don't leave much for anythin' else out here. An' when they're done with that, they come out of the woods, start raidin' farm crops, goin' through people's garbage…whatever they can find. Hungry lil' peckers."

He shakes his head. "I dunno what people find cute about 'em. You wanna good pet, you go get yourself a dog or a cat. Hell, a fish or a lizard, if that's your thing. But there's something jus' not right 'bout tebs. I mean, if God had meant animals to talk, he would'a…" He thinks about this a moment, dredging the depths of his intellect. "I dunno. Given 'em a dictionary or sum'pin."

Jimmy Ray's not particularly careful about avoiding the dry leaves that have fallen across the trail, even though they crunch loudly beneath the soles of his boots. It's almost as if he wants the tebs to know he's coming. "Talked once to an environmentalist from the state wildlife commission," he says after awhile. "Said that tebs are what you call a weed species…something that gits transported into a diff'rent environment and jus' takes over. Like, y'know, kudzu or tiger mussels, or those fish…y'know, the snakeheads, the ones that can walk across dry land…that got loose up in Maryland some years ago. Tebs are jus' the same way. Only diff'rence is that they were bio…bio…whatchamacallit, that word…"

"Bioengineered."

"Thas'it. Bioengineered…so now they're smarter than the average bear." He grins at me. "'Member that cartoon show? 'I'm smarter than the average bear.' I sure loved that when…"

Suddenly, he halts, falls silent. I don't know what he's seen or heard, but I stop as well. Jimmy Ray scans the forest surrounding us, peering into the sun-dappled shadows. At first, I don't hear anything. Then, just for a moment, something rustles within the lower limbs of a maple a couple of dozen yards away, and I hear a thin, high-pitched voice:

"Come out and play...come out and play..."

"Oh, yeah," Jimmy Ray murmurs. "I gotcher playtime right here." He absently caresses his rifle as if he's stroking a lover, then glances back at me and grins. "C'mon. They know we're here. No sense in keepin' 'em waitin'."

A few hundred yards later, the trail ends in a small clearing, a meadow bordered on all sides by woods. The morning sun touches the dew upon the autumn wildflowers, making the scene look like a picture from a children's storybook. And in the middle of the clearing, just where it should be, is a small wooden table with four tiny chairs placed around it. Kindergarten lawn furniture, the kind you'd find at Toys R' Us, except that the paint is beginning to peel and there are old bloodstains soaked into the boards.

"Hauled this stuff out here two seasons ago," Jimmy Ray says, pushing aside the high grass as we walk toward it. "Move it around, of course, and clean it off now and then, but it works like a damn." He smiles. "Learned it from *Field and Stream*, but this part is my idea. Wanna gimme that beer?"

I hand him the six-pack; he rips the tops off the cartons and carefully places the them on the table. "Book says you should use honey," he explains, his voice a near-whisper, "but that's expensive. Bud works just as well, maybe even better. They can smell the sugar, and the alcohol makes 'em slow. But that's my little secret, so don't tell anyone, y'hear?"

The bait in place, we retreat to a small shack he's put up on the edge of the clearing. No larger than an outhouse, the blind has a narrow slit for a window. The only decoration is a mildewed girlie poster stapled to the inside wall. Jimmy Ray loads his rifle, inserting four rounds in the magazine and chambering a fifth, then lines up five more sounds on a small shelf beneath the window. "Won't take long," he says quietly, propping the rifle stock against the window sill and focusing the scope upon the table. "First one saw us, so now he's tellin' his friends. They'll be here right soon."

We wait silently for nearly an hour; Jimmy Ray turns his head now and then to spit into a corner of the blind, but otherwise he keeps his eye on the table. The shed is getting warm and I'm beginning to doze off when Jimmy Ray taps my arm and nods toward the window.

At first, I don't see anything. Then the tall grass on the other side of the clearing moves, as if something is passing through it. There's a soft click as Jimmy Ray disengages the safety, but otherwise he's perfectly still, waiting patiently for his prey to emerge.

A few moments later, a small figure crawls into a chair, then hops on the table. The teb is full-grown, nearly three feet tall, its pelt black and soft as velvet. Its large brown eyes cautiously glance back and forth, then it waddles on its short hind legs across the table until it reaches the nearest beer. Leaning over, the teb picks up the carton, sniffs with its short muzzle. Then its mouth breaks into a smile.

"Honey!" it yelps. "Oh boy, honey!"

Jimmy Ray steals a moment to wink at me. Honey is what tebs call anything they like; either they can't tell the difference, or more likely their primitive vocal chords are incapable of enunciating more than a few simple words which they barely understand, much the way a myna bird can ask for cracker without knowing exactly what it is.

Now more tebs are coming out of the high grass: a pack of living teddy bears, the result of radical reconfiguration of the DNA of *Ursus americanus*, the American black bear. Never growing larger than cubs and bred for docility, they're as harmless as house cats, as friendly as beagles. The perfect companion for a child, except when people buy them for all the wrong reasons. And now the woods are full of them.

"Honey! Oh, boy, honey!" Now the tebs are clambering onto the chairs, grabbing the beer cartons between the soft paws of their forelegs and draining them into their mouths. A perfect little teddy bear picnic. They're happy as can be, right up until the moment when Jimmy Ray squeezes the trigger.

The first bullet strikes the largest teb in the chest, a clean shot that kills it even before it knows it's dead. The teb sitting in the next chair hasn't had time to react before the back of its head is blown off; the first two gunshots are echoing off the trees when the other tebs begin throwing themselves off the table, squeaking in terror. Jimmy Ray's third and forth shots go wild, but his fifth shot manages to wing a small teb who was a little too slow. It screams as it topples from its chair; by now the rest of the pack are fleeing for the woods, leaving behind the dead and wounded.

"Damn!" Jimmy Ray quickly jams more four more rounds into the rifle, then fires into the high grass where the tebs are running. "Quick lil' bastards, ain't they?"

He spits out his chaw, then he reloads again before slamming open the shed door and stalking across the clearing to the table. He ignores the two dead tebs, walks over to the one he wounded. It's trying to crawl away, a thick red smear against the side of its chest. Seeing Jimmy Ray, it falls over on its back, raises its paws as if begging for mercy.

"I...I...I wuv you so much!" Something it might have once said to a six-year-old girl, before her father decided that keeping it was too much of a hassle and abandoned it out here.

"Yeah, I wuv you too, Pooh." And then Jimmy Ray points the rifle muzzle between its eyes and finishes the job.

We spend another half-hour stalking the surviving members of the pack, but the other tebs have vanished, and before long Jimmy Ray notices vultures beginning to circle the clearing. He returns to the picnic table and checks out his kills. Two males and a female; even though he's disappointed that he couldn't have bagged any more, at least he's still within the season limit.

So he ties their legs to a tree branch, and together we haul the three dead tebs back his truck. Jimmy Ray absently whistles an old Lynyrd Skynyrd song as he dumps two of the corpses in the back of his truck; for the hell of it, he lashes the body of the biggest one to the front hood, just to give him bragging rights when he drops by the bar for a quick one on the way home.

He's pleased with himself. Three pelts he can sell to a furrier, some fresh meat for his dogs, and another head for the collection in his den. Not bad, all things considered. He climbs into the truck, stuffs some more Red Man into his face, then slaps a CD into the deck.

"But y'know what's even more fun?" he asks as he pulls away. "Next month, it's unicorn season. Now there's good eatin'!"

Then he puts the pedal to the metal and away we go, with a dead teddy bear tied to the hood and "Sweet Home Alabama" blasting from the speakers. It's a great day to be alive.

MOREAU²

Carson and Mariano were the sole survivors of the crash; everyone else was killed. Upon later reflection, Phil would realize that the only reason why he and George made it through was that they had been in the back of the spacecraft; the military lander had come down nose-first, so the pilot and co-pilot died instantly, and the two Marines from the 4th Space riding in the forward section of the passenger compartment were crushed when the cockpit bulkhead collapsed upon them.

So it was all a matter of luck, really. If the seating arrangements been reversed before they departed Olympus Station, if the Pax Astra heatseeker the pilots were trying to avoid before they lost control had made a direct hit, if the craft had rolled over upon impact, if its fuel tanks had exploded...no sense in trying to second-guess fate. They were alive, and that's all there was to it.

But Mariano was unconscious, and when Carson pulled him from the wreckage he noticed that his right leg was twisted at a bad angle. Phil didn't know enough first-aid to help him even if he wasn't wearing a moonsuit; at least his suit was still intact, and when Phil pushed back George's helmet visor, he saw a white smudge of vapor against the faceplate. That's when he knew for certain the photographer was still among the living.

Burying the dead was pointless. The pilots were entombed within the craft, and he would have wasted precious air attempting to dig graves for the two Marines in the lunar regolith. When Phil climbed back into the lander to see if he could salvage anything useful, he found a helmet resting a couple meters away from the moonsuit to which it had once been attached. It took a few moments for him to realize that the helmet wasn't a spare, and the significance of the red ice frozen around the suit's collar ring. He turned away and took several deep breaths, and somehow managed not to get sick.

Some reporter he was: he couldn't remember the names of the soldiers who'd died.

Pulling a seat cushion out of the ship, Phil lashed George to it with a safety belt, then found some severed electrical cables and used them to fashion a crude harness. He also found an undamaged carbine, but decided against taking it; if he was picked up by a Pax squad, carrying a weapon might invalidate his status as a non-com. He located Mariano's camera bag, and as an afterthought he looped its strap around the photographer's neck. If he knew George, he'd throw a fit if he woke up to find that his rig had been left behind.

The electronic compass on his helmet's heads-up told him which direction was west. He pulled up a map overlay, and discovered that the dead volcano upon the horizon was Sosigenes. He had no idea how far away it was; he'd already been warned that ground distance was difficult to determine on the Moon. With any more luck, they might be able to reach it before their air ran out. And, after all, Sosigenes had been their destination in the first place....

So off he went across the Sea of Tranquility, trying to avoid the larger rocks in his way as he dragged Mariano behind him. One-sixth gravity helped a little bit, but not much; the stretcher prohibited him from making bunny-hops, and after awhile it didn't seem as if there was any real difference. At first he maintained radio silence, for fear that any transmissions might bring another missile down upon him, until he realized that the radio was his only real hope of being rescued before his air supply was used up. So he switched it back on and toggled to the emergency band. No one responded to his calls for help, though, and soon he was singing "Little Red Rooster" over and over, just to keep him himself company. It was the only song he could remember offhand, but his father had sung it with his platoon during Gulf War II, and just now it seemed appropriate.

About an hour after he left the crash site, Phil caught a faint flicker from the corner of his eye. He turned to look, and saw a bright starburst above the southern horizon. A moment later, he spotted another one, like distant fireworks on the Fourth of July. Then he glimpsed tiny pinpricks of light racing across the sky, low to the ground in the approximate direction of Arago Crater, and realized what he was witnessing: a battle between the Pax Astra Free Militia and the 4th Space Infantry.

Too bad he didn't know how to operate George's camera. It would have made an excellent shot to accompany his dispatch from the front. If he lived to write it, that is.

Phil was within sight of the long, deep rill separating him from Sosigenes, and was beginning to wonder how he was going to get around it (and trying to forget the fact that he had less than fifteen minutes of oxygen left; he hadn't checked Mariano's suit lately, so he had no idea whether his companion was alive or not) when he saw something moving several kilometers away. At first he thought it was a sunlight reflecting off the silver-gray dust that marred his visor, but as he watched it became a white object, kicking up fantails of regolith as it skirted boulders and small impact craters.

A rover.

Dropping the stretcher, Phil began jumping up and down as high as he could, waving both hands above his head. That wasn't a good idea; besides the fact that he used up more air that way, he was also exhausted. As the rover swerved toward him, the sole of his left boot came down on a rock; Phil lost his balance tumbled to the ground.

The back of his head smacked the inside of his helmet, and that was the last thing he felt for a good long while.

✦✦✦

Like so many conflicts before it, the Moon War began with a press conference.

The OTV from the Cape carrying the twenty members of press pool arrived at Olympus Station at 1100 hours. Phil was already there, of course; as a UMI stringer, he had living aboard Skycan for the past four months, filing stories about the breakdown of diplomatic relations between the Pax Astra and the spacefaring Earth nations. Fat lot of good it had done him; as soon as the U.N. Security Council voted in favor of the U.S.-backed resolution authorizing military action against the Pax, orders came down from the Civil Space Administration to quarantine the operations center in the station's hub.

Joni Lowenstein, Skycan's general manager, had been apologetic about the whole thing. "Nothing personal, Phil," she'd said during their brief discussion after he'd discovered he was no longer welcome in MainOps. "It's just that CSA…" she pronounced it as *see-saw* "…doesn't want any leaks. Don't worry, you'll get the details when your buddies show up."

The clampdown blew away any chance of him scooping the competition. The only people who knew exactly what was going on were sequestered from the rest of the station, and when Phil tried logging into Olympus's computer from his bunk terminal, he found that the back door he had secretly installed eight weeks ago had been deleted. Joni probably knew about it all along.

So he filed a brief dispatch describing the news blackout, a story which someone allowed to be sent because it contained nothing really new, and a half-hour later a desk editor at UMI's Washington bureau replied with a terse message: *Story thin. Try harder. Understand situation, but you've got the ball. Mariano arriving soon: hook up with him.*

So he monitored the net, which told him little that he didn't already know—the Pax Astra embargo against shipments of He³ in retaliation against the U.N.'s refusal to formally recognize the Pax as an independent nation, followed by the shoot-down of an American lunar spysat, which in turn lead to an emergency meeting of the Security Council and the subsequent declaration of hostilities—and impatiently waited until, eighteen hours later, twenty journalists who'd won the straw-pull to represent the hundreds of reporters, photographers, cameramen and talking heads left behind came climbing or falling down the ladder into Module 39, one of the station's two rec rooms.

Phil watched their arrival with quiet amusement. His buddies. Right. There were perhaps two dozen reporters working the space beat these days, but most were posted either in Descartes City or in Clarke County, the big Lagrange colony. Of all the major net services, UMI alone had decided to put someone on Olympus. The station had once belonged to Skycorp, but when the powersat construction program had ended, the company had sold the station to a Japanese consortium, and when Uchu-Hiko failed to make it work as an orbital hotel, they had passed it off to CSA; the station was too big to deorbit, but too expensive to properly maintain, and so now it was just a ring-shaped hulk wasting away in geosynchronous orbit. His colleagues thought he was nuts for taking this backwater assignment; the real action was clearly further out in system, with the Mars colonies being the assignment everyone wanted. But Mars was claiming neutrality, and now the Pax was deporting correspondents from Descartes and Clarke County while censoring dispatches from the small handful allowed to remain.

So UMI had something of jump on the competition. With the rest of the space press sent packing, the only reporters able to cover the story were groundsiders hastily mustered from bureaus in Washington, London, and Rio. Not only was UMI's man already on the scene, but he was also long-since acclimated to Olympus. And even though he was out of the loop, at least Phil had the pleasure of watching his "buddies" come aboard.

If the thunder and shudder of the shuttle launch, or the long ride to GEO aboard an orbital transfer vehicle, hadn't been enough already to blow their professional cool, the gentlemen of the press were thoroughly rattled by Skycan's one-third gravity. Some looked distinctly green, while others experienced the wonders of Coriolis effect for the first time; Phil watched as a woman absently dropped her data-pad on the nearest table, then gape in surprise as it missed the table completely and fell to the carpeted floor below.

One of the last people to clamber down the ladder was a squat, thick-set guy with a heavy gray beard, wearing a photographer's vest over a New York Dodgers sweatshirt. A little less ruffled than the rest of the pack, he was still noticeably pale, the sparse hair on the crown of his skull slick with sweat. Phil had to stare at him for a minute before he was sure who he was.

"George!" He whistled and raised a hand. "Hey! Mariano!"

The photo glanced around, spotted him, trudged over to where Carson was seated. "Phil Carson," he said, dropping his camera bag in an empty chair. "How the hell are you?"

"Better than you, I think."

"No kidding." George picked up his bag again, sat down. "What am I doing here?"

"Covering another war. Didn't they tell you?"

"Oh, yeah. Right." George grimaced. "Swear to God, I had to fight my way onto this junket. Arm-twisting, extortion, major bribes...and what happens soon as we reach orbit?"

"You threw up."

"Threw up, threw down, threw out..." He pulled a bandana out of a vest pocket, swabbed his forehead. "Turned fifty last week. Haven't been up in nearly six years. Man, I'm too old for this shit."

Phil grinned. When he met Mariano shortly after he started working for UMI, George had already been an old space hand, covering stories both on Olympus and the Moon. Mariano had shown him the ropes, then asked for reassignment to the Florida bureau. Now here he was, a few kilos heavier and a few less hairs on his head, called back into the saddle one last time...

"Jeez, it's nice to see you again."

"Yeah, yeah." George glared at him. "Knock it off. I hear you're having trouble."

"Max Q. News blackout as soon as the story broke."

"Pentagon?"

"I'm told it's CSA who set the rules."

"They don't call the shots in something like this. At least not directly."

"Well, whoever it is, they're not saying word one. Not until the briefing, at any rate."

"Screw the briefing. I want meat." George unsnapped the top of his bag, found a tiny valve, and gave it a twist. An airtight membrane deflated with a soft hiss and the bag sagged slightly, then he unzipped the inner cell. "Get me to where the action is, that's all I want. When do we ship out?"

Phil shrugged. "Your guess is as good as mine. The military hasn't arrived yet, so my guess is that the GM will handle the briefing."

"Lenny Baskin?"

"Uh-uh. He got replaced a long time ago. The new boss is Lowenstein. Joni..."

"I know Joni. Nice lady. Have you heard anything?"

"Nada. You?"

"A little." Mariano pulled out a Nikon, fitted a 50mm lens onto its body, unwrapped a disk and slid it home. "4th Space mobilizing at the Cape, 2nd Space on Matagorda Island. Nothing confirmed, of course, but we've got reports that they're about to launch, if they haven't already. My guess is that they'll go for a..."

"Here comes Joni now."

The GM descended the ladder. An old Skycorp vet, Joni Lowenstein was in her mid-sixties, but only her butch-cut gray hair and the crows-feet around her eyes revealed her years; otherwise, she could have been a woman half her age. Conversation died off as she strode to the end of the compartment room and sharply clapped her hands. "If I can have your attention, please," she called out, "we'll begin the briefing."

Cameras whirred and clicked, reporters switched on datapads. A TV crew jostled their way to the front of the room and hastily set up their equipment. Joni obviously didn't want to be here; she shuffled her feet, looked like she wanted to disappear, yet she patiently waited for everyone to find their places before opening her pad and reading aloud a formal press statement.

Most of the facts were already known. At 1800 hours GMT, Tuesday, January 16, 2052, a surveillance satellite placed in low orbit above the Moon by the United States was destroyed by a missile launched from Descartes City in the lunar highlands. This was followed by a communiqué from the Pax Astra stating that the spysat constituted unlawful infringement of its territory. Since the U.N. hadn't recognized the Pax Astra as a sovereign nation, the Security Council had invoked the 1967 Space Treaty and unanimously approved the American resolution proposed that the embargo and shootdown constituted an act of aggression against the signatory nations.

"So the situation is as follows. The United States, under U.N. authorization, has decided to reclaim Descartes City." Joni checked her notes again. "Five hours ago, one hundred troops from the 4th Space Infantry, U.S. Marines, were mobilized from the Kennedy Space Center, with forty more troops from the 2nd Space on standby at the

ConSpace launch site on Matagorda Island. The assault will be staged from here, Olympus Station, where the forces will be loaded aboard lunar landing vehicles provided by various American and Japanese corporations, with logistical support from the European Union. The LLVs are scheduled to depart GEO within a launch window which is still classified. The objective is a frontal assault against Descartes City within a time-frame that is also classified at this time."

Joni lowered her pad. "I'll take questions now," he said. "Please identify yourself and the news organization you're representing."

There was the usual coughing and shifting through scribbled notes before the first reporter stood up. "Dale Hale, *Time-Global*. It hasn't been adequately explained why the Pax Astra would shoot down a U.S. spysat. Have they yet explained their reasons for doing so?"

"The Pax government stated that the satellite was an incursion of the…um, airspace, for lack of better term… above Descartes. They stated that the sat was put there with the sole intent of monitoring their movements in preparation for a military attack. The Pentagon has categorically denied this. Next question."

Fingers gently tapped keypads. The compartment grew warm under the glare of camera lights. Joni swabbed sweat from her forehead; she seemed too aware that, even as she spoke, her image was being transmitted in real-time to hundreds of thousands of websites. The handful of reporters gathered here were little more than data-collectors and question-askers, acolytes of the church of information. With only the most insignificant of delays caused by satellite downlink and AI-augmented language translation, her words were being disseminated to billions of terminals scattered across the world below. For a few brief minutes, she'd become the most visible person on Earth. Phil felt sorry for her. He liked Joni, yet even if he didn't, no one should have to endure this sort of exposure except a trained PR person. Most of them were professional liars; Joni wasn't.

"Ellie Horowitz, *San Francisco Chronicle-Examiner*. Why is the U.S. task force concentrating on Descartes when the Pax Astra government is based in Clarke County?"

"I don't know the reasons and…um, I'm not in the position to speculate."

"Does this have anything to do with the fact that Clarke County is reported to be in possession of a nuclear weapon?"

"I'm sorry, but I can't comment on that. Next question, please."

Mariano leaned over. "Geez, lady, do a little research, why don'cha?"

Phil nodded. A direct assault on Clarke County was out of the question; all the colony had to do was close its airlocks and docking bays, and it was virtually invulnerable, unless the U.S. was willing to kill ten thousand civilians by blowing the windows of its habitat sphere. Besides, the colony had a ten-megaton nuclear warhead it had salvaged during the revolution from a low-orbit satellite intended to deflect the Icarus asteroid several years earlier. The Pax only had to lob its nuke at any approaching spacecraft, and the 4th Space was toast. Descartes City was far more vulnerable. Clarke County's lifeline was lunar oxygen and water; if Marines seized Descartes, then the Lagrange colony would have little choice but to surrender.

"Bet they're going use Tranquillitatis as the LZ," Phil murmured, and George nodded. No argument there. Mare Tranquillitatis lay just west of the highlands: a vast, flat plain, perfect for a large-scale troop deployment. But, of course, the Pax would know this…

The press briefing lurched on. Skycan would be used as the command-and-control center for the invasion— now officially called Operation Lunar Freedom—until a beachhead was successfully established on the Moon. Beyond that, nothing new was disclosed. Joni answered questions one of two ways: *no comment*, or *we can neither confirm nor deny this information*. Phil impatiently waited for someone else to ask the most obvious question. When no one did, he finally raised his hand. Joni seemed reluctant to acknowledge him, but she pointed his way

"Phil Carson, United Media," he said, rising from his chair. "When will the press be allowed to visit the landing site?"

Joni looked as if she'd like to toss him out the nearest airlock. "Under the current conditions, there are no plans to let the press accompany the strike force. We can't allow…"

Everyone in the room groaned. "We can't allow civilians to place their lives in jeopardy," she continued, raising her voice. "All members of the press will remain aboard

Olympus, where it will observe the operation from the closest safe-distance possible. We'll accommodate any reasonable request..."

"So far you're doing a hell of job!" someone shouted from the back of the room.

"Why don't you let us decide whether we're capable of taking that risk?" someone else asked.

"Ladies, gentlemen, please..." Joni raised a hand. "I realize that many of you are accustomed to covering wars, but you've got to understand that this isn't South America or the Middle East. This is the Moon we're talking about here, as hostile an environment as you're going to find. You're simply not trained for this, and we don't have the time to teach you how to wear moonsuits or handle an emergency like a blowout."

Low murmurs. She had a point; they were all groundsiders; for many this was their first trip into space. "Then send me," Phil said. He felt Mariano nudge the back of his leg. "George, too," he added. "Both of us are EVA certified. We've moonwalked before."

"Will you work under pool rules?" This from Horowitz of the *Chronicle-Examiner*.

Phil glanced at George. The photographer shrugged. "Sure," Phil said. "We'll share any interviews or photos we get to the rest of the pool." He looked back at Joni. "That way you only have to send down two guys, but everyone up here gets a piece of the action."

"Fair enough," said Hale from *Time-Global*, and the rest of the poll murmured their assent. "How 'bout it, Ms. Lowenstein?"

Joni shook her head. "Sorry, folks, but the military's pretty clear about this. Absolutely no one goes out who isn't combat personnel or support crew."

"Ah, c'mon!"

"It's not my call. You want to fight this, take it up with the Pentagon PAO when he gets here." She closed her pad. "That's all for now. Next briefing will be here at 0800 tomorrow. This compartment is now designated the newsroom, and Modules 36, 37, and 38 have been set aside as your quarters. You may link your pads with the terminals here or in the bunkhouses, and the com officer will transmit your reports when sat time is available. All meals will be served in the mess deck, modules 25 through 28. All other areas of the areas of the station are open to you except the data processing center and MainOps. I should warn you that, if you attempt to visit these areas without authorization, your credentials will be voided and you'll be sent groundside on the next available OTV. Do you have any questions about these policies?"

Some rumbles, a few obscene comments, but no arguments. Nor was Phil surprised. No one was going to buck the system. Getting shipped home during a breaking story was worse than humiliating; reporters have been fired for less. One of the eternal problems of war correspondence is that the military draws the line wherever it damn well pleases, and there's little anyone can do about it.

"Nice try," George said when the briefing was over. "I could have told you she wouldn't go for it."

Joni had climbed back up the ladder, dogged by a couple of die-hards desperately trying to catch any crumbs of information she might drop. Others hastily typed up their dispatches; lines were already forming in front of the terminals scattered around the room. The TV crew was breaking down their equipment. Someone complained about not being able to smoke.

"Maybe we can get the PAO to change his mind." Phil wearily took his seat again. "If we talk to him when he gets here…"

"Ever dealt with a Pentagon public affairs officer?" George asked, and Phil shook his head. "Don't count on it." Then he dropped his voice. "Look, I've got some connections. I'll fire off a squib, see if I can shake something loose. Are you going to be around?"

As if he was going to skip out to the nearest deli for a Reuben and a beer. "Naw. I think I'll head down to my bunk. Send a memo to New York, catch a few winks. I've been up for the last twenty hours straight."

"Okay. If I learn anything, I'll find you."

"Module 38, bunk 6." He stood up. "I've got a private link. Carson-386. Got it?"

"Uh-huh. Get some sleep, kid. It's going to be a long war."

He had been in bed only four hours when his node buzzed. Rolling over in his curtained bunk, he fumbled for the wall terminal. "Carson."

"Phil, it's Joni." No image on the tiny flatscreen, just her voice.

He pushed back the blanket, sat up as much as he could
without banging his head on the ceiling. "What's up?"

*"Can you come up to MainOps? I want to talk to
you about something."*

"Sure. Be there in five."

*"Okay. The guy at the hatch knows you're coming.
And Phil...? This is on the Q.T."*

Five minutes later, he was floating weightless in the
core shaft of Olympus's hub module, clinging to a handrail and waiting for the command center hatch to open.
Ten meters below his feet, he could see the airlock module. An orbital transfer vehicle had docked a few minutes
earlier, just as he was coasting through the access tunnel
from the rim modules; a couple of Skycorp crewmen were
helping several men in cammies crawl through the hatch,
and he had passed two military officers while climbing up
the ladder from the rim. The Marines had landed.

The hatch opened and a soldier with sergeant's chev-
rons on the shoulders of his jumpsuit peered at him. There
was a taser holstered to his belt, and he looked mean
enough to chew nails and pissed off that he had none.

"Phil Carson, United Media."

Without a word, the Marine moved out of his way, and
pushed the hatch shut behind him. MainOps was a long
cylindrical compartment designed without deference to
gravity: duty stations above one another, with chairs fixed
on either side of open-grid decks so that one crewman's
head was often upside-down next to another's shoulders.
The command center was dimly-lit by flatscreens and
recessed fluorescent tubes; the only sounds were the

electronic chitter of computers, and the soft voices of men and women strapped into chairs before workstations.

"Carson. Up here."

Phil looked up, spotted Joni seated in her alcove. Someone was with her, but he couldn't tell who it was. "Coming up," he replied, then he grabbed the fireman's pole running through the center of the compartment and pulled himself along it. It wasn't until he reached her station that he saw who else was there.

"What took you so long?" Mariano asked.

"Rush hour." He was mildly surprised to see George. "What, there's a shortcut I don't know about?"

"I was shooting the soldiers coming aboard when I got the call." He gently pushed aside the camera dangling loosely on its strap; Phil noticed the lens was capped. "Nice to be here," he said to Joni, "but I wish you'd relax the rules a bit."

Joni shook her head. No apology offered, no explanation required. No one wanted to risk a net photo of MainOps being enhanced and studied by the opposition. "You'll get all the pictures you want," she said. "If you cooperate, of course."

"What sort of cooperation are you talking about?" Phil asked.

"Just a moment." Joni cupped a hand around her headset mike, murmured something. "We'll have company in a second," she said. "Make yourselves comfortable."

Phil found an unoccupied foot restraint, slipped his feet within its stirrups. A few meters away was the traffic control station; peering over the shoulder of the duty officer, he noticed a half-dozen or more blips moving slowly around the three radial bars of the radar screen. Military OTVs, no doubt, holding orbit around Olympus while men and materiel were transferred aboard the station. Operation Lunar Freedom was shifting into high gear.

Someone floated next to him; Phil turned to see a thin, fox-faced man in his late fifties. The shoulder patch of his cammies bore the rocket-and-lightning bolt insignia of the 4th Space, but the four stars sewn to his collar was what caught his attention.

"Gentlemen," Joni said quietly, "General Errol Ballou, the CO of this operation. General, this is Phil Carson and George Mariano, both from United Media."

Carson and Mariano caught each other's eye. The commanding officer in charge of Lunar Freedom. Whatever this was about, it wasn't going to be on the same lines as the press conference a few hours earlier.

Gen. Ballou didn't smile as he shook their hands in a perfunctory way. "Gentlemen, this meeting is off the record. Anything we discuss here is on deep background. No publication, no attribution. Mr. Carson, I trust you're not recording this."

"Uh...no. No, I'm not." He pulled his datapad from his pocket, held it up to show that its LED was dark. Joni extended her hand; Phil hesitated, then surrendered the pad to her. She checked to make sure it was switched off, then gave it back to him.

"Thank you, sir," Ballou said. "We're on a tight schedule, so let's make this short. I'm told that you've volunteered to cover the ground phase of the operation."

"Yes, sir, we..." Phil's voice was a dry croak; he cleared his throat. "Excuse me. George and I have been on the Moon before, both of us, so we've been certified for..."

"I know. We've checked your records just to make sure that you weren't trying to put one over. At least thirty hours of moonwalks, each of you."

"So I...uh, I take it you're interested in our proposal," Mariano said.

"More or less." A short silence; Ballou seemed to be sizing them up. "You're better qualified to cover the ground phase than your colleagues," he said at last. "But I'm still unwilling to put the two of you into a combat situation. When our forces touch down at Mare Tranquillitatis we're not expecting a quiet stroll. Our intelligence indicates the Pax will be expecting us, and we'll probably have to fight our way to the Descartes highlands."

So Phil's guess was right; they were planning to make Mare Tranquillitatis the landing zone "However," the general continued, "I'm put in the position of having to balance your personal safety against the public's right to know why we're doing this. You two are best suited for the job, and you've offered to represent the press, and that's why I'm sending you to the Moon."

"Thank you, sir," Phil said. George murmured the same.

Ballou shook his head. "Don't thank me yet, guys. You haven't heard the rest."

✦✦✦

Warm darkness. The low background hum of a air-circulation system. The sound of bare feet padding across plastic tiles.

He opened his eyes in time to see something move past tiny red and blue lights. A door opened, allowing a shaft of light to enter the room, then a small figure—a child?—darted through the door. It closed again, and once more he was alone.

Phil felt around himself; his hands moved across a thick blanket until they found the edge of the bed. He raised his left hand to his chest, discovered that he was naked under the covers. He focused on the tiny lights: the readouts of a medical monitor.

"Lights on," he murmured, and ceiling panels flickered to life. He squinted, raised a hand to his eyes. He appeared to be in an infirmary: white-painted mooncrete walls lined with cabinets, a small sink in the corner, an oxygen mask dangling from a hook above his bed. There was a slight soreness in the crook of his left arm; looking down, he noticed a small bandage on the inside of his elbow. Yet there seemed to be nothing wrong with him; he was weak, but otherwise uninjured.

Phil carefully climbed out of bed. The room was much colder now that he was out from under the covers. Rubbing his goosepimpled arms, he looked around for clothing of any sort, even if it was only a surgical robe. Finding nothing, he pulled the blanket off the bed and wrapped it around himself.

Next order of business was finding the head. A door on the other side of the room led to a tiny water closet; he relieved himself in a bare steel commode, and noted that, when he stepped away, only a minimal amount of water was squirted into the bowl as it automatically flushed.

He stepped out of the w.c., went to one of the cabinets, opened it and found a pack of bandages. He held it at shoulder height, then let it go. The pack fell straight down, but slowly; it took almost two seconds to hit the floor.

"I wish you wouldn't play with the medical supplies, Mr. Carson. They're rather scarce just now, and can't be easily replaced."

He looked around. In the small room, the filtered voice sounded as if it was coming from everywhere at once. "Sorry. Just trying to figure out if I was still on the Moon." He scanned the ceiling, searching for the lens of a hidden camera.

"You've deduced that fact by yourself." The voice was male, somewhat young, but with a European accent and not the quasi-Southern drawl of a loonie. It came from a small grid near the door. Phil still couldn't find the lens.

"Well, thanks for bringing me here...wherever here is." Although he had a good idea.

"You're welcome. Oh, stop looking for the camera. It's located behind one of the ceiling panels...I forget which one, but it's there."

"Sort of figured as much."

"If you'll be patient, I'll come meet you. I imagine you want some clothes, too."

"If it's not too much trouble."

"None at all. Be there soon."

"Sure. Okay." He sat down on the edge of the bed. As an afterthought, he picked up the bandage pack and put it back where he'd found it. A few minutes later, he heard footsteps coming down the corridor. The door opened again, and his benefactor stepped into the room.

Tall, slender, only a few years older than Phil himself. Narrow-boned face, sallow complexion, thin blond hair brushed straight back from his angular forehead and tied behind his neck in a short ponytail. Wearing a white lab coat over an old brown sweater. There was a bundle of clothes beneath his arm.

"Good morning. I trust you're well rested."

"Can't complain. Is it morning?"

"Only in a manner of speaking. It's still midday local time, but the last time I checked the clock, it was 0900 GMT." A quick smile. "Time's not something I much pay attention to down here." He dropped the clothes on the bed next to him: drawstring trousers, a pullover shirt, underwear, moccasins, a pair of 10-kilo anklets. "Hope they fit. I had to guess your size."

"Thanks." Phil picked up the trousers; a little long for him, but better than wearing a blanket. "Guess you're the guy who found me...found us, I mean. Where's...?"

"Your friend? Safe and sound." He nodded toward the clothes. "Get dressed, that's the first step."

Carson stood up, picked up the underwear. He half-expected the other man to modestly turn away, but he didn't. "So...uh, where am I?"

"Sosigenes Center. A small research facility near Sosigenes Crater, maintained and staffed...at least until recently…by a certain Earth-based company. Don't you want to get dressed?"

"Yeah, sure." He turned his back, shrugged off the blanket, stepped into the underwear. He felt the stranger's eyes upon him. "Located underground, I guess."

"What makes you think that?"

Phil felt his face grow warm. He was glad that he had turned away from the other man. "Nothing. Just a hunch."

"Ah. So. Yes." Each word a distinct syllable. "Yes, we're located underground. Thirty meters, to be exact. This facility was built within lava tubes, with only a few components on the surface. Airlock dome, garage, solar farm, and so forth…everything else is down here."

The trousers fit better than he expected, although he had to roll up the cuffs a few centimeters to keep them from dragging on the floor. "What sort of research?"

"Biological. Aren't you concerned with other things first?"

A bio-research lab. Ballou's information had been correct. Phil turned around, picked up the shirt. "My friend. His name's George Mariano, and he's…"

"A news photographer, yes. Just as you're a journalist." A small nod. "George is safe. He's in the next room, being treated for his injuries. A broken leg, mild concussion, shock…. he's undergone nanosurgical therapy, though, and he's regained consciousness. We'll soon be joining him soon."

"So you know who we are."

The other man chuckled. His discomforting gaze didn't waver as Phil pulled the shirt over his head. "Of course. The first thing I did after bringing you down here was download your suits' memory chips. You're both correspondents, covering the war for United Media International. I take it that you were separated from your unit."

"Our lander was shot down. It crashed about thirty klicks west of here. George and I were the only survivors." The shirt fit better than the pants. "So you were driving the…?"

"The rover you spotted, yes. It wasn't necessary for you to jump and down like that. I saw you as soon as you entered the outer perimeter. You're quite brave, hauling your friend on a stretcher all that way. Very commendable, given the circumstances."

"Circumstances?"

"Neither of you had more than fifteen minutes of oxygen left. You wouldn't have made it here on your own. It was only fortunate I happened to be scanning the area. When I picked up your radio signal, I came out to retrieve you." He paused, and then added: "If you'd left him behind, you wouldn't have used up so much oxygen."

"Never occurred to me."

"Indeed."

Silence fell between them as Phil pulled on the moccasins and fastened the ankle weights. The more he thought about what his benefactor had just said, the less he liked him. Nor did he appreciate being studied; at first he thought it might be sexual interest, but now he realized that it was more clinical in nature, as if he was an interesting specimen.

"What's this about?" Phil gently peeled aside the bandage he'd found on his arm; there was a small puncture mark within his elbow, surrounded by a yellow disinfectant stain. "Did you inject me with something?"

"Only glucose. You were rather dehydrated when I found you. I took you off IV a while ago."

"Uh-huh." Glancing around, he spotted a post with an empty plastic sack dangling from it. "Since you know our names, maybe you'd like to tell me yours."

Hesitation. "Moreau. You can call me Moreau."

"Just Moreau?"

"Yes."

"So, Mr. Moreau…"

A dry chuckle. "Dr. Moreau, if you please."

Something tugged at his memory, but he couldn't quite place it. "Dr. Moreau, how many people are at this facility? Besides yourself, I mean."

"I'm here alone." For the first time since he entered the room, Moreau turned away. "Sosigenes usually supports a staff of fifty people…researchers like myself, for the most part…but when the Pax learned that an invasion was imminent, the others were evacuated to Descartes. I volunteered to remain behind and make sure that none of our ongoing experiments were disturbed."

Phil frowned. "You know, I could be wrong, but…"

"Yes?"

When I woke up, I thought I saw a child leaving the room. Didn't you just say that you were alone? But he didn't voice his thoughts. "Never mind. Do you have any idea what's going on out there? The invasion, I mean. I saw something that looked like a battle…"

Moreau kept his back turned to him. "I'm afraid it's come out badly. Most of the Marines were killed, the rest routed from Mare Tranquillitatis. Major casualties among the Free Militia as well, but the Americans suffered worse."

"Damn." Then he remembered where he was. "Of course, that means your side won. Shouldn't you be…?"

"Pleased?" A long sigh; Moreau folded his arms across his chest, lowered his head. "War isn't a game, Mr. Carson, regardless of however much we may pretend otherwise. Our violent tendencies are the worst attribute of the human species. You might view it otherwise, but personally, I grieve for the lives lost today, regardless of whose side they were on."

It was the first thing Moreau had said in the last few minutes that Phil believed. The man might be a liar, yet first and foremost he was a humanist. "No argument there. There's stories I'd rather cover than a war."

Moreau glanced over his shoulder. "Really? A story more significant than war?"

"Is there something more significant?"

Moreau smiled. "Let's look in on your friend. Perhaps he's ready for a bite to eat. After that…well, we'll see."

Mariano was in the next room, sitting on an examination table as he carefully pulling his drawstring trousers over the semirigid plastic cast that encased his right leg. Moreau took a few moments to examine him. "The compound fractures in your femur and patella have been rejoined," he said, "but it's still new bone. You'll need to avoid putting any weight on your leg for a couple of days. I'll see if I can find something for you to use as a cane."

He left the room, leaving Phil alone with George. There was an uneasy silence; George didn't seem to want to look at him. "Guess I should say thanks," he murmured. "I'd probably be dead now if it weren't for..."

"Forget it. You would have done the same for me."

"Don't count on it," he replied, but it was with a wry smile. George winced as he pulled a shirt over his head, then peered at the bandage on his left arm. "What the hell?"

"Glucose on IV. He said we were suffering from dehydration."

"Swell. So what do you make of this place? Think this is what Ballou was talking about"

"Could be. It's in the right location, near Sosigenes Crater. Or at least that's what Dr. Moreau just told me."

"Who?" Phil repeated it, and George shook his head. "Yeah, right. I'm sure that's really his name."

"Why don't you think so?"

"Haven't read H.G. Wells, have you?" George raised an eyebrow. "And you call yourself a writer. But it does give us a clue as to what's going on here."

"He said it was bio research, but he didn't..."

Footsteps outside the room. Mariano raised a finger to his lips just as Moreau reappeared, carrying an titanium walking stick of the sort used by lunar hikers. "This should help a bit," he said, handing it to George. "I imagine you're both hungry. If you'll follow me, I'll take you to the commissary."

The corridor was narrow and circular, winding its way around what appeared to be a central core. It was deserted, or at least so far as Phil could tell; all they could hear was a low hum from the ceiling air vents. The doors they passed were shut, but he noted that they were all coded with numbers that began with the digit 3. Moreau noticed his curiosity. "Sosigenes Center is a new facility," he explained. "My company built it just a few years ago, and until now it's been...well, not that well known."

Carson glanced at Mariano; the photographer gazed back at him, his eyes wide. As General Ballou had told them, the lab was secret. Yet if it was, Moreau was being unusually candid about its existence, particularly in the presence of two journalists. "So what sort of work have you been doing here?" Phil asked, wondering just how far he could take the line of query.

Moreau didn't say anything at first. He strolled ahead of them, slow enough for George to keep up with him. "At first it was principally agricultural," he replied after a moment. "We were developing ways of genetically engineering new species of various crops...corn, wheat, soybeans, and so forth...for easier cultivation in a low-gravity environment." He plucked at the sleeve of his sweater. "Our first success was with *Cannabis sativa*. We managed to develop a new strain that yields taller plants in lunar conditions. Your clothes, for instance, are made from lunar hemp."

"Superpot." Phil nodded. "I heard of it. Raised a ruckus back on Earth."

"Back in America, you mean. Your country has such idiotic drug laws..."

"So this place is owned by GenSyn."

Moreau turned to look back at him. "Yes. Sosigenes Center was built by GenSyn. I take it you've heard of us."

Too late, Phil realized that he'd tipped his hand. "I remember the net stories," he replied. "Some people think you...your company, I mean...want to export drugs to Earth."

Moreau chuckled. "If that was our intent, then we would have made more money than we did from raising superpot. Please, Mr. Carson, put away your tabloid mentality. This isn't some redneck meth lab."

Ballou thought it was; that was why he'd allowed them to accompany the advance team, to check out intelligence reports of a GenSyn facility near Sosigenes that was manufacturing illegal drugs for the Pax, which in turn was smuggling them to Earth in order to finance the revolution. Since GenSyn was based on Clarke County, then it was the sort of thing that the military wanted the media to show to the folks back home. Bad enough that the Pax was stopping the supply of He^3 to fusion tokamaks on Earth; now they were also involved in drug trafficking.

He only had Moreau's word to go on, yet Phil had no reason to believe that he wasn't telling the truth.

Otherwise he wouldn't have brought them here. "My apologies. I was only…"

"Accepted." Moreau continued walking down the corridor. "At any rate, Sosigenes was quite small then, but then we began to branch out into investigating certain aspects of the human genome, and so it became necessary to expand our facilities. This is the third-lowest of four subsurface levels, and it was completed just three years ago…ah, here we are."

He stopped at a door marked COMMISSARY. Pushing it open, he called for the lights; the ceiling illuminated, revealing a large room filled with tables and chairs. "I'm afraid the menu isn't very good," Moreau said as he led them to a dispensary along one wall. "Shipments of fresh food stopped a couple of weeks ago, and we've…I've had to make do with what's already in stock."

Phil wasn't about to complain. His last decent meal had been aboard Olympus; the only food he'd had since then had been cold-ration packs aboard the military lander. He inspected the glass doors of the dispensary until he found a vacuum-wrapped tomato and cheese sandwich and what looked like a slice of apple pie.

"Looks like you've had company lately," George said.

At first he didn't see what George was talking about, then Phil saw what he'd failed to notice before. Halfway across the room, a table was littered with discarded wrappers and empty juice cartons. The chairs had been pushed back, as if the people sitting there—six at least, perhaps more—had suddenly left, without bothering to clean up after themselves.

"I thought you told me you were alone," Phil said.

Moreau quietly stood off to one side, either unable or unwilling to reply. Phil walked over to the table: fresh bread crumbs, and one of the juice cartons was half-empty and still cool to the touch. It looked like the sort of mess a bunch of kids might leave behind, as if expecting an adult to come along later and pick up for them.

"I hope you're not going to tell me this is all yours," George said. "You don't look like the sort of person who can't keep the place clean."

"No," Moreau said quietly, "I'm not."

"So who else is here?" George hobbled over to the nearest table; leaning his stick against a chair, he sat down and began unwrapping the sandwich he'd selected. "Don't mean to be rude, but..."

"All the same, I'm afraid you are." Moreau folded his arms across his chest. "Gentlemen, there's a limit to my hospitality. I think I've answered all the questions I care to, at least for now. Please eat, then I'll escort you to your quarters."

Phil glared at George. For a little while there, it seemed as if Moreau was going to open up, tell him the truth. Then Mariano had come in with a hard line of questioning; caught in a lie, Moreau had retreated into silence.

George refused to look at him; he realized his mistake. The two men ate in silence, while Moreau stood quietly nearby, not saying anything to either of them. Perhaps GenSyn wasn't making drugs. Nonetheless, Moreau was hiding something.

+ + +

Down the corridor from the commissary were a row of dorm rooms. Small and tidy, nonetheless they appeared to have been recently vacated. Pieces of tape on the walls above the desk in Phil's room showed where the last occupant had hung up photos, and in the drawer he found a few pens and some scrap paper. Although the closet was empty, the bed was still made, and there was toilet paper and a half-dissolved bar of soap in the adjacent bathroom.

The desk held a comp terminal. Once Moreau left, bidding him a good night, Phil did his best to keep awake for a little while longer. His eyelids itched and his body craved sleep, yet there were too many questions that needed to be answered, so he sat down at the desk, pulled out the keypad, and began a line of inquiry.

Moreau must have figured that he would do this, because every keyword he typed into the search engine drew unhelpful results. SOSIGENES gave him an orbital photo of the crater itself and nothing more, and GENSYN rendered standard P.R. material such as annual company reports and recent press releases, none of which mentioned a lunar research lab. He tried to access the net, only to find that he was completely locked out; UNAUTHORIZED USER appeared when he tried to patch into the LunaNet server. So there was no way he could send email, or even logon to a news site to find out what was going on.

Finally, he typed in another word: MOREAU. The response was a link to a text within the library system:

THE ISLAND OF DR. MOREAU, by H.G. Wells. So Mariano was right; Moreau had borrowed the titular name of a character of a novel published in the late nineteenth-century. Yet perhaps might be a clue here; moving his chair a little closer, Phil began to read:

I do not propose to add anything to what has already been written concerning the loss of the Lady Vain. *As everyone knows, she collided with a derelict when ten days out from Callao...*

He tried to keep up with the story for as long as he could, yet it wasn't long before his vision began to blur. He was more tired than he thought. Phil book-marked the text and shut down the terminal, then undressed and removed his anklets before crawling into bed. He was asleep as soon as he told the room to turn off the lights.

How long he slept, he didn't know; he might have remained asleep for many more hours if the door hadn't creaked open, if a ray of light hadn't passed across his face, if he hadn't felt a small, warm hand upon the side of his neck...

He jerked awake, flopped over on his back to see a small form standing next to the bed, captured in silhouette by the light from the corridor.

"Lights on!" he yelled.

The figure squealed in terror, then Phil's eyes were dazzled by the abrupt glare from the ceiling. In that half-instant, he saw what appeared to be a child—long-haired, almost naked, with strangely elongated arms and legs— dart from the room.

Phil whipped aside the covers, lunged for the door. Too late, he remembered that he wasn't wearing his weights; in one-sixth gravity, he sailed out the door into the corridor. He yelped as his left shoulder hit the wall; from somewhere just ahead he heard high-pitched laughter.

Looking up, he caught a brief glimpse of the intruder: no more than a meter in height, wearing nothing more than a pair of briefs. A pair of large eyes peered at him from beneath a mane of hair, then the figure turned and fled, chortling as it dashed down the corridor. Just before it vanished around the bend, it performed a cartwheel, like a mischievous child showing off...

"The hell?" Mariano appeared in the doorway of the next room, holding himself erect with his stick. He squinted against the light. "What are you...?"

"C'mon!" Ignoring the fact that he was wearing only skivvies, Phil scrambled to his feet and rushed down the corridor.

This time he was careful not to bound, but instead kept his momentum in a forward direction, taking advantage of lower gravity to turn his run into a headlong sprint. He reached the place where he'd last seen the child, just in time to see a door on the inner side of the corridor slam shut.

Phil skidded to a halt. George came up behind him, hobbling on his stick. A sign on the door read AUTHORIZED PERSONNEL ONLY—DO NOT ENTER, yet the knob turned freely when he tested it. He glanced back at Mariano, and the photographer shrugged. "Your call," he whispered. "I'll say we didn't see it."

Phil nodded, then he opened the door and they stepped inside.

A vast, well-like atrium, one so large that they could barely make out the far side. A volcanic bubble, Phil guessed, restructured to form the station's core. Twenty meters above them, earthlight slanted down through thick panes of polarized glass, illuminating a miniature rain forest. Palmettos crowded each other for room, their fronds casting shadows across the ferns and tall grass that grew upon the atrium floor, their vines curled around the supports of upper-level walkways. From somewhere within the branches, they could hear the disturbed cries of songbirds.

Phil's eye caught something resting in the grass, a spherical object. Stepping closer, he kneeled down to examine it: a red-and-white rubber ball, the sort of thing one might find in a kindergarten playroom. And not far away, another toy: a stuffed koala bear, missing one of its eyes.

He reached down to pick it up, and something struck the back of his head.

"Hey!" he yelled, then looked around to see a stick lying next to him. From somewhere up in the trees, a muffled giggle, followed by another one from close by.

A palm nut hit the ground near George. "Man, I don't like this," he murmured as he stepped back toward the door. "This place is giving me the…"

"Hush." Phil slowly stood up. "They're just kids. All they want to do is play." That gave him an idea. "Go over there," he added, motioning toward a clearing a few meters away. "Don't act frightened…just do it."

George gingerly walked in that direction, his eyes never leaving the dense foliage around them. Phil bent over, picked up the ball. Some murmurs from the tree-tops. "Okay, catch," he said, then tossed it to George.

Mariano caught it one-handed, still leaning heavily upon his stick, then glanced anxiously at the sound of muted laughter from just behind him. "All right," Phil said, "now throw it back to me. And smile...we're having fun."

George reluctantly returned the ball to him. Now there was more laughter, a little closer this time. Another palm nut landed on the ground, but this time it wasn't close enough to be threatening. "That's right," Phil said aloud. "Just a couple of goofy ol' guys, having a game of catch. Here y'go..."

He threw the ball to George again, but this time he fumbled and the ball dropped to his feet. George started to lean down to pick it, then stopped. "Phil," he said softly, nodding to his left, "behind you..."

Phil slowly peered over his shoulder. A child was swinging upside-down from a tree branch. At first he thought it was the same one he'd seen in his room, but then he noticed that its hair was lighter in color, almost blond...

No. *It* was definitely a *she*. About five or six, judging from her height. Yet other anatomical differences weren't nearly so subtle. Her arms were almost as long as her legs, and her toes were nearly as long as her fingers; they were wrapped around the branch, allowing her to suspend herself upside-down. Although her rib-cage looked larger, her frame was so slender that Phil could have wrapped his hands around her stomach and been able to touch his thumbs and forefingers.

Yet it was her eyes that surprised him the most. Twice normal size, with dark-blue irises nearly the size of quarters; when she blinked, he caught a glimpse of nictitating membranes, like a second pair of eyelids.

Utterly alien...and yet, without question, a little girl, and a charming one at that. "Throw!" she demanded, and grinned as she extended her hands. "To me! Throw!"

Phil looked back at George. "You heard the lady," he said, stepping aside. "Throw her the ball."

At first, it seemed as if George hadn't heard him. He was frozen in place, staring at the girl with eyes almost as large as her own. Behind him, another child appeared upon a low branches: nearly identical to the first, except this one was a boy, possibly the one who'd visited Phil's room. George didn't see him; he retrieved the ball and tossed it to the girl, but it was a clumsy pass and she shouldn't have been able to catch it.

Yet she did. Even before the ball was halfway to her, she swung herself off the branch, performing a somersault so graceful that it would have awed an gymnast, and touched down in plenty of time to catch it. She laughed with glee. "Thank you!" she cried, then she spun around to pitch the ball high into the air, in what seemed to be a random direction.

Another child hurled himself from the top of a palm. He grabbed the ball, yet for a moment it seemed as if he was going to fall to his death. "Got it!" he yelled, then his left foot snagged a vine, and he whipped around to hurl the ball toward a second girl, who shrilled laughter as she deflected it with her right foot, straight into the hands of the boy who'd been lurking behind George.

He dropped to the ground in front of the astonished photographer. "Again!" he yelled. "Harder! Too easy!"

George was barely able to catch the ball. "I don't...I don't..." He stared at Phil. "What...I don't...who the hell are...?"

"They're my children, Mr. Mariano." Moreau's voice echoed down from above the jungle, where he stood upon a walkway near the ceiling. "So to speak. If you wish, though, you may call them Superiors."

The fourth level of Sosigenes Center was inaccessible except by a single elevator, which could only be opened by keycard and retinal scan. Once they were dressed, Moreau led Carson and Mariano to the Advanced Genetic Engineering Facility; much to their surprise, he requested that Phil bring his pad and George his camera.

"Why are you doing this?" Phil asked as Moreau escorted them down an empty corridor. "Why tell us now?"

"No point in denying it, is there?" Moreau's hands were clasped behind his back. "It wasn't my intent to reveal this to you, or at least not when I brought you here. In fact, I'd hoped that, once Mr. Mariano..."

"George." Mariano was loading a fresh film disc in his camera. "Call me George, please." He hesitated, then added, "And what should we call you, Dr. Moreau? And don't tell us that's your real name."

A smile brushed his lips. "Sorry. I should have known better." He glanced at Phil, making sure that his pad was turned on. "Dr. Laurent Marquand," he said, and spelled it for him. "Director, Project Tango Red."

"Uh-huh. And what is Project...?"

"One question at a time, please." Moreau—or rather, Marquand—held up a finger. "First, why am I doing this? As I was saying, I have no choice. I thought that once Mr. Mariano's leg healed, I'd be able to have you out of here before you saw anything you shouldn't. In fact, I've already summoned a rover from Descartes. It's on its way now, and should be arriving within a few hours."

"That's...very gracious of you." Phil had no idea how they'd be treated by the Pax. Hopefully not as prisoners of war. "But if you didn't want us finding out..."

"But alas, you did." Marquand let out his breath. "One of my children...figures it would be Vladimir, since he's always been the most inquisitive...saw to that when he disobeyed me by paying you a visit. Twice, in fact."

"Guess he was curious." Phil couldn't help but grin. "Typical six-year-old."

"Six?" Marquand gave him a sidewise look. "Is that how old you think he is? What would you say if I told you that's he's little more than two years old?"

Phil stopped walking. "That's impossible. I was playing ball with him just a few minutes ago. He was..."

"The size of a child three times his age, and with the reflexes of a teenager." Marquand made an impatient gesture. "We're getting ahead of ourselves again…I hoped you'd leave before you saw any of them, but you did anyway. That limits my options, doesn't it? The only choice I have is to tell you everything, and hope that you'll use that knowledge in the responsible manner."

By now they'd arrived at a door marked with an alphanumeric sequence: GHS-413. Marquand slipped his card into the slot, then bent a little closer to let the scanner examine his right eye. A double-beep, then the door slid open. "Gentlemen, if you will…"

They entered a small alcove, a viewing area just large enough for the three of them. A vault door was on the opposite wall, but Marquand walked instead to a large, double-paned window. The room on the other side was pitch-black, save for tiny red and white lights of instrument panels and the faint blue glow of flatscreens.

"The great problem of the exploration of space isn't hardware-related," Marquand continued. "For a long time, it seemed that way…we had to invent efficient means of leaving Earth, and once that was done we had to learn how to build space stations, and then how to use the resources of the Moon and Mars to keep ourselves alive. And so we did so, step by step, over the course of generations, yet the greatest single obstacle hasn't been development of reliable spacecraft, but something much more obvious, yet nonetheless so subtle that we overlooked it for nearly a century."

Marquand patted his chest. "It's this…the human body itself. *Homo sapiens* are perfectly suited for life on Earth, but our flesh betrays us once we venture in space.

Our bones become brittle, our muscles too weak to sustain once we return to Earth unless we constantly exercise or build ships that spin to provide artificial gravity. Our eyes are adapted for only a narrow spectrum of light, and our lower limbs are almost useless in microgravity. So we surround ourselves with redundant layers of technology, praying that none of them fail, hoping that one day we..."

He stopped himself, briefly shutting his eyes as if to gather his thoughts. "Hundreds of millions of years ago," he went on, "an aquatic animal squirmed out of a stream somewhere on Earth and, for a brief seconds, learned how to breathe open air. Over the course of time, other creatures learned to do the same thing. All well and good, yet evolution is a slow process, taking eons to achieve its most favorable results. Yet we have the way to accelerate the process..."

"And this is what you're trying to do here," Phil said. Behind him, he heard the click of George's camera.

"No." Marquand shook his head. "We're not trying anymore." And then he touched a button on the console beside him.

Ceiling panels on the other side of the window flickered to life, revealing row upon row of horizontal glass tanks. The closer ones were empty, their instrument panels dull and blank, yet the ones farther away were filled with a milky substance, and suspended within them were fetuses in various stages of development.

"Superiors," Phil murmured.

"Personally, I prefer the term *Homo astronauticus*, but the rest of the team thought that *Homo superior* was a more apt term, so...well, yes, that's their species name now. Or Superiors, for short."

"Oh, Christ..." George moved closer to the window, shooting from as many angles as possible. "I don't believe this...I don't friggin' believe this..."

"What don't you believe?" Marquand asked. "That we've accomplished this?"

George lowered his camera; there was horror and disgust in his eyes as he regarded the tanks. "That you'd take...that you'd take babies and turn them into...into these freaks..."

"I don't think you understand," Marquand seemed puzzled. "These specimens were created *in vitro*...cloned from tissue samples donated by team members. They're not the result of normal human procreation."

"Even worse," George murmured.

Phil was surprised. For as long as he'd known George, he'd never heard him express any anti-cloning sentiments. Perhaps he'd simply never expressed them to him. Marquand stared at them both, more appalled than embarrassed. "Go on, please," Phil said. "You began with tissue samples..."

"DNA restructuring began in the cellular stage of development, long before the specimens reached fetal stage. We spent the first three years designing a genetic blueprint, gradually perfecting it until we obtained the desired results." Marquand typed into a keypad; anatomical charts appeared on the window. "Lighter bones with much less potential for long-term calcium loss. Skeletal changes such as double-jointed limbs and greater dexterity for the hands and toes. Greater respiratory capacity coupled with an improved cardiovascular system. Increased resistance to cancer, diabetes, rhinoviruses, and other common illnesses." He pointed to a three-dimensional cutaway of an eye. "The eyes, of course, are an obvious feature...the cones of their retinas are more sensitive, their irises expanded significantly, making them capable of seeing in the dark."

"I saw one of them blink. It...she...looked like she had a second pair of eyelids. Is that to protect their eyes in strong light?"

Marquand smiled. "Yes, but that's only a secondary consideration. This is actually our most revolutionary achievement." He pulled up another image; fine wires led through a tiny socket in the nape of the neck, connecting to a tiny package within the back of the skull. "See this? A microprocessor nanosurgically implanted within the cerebral cortex. Technically, it's called a MINN...Mnemonic Interfaced Neural Network...but we call it an associate."

"A computer in the brain?"

"Yes. One gigabyte onboard memory. But more importantly, it enables the children to interface with computer systems within their environment...Sosigenes's own AI, for instance. We've just begun tutoring them in how to use them. Once they become proficient, they'll be able to converse with AIs in two ways. A subcutaneous vocal implant in their inner ear and lower jaw...we've already begun testing those, with positive results so far...and also what we call an eyes-up display."

Marquand's hand moved to his own eyes. "When they blink rapidly three times, as they're learning how to do, the inner eyelid comes down and they're able to see what appears to a hologram. In reality it's a personal computer screen, displaying information relayed to them from their associate. Coupled with subcutaneous implants, this gives them direct verbal contact with any computer linked to MINN system."

"So, you mean if I had one of these..."

"You can't. It has to be installed in the brain while its still the early fetal stage."

"Okay, but if I did, and I asked...oh, say, which way to the men's room..."

"And then you'd blink three times, and the associate would show you a map on the eyes-up. Or it could display a spacecraft control system and lead you through a step-by-step procedure of how to use it. You can even load information into a terminal, and the children will be able to call it up at will, then download it to wherever they want." He pointed to Phil's pad. "Like having one of them imbedded in your brain, ready to be used at any time."

"Sick." George took another picture of the lab. "This is really sick."

"Why do you say that?" Marquand peered at him. "Because we've tinkered with the human body?"

Mariano didn't look at him. "You said it. I didn't."

"But we've been doing much the same thing for nearly a century, beginning with the advent of cardiac pacemakers. " Marquand shook his head. "We're on the verge of a new era...a time when humanity will be able to live in space as if it evolved there. Within two or three generations, humankind will be utterly transformed."

"Uh-huh." George turned to aim his camera at Marquand. "So I take it that you think Wells was on the right track. With *The Island of Dr. Moreau*, I mean."

"Wells was ahead of his time." At first, Marquand seemed reluctant to having his picture taken; then he relaxed, and struck a pose next to the window. "But he couldn't have foreseen what we're doing here. This is Moreau raised to the next level."

"Sure. Moreau to the second power." George snapped the picture. "But you're forgetting how the story ends, aren't you? Moreau's creations..."

"I think that's enough for now." Marquand's smile faded. "No doubt you'll want to rest before the rover gets here." Stepping past them, he opened the door. "If you'll follow me, I'll take you back to your quarters."

Phil was tired; he hadn't slept very long before Vladimir had awakened him, and he knew he had to get some sleep. Yet as soon as he was alone again, he found himself sitting cross-legged on the bed with his pad in his lap, working on his lead:

Mare Tranquillitatis, the Moon; Jan. 27, 2052 (UMI)—The existence of a new race of genetically-engineered humans was made public today by a senior scientist involved with the project. Known as homo superiors, *or "Superiors" for short, they are the result of a secret three-year program aimed at developing...*

There was a quiet knock upon the door. Phil barely had time to fold the pad and shove it beneath the covers before the door opened and Laurent Marquand stepped in. "I hope I'm not disturbing you," he said. "I saw your light still on, and thought this might be a good time to have a talk."

"I was about to take a nap, but...sure, what's on your mind?" Phil shifted a little on the bed, making sure that the bulge made beneath the covers by the pad was hidden by his body.

"I was wondering what you plan to do with what I've told you." Although Phil gestured to the chair, Marquand preferred to remain standing. He closed the door behind him. "I hope you don't intend to write a story about this."

"Well..." Phil was glad he'd taken precautions. "You invited me to bring my pad and George to bring his camera, and what you told us constitutes an interview. Little late to be having second thoughts, isn't it?"

"I'm not sure it is." Marquand crossed his arms. "I believed that you'd treat this with an open mind. And to your credit, you have. But your colleague didn't take this very well. It's not hard to see that he thinks this is immoral."

"George isn't writing the story." Too late, Phil realized that he spoken in the present tense. "Or at least he won't be," he quickly added. "He just takes pictures...it's going to be my byline."

"I understand. All the same, it makes me wonder if public disclosure may be premature, at least at this time." As he spoke, Marquand's gaze drifted around the small room; Phil wondered if he was searching for his pad. "Once news of this gets out, quite a few people may share his reaction. And although we're quite some distance from most of your readers, I have to take the children's safety into consideration."

"You don't believe the Pax will protect you?"

"Only a few of their leaders know about this. Tango Red was undertaken by GenSyn, not the Pax, and they may feel threatened by this." Marquand raised an eyebrow. "After all, this is the next stage of human evolution. Image what might have happened if Neanderthals had opened the morning paper and discovered that Cro-Magnon man had suddenly arrived on the scene."

Phil couldn't help but chuckle at the mental image of a caveman squinting at a pad, perhaps with a cup of coffee in his hairy hand. A dark frown appearing on Marquand's face. "I'm sorry you find this so humorous," he went on, "but you must realize that you share some responsibility for this."

Phil stopped grinning. "No, I don't. Not at all. I'm a journalist. It's my job to report the news. My only responsibility is to be as fair-minded and objective as I can be. I didn't set out to produce a new race, you did, and now that I know about it, it's my duty to report it."

"But it wasn't my intent to let you know…"

"It wasn't? I wonder about that. When we first met, you hinted that there were stories more significant than war. Maybe you were just making conversation, but you knew you were talking to a reporter...didn't you think that would get my attention? And on two different occasions, one of your Superiors...your children, as you call them...got loose and visited me. If you're so concerned about their safety, why did you leave their door unlocked? And isn't it odd that you just happened to be around when George and I found them..."

"These were accidents."

"No...no, I don't think so." Phil shook his head. "A secure research facility, and you let two reporters wander around. No, these weren't accidents. You saw a chance to stage a news event...I saw the way you posed for George when he took your picture...but now you think you may have made a mistake, and so you want to put everything in reverse."

Marquand said nothing. His arms folded across his chest, he looked down at the floor. "I see...and you don't think you owe me anything? Not even after having saved your life?"

"I owe you fair and unbiased coverage. I would have done that even if you hadn't rescued George and me."

"And there's nothing I can say that would convince you to forget what you've seen? Just claim that this is an agriculture research lab?"

"We're way beyond that now. Like you said yourself, this is more important than the war." Phil hesitated. "Since we're laying down our cards, I'll put down an ace of my own. It's no coincidence that we crashed near here. George and I were accompanying an advance team of Marines assigned to check out this facility. They had intelligence reports about something at Sosigenes, but they thought..."

"We were making drugs." A faint smile that quickly disappeared. "How ironic. If I'd known, I might have shown you the labs on Level Two and dropped hints that they were being used for that purpose. The lie would have been less harmful than the truth," He sighed, tucked his hands in his coat pockets. "But what if I were to tell you, in all truthfulness, that you *are* involved? That you do indeed have a personal stake in the outcome of this story?"

"I...I don't understand."

"I've deceived you more times than you realize, Mr. Carson. When you asked me about the bandage on your arm..." Phil glanced at his left elbow "...I told you, just as I told Mr. Mariano, that you've received intravenous glucose as treatment for dehydration. That's an untruth. The fact of the matter is that I took something from you instead..."

Phil felt his face grow pale. "Tissue samples."

"Only a few dozen people have worked on this project, and for various reasons not all of them were suitable donors. One of the problems we've had in working in such a remote location has been securing tissue from a wide gene pool. So when the opportunity presented itself..."

"You're out of your mind!"

"A mad scientist?" A corner of Marquand's mouth ticked upward. "Oh, please...but keep in mind that the next Superior born here may be your own genetic off-spring, or George's, just as much as Vladimir is mine."

Now he looked straight at Phil. "Do you feel as objective as you did before? Do you still think that what happens to them is none of your concern?"

Without realizing what he was doing, Phil absently let his hand drift toward the lump beneath the bedcovers. "You're right," he admitted. "It is my concern...more than before." Pulling aside the covers, he picked up his pad. "Which is why it's important that I finish this story, and file it as soon as possible."

"I see." Marquand let out his breath. "And the fact that I've locked out your net access..."

"The rover will be here soon. Soon as George and I reach Descartes and we clear things with the locals, I'll use their dish. It may take a while, but..."

"UMI will still get their story. Of course." Marquand walked over to the door, opened it. "I have to admit, Mr. Carson, you're a man of integrity."

"Just a guy doing his job, Dr. Moreau...Marquand, I mean."

Again, the elusive smile. "So am I, whether you care to believe it or not." And then he left, closing the door behind him.

Phil slowly stood up, groaning as sensation returned to his cramped legs. He should have been relieved, but he wasn't. It might have been a mistake to be honest with Marquand; he might not be mad, yet he was clearly committed to his cause. Even if he allowed him and George to leave Sosigenes, he could still prevent the story from getting out. He had contacts in the Pax, and they would be able to stop them.

Yet Phil had to find a way to send a dispatch back to Earth. If only there was...

He glanced at the desk terminal, and an idea came to him. It might not work, but it was the only shot he had. Ignoring his exhaustion, he sat down at the desk and continued writing his story. This time, though, he didn't use his pad, but wrote on the terminal instead.

If he worked fast, he might be able to finish before the rover arrived.

Phil heard the atrium door open, but didn't turn around to look. Squatting in the grass beneath a dwarf palm, he kept his attention upon Vladimir. The little Superior boy stood before him, waiting for Phil to throw the ball back to him. He would, but first they had to finish their game.

"Simon says, 'Send.'" Phil kept his voice low, hoping that he wouldn't be overheard.

"Mr. Carson..."

"Send!" Vladimir chirped, and his eyes blinked rapidly three times.

Phil let out his breath. He hoped Marquand didn't hear that. "Catch!" he said, then tossed the ball into the air. Vlad raised his hands to catch it, then realized that he'd been duped and let it fall. "Ah-ha!" Phil laughed. "Simon didn't say 'catch'!"

"No fair! Tricked me, you did!" Vlad bent down to pick up the ball. "Now my turn. Simon says…"

"I'm sorry, Vladimir. Mr. Carson has to leave now." Marquand stood at the edge of the clearing. "That's a good game, though. We'll play it again sometime."

Vlad frowned, holding the ball in his hands. "Play no more? Away, you go?"

"Afraid so, kiddo. Gotta head back to where I came from." Phil pointed to the crescent Earth hovering in the black sky above the atrium windows. "Earth? You know that place?" Vlad nodded solemnly; it was a world he'd never visit, but he saw it every day. "Don't worry…when I come back, you can show me all the games you've learned."

The boy beamed at him. "Simon says…!"

"Another time, Vladimir. We have to go." There was impatience in Marquand's voice, yet Phil was secretly relieved. If Vlad had repeated everything Phil had said during their game… "The rover has arrived, Mr. Carson. And I think your companion would like to depart."

"Sure. No problem." Phil took a moment to ruffle Vlad's hair, then he stood up and followed Marquand out of the atrium. He heard a vague motion behind him, but when he looked back, Vlad had disappeared into the trees, leaving his ball behind.

Mariano was waiting for them in the corridor, his rig slung across his shoulder, an annoyed look on his face. "You could have told me where you were going," he murmured as they joined him. "We had to look all over for you."

"Sorry. Just wanted to spend a little more time with the children." And he couldn't take a chance on Marquand finding both of them missing. He looked at Marquand. "Vlad's a great kid. You say he's your...I mean, he's cloned from your genes?"

"Yes, he is." Marquand seemed to take a certain paternal pride. "And you shouldn't hesitate to call him my son. I consider him as such." He paused. "Obviously he likes you, too. It never occurred to me to teach him that game."

"Try it some time. He's pretty good at it." *More than you know*, he silently added.

They'd just stepped aboard the elevator when Phil realized they had missed a step. "Our suits," he said. "We're going to need our suits if we're going to leave."

"Not necessary." Marquand touched the top button. "The rover's fully pressurized, as is the ramp. Besides, Mr. Mariano's is ruined. I had to cut it off him in order to treat his injuries."

George gave Phil a wary glance, but neither of them said anything. A few seconds later, the doors opened, and Marquand led them into the airlock dome. There were plenty of moonsuit lockers, yet through a window they could see a rover parked just outside, an accordion walkway extended to meet its aft boarding hatch. No reason for them to put on suits.

"Looks like they sent out the stretch limo," George remarked, and now Phil saw that the vehicle was a long-range rover: an eight-wheeler segmented into two sections, the kind used for major expeditions. Yet Descartes

City was less than a hundred miles away, and this wasn't the sort of vehicle sent out for a brief sortie.

"I think they're short of equipment just now," Marquand said, then he turned to Phil. "There's nothing I can do to change your mind? Nothing I can say that will make you reconsider reporting what you've seen?"

"We talked about this last night. We do what we have to do...that simple."

"Even if it means putting the children at risk?" Marquand raised an eyebrow. "Or is the public's right to know more important?"

"I think the public..." Phil hesitated. "I believe people are smarter than you think they are. If you just tell them the truth and let them make up their own minds, then they generally do the right thing."

"I wish I could believe you, but..." Marquand touched a button on the wall, and the ramp hatch irised open. "As you say, you do what you have to do."

"We'll be in touch." Phil ducked his head and entered the hatch.

"What was that all about?" George said quietly as they marched down the ramp.

"Later," Phil murmured. "Let's just get out of here."

They had been traveling for nearly an hour when Phil felt the rover suddenly hit tough terrain. Until now, the vehicle had been moving along a graded road leading from the edge of Mare Tranquillitatis into the Descartes highlands. George had crossed his arms across his chest and closed his eyes to take a nap, yet Phil had remained awake, and with the first hard bump he looked up from the H.G. Wells novel he'd been reading on his pad.

Glancing out the window, he saw that the landscape had changed. Small hills, bleached by raw sunlight, rose around them. Another sharp lunge, and he realized that the rover had just gone across a small boulder. Its oversize wire-mesh tires and independent suspension were usually enough to take on rocks and micrometeorite craters, which meant...

"Huh? Wuz'happenin?'" George woke up, grabbed for a safety strap. "What's going on?"

"I think we've left the road." They were in the rear passenger compartment, surrounded by ten empty seats. They'd met the driver only briefly—a dour young man, wearing a scalplock of the kind favored by loonies—before he'd shut the inner hatch leading to the forward tractor. Phil reached up to the com panel above him. "Hello? What's happening up there?'

Another bump, then the rover came to an abrupt stop, hard enough to throw them out of their seats. "Oh, for chrissakes..." George stabbed at the button above his seat. "Hey, what's the deal? Run out of gas or something?"

No response. Phil got up, walked forward to the hatch. He was about to grab the locklever when he felt a sudden jolt. A second later, the lights went out.

"Hey! What the...?" George angrily hit the intercom once more. "Yo! Moondog! You got a problem or what?"

There was a silence that he'd never heard before... or at least not in space. The sort of stillness one takes for granted on Earth, but not out here. Feeling a chill, Phil raised a hand to a ceiling vent. No air was coming out.

"Oh, God!" George was peering out the window next to his seat. "Oh, man, look...he's cut us off!"

"I know." Phil didn't need to look outside to know that the tractor had just detached itself from the trailer. When it had done so, it had also severed all service lines leading to the rear half of the rover.

No power. No air.

Phil slumped into the nearest seat. In a few moments, the temperature would start to rise. Or maybe it would fall? No...the sun was up, so that meant they were going to sweat awhile. Or at least until the air ran out.

"Mayday! Mayday!" Lurching on his stick, George had gone to the back of the trailer to open the panel leading to the emergency radio transmitter. "Rover down! Repeat, to all stations, rover down, at..." He looked at Phil. "Where are we, anyway?"

"Doesn't matter." There were suit lockers across the aisle from him. In frustration, he raised a foot and kicked one of them open, and wasn't at all surprised to discover that it was empty. "Give up. The short-range is disconnected. Probably pulled the plug on the sat dish, too."

Marquand was a smart man; he wouldn't have left anything to chance. Phil gazed out the window again; the tractor had disappeared, but it probably lingered somewhere nearby, perhaps just beyond that range of hills. It would remain there for a few hours, then the driver would return.

All he needed to do then was fit their bodies into a couple of moonsuits, then take a trip out to the crash site. Two corpses found near the wreckage of crashed lander, one with a broken leg. Waiting for rescue until their air ran out.

Just two more reporters to die in a combat zone…

Phil chuckled, shook his head. "What's so goddamn funny?" George demanded.

"Y'know that kid? Vlad, the one I was playing with?" Phil wiped his eyes with his fingers. "I taught him a game. Simon says…"

"I don't give a…"

"No, really. It's a great game. Especially if he's got a MINN implant and voice-activated computer access. All you have to do is get him to go eyes-up and repeat everything you say. Simon says, 'Search for file Carson-slash-urgent.' Simon says, 'Open Luna-dot-net.' Simon says, 'Open email to editor-at-UMI-dot-com.' Simon says, attach file Carson-slash-urgent. Simon says, 'Send…'"

"You didn't tell me." George stared at him from across the compartment, his voice becoming harsh in the thinning air "Why didn't you tell me? I could have attached my…"

"Simon says, 'Stop being such an…'" Phil stopped himself. "Naw, forget it." The compartment was becoming warm, his head getting thick; all he wanted to do was close his eyes, take a nap. "Shut up and sit down. It'll be over soon."

He laid his head against the seat cushion, gazed up at the distant sliver that represented home. A lousy assignment, but at least he'd filed one last time.

One day, his children might thank him for this.

HIGH ROLLER

We came into Nueva Vegas through the service entrance on the crater's north side. Our hiding place was a pressurized cell inside a water tank carried by a cargo hauler. We played possum while the vehicle came to a stop and casino security scanned the tank; the water surrounding us blocked the neutrino sweep, and our skinsuits stealthed everything else. The tractor began moving again; we felt it enter the vehicle airlock, then it stopped once more and there was another long wait while the airlock pressurized and electromagnetic scrubbers whisked away the dusty regolith. We rolled forward again; another minute passed, then we came to a halt and I heard JoJo's voice through my headset:

"Clear."

About time. I'd been flat on my back during the forty-kilometer ride down the Apollo Highway from Port Armstrong, and my arms were beginning to cramp from holding the equipment bag against my chest. I reached up, found the hatch lockwheel, twisted it clockwise and pushed it open, then sat up and squirmed up through the half-meter manhole. Jen was right behind me; I crouched on top of the hauler and took her bag from her, then helped her out of the tank.

As we'd expected, we were in the garage beneath the crater. Rovers, buses, and various maintenance vehicle were parked all around us. No one in sight; the day-shift workers had long-since clocked out and the night-shift guys had already clocked in. JoJo was the only guy around, and he didn't count.

In fact, JoJo wouldn't count for much of anything until I reactivated him. Once Jen and I pulled our masks out of our bags and put them on, I climbed up to the hauler's cab, turned a valve to bleed off the air, and un-sealed the hatch. He sat behind the yoke, two meters of ceramic polymer, dumb as a moonrock. Had to be that way; if he'd retained his programming during the ride to the casino, it might have been downloaded at the security checkpoint and searched by the local DNAI. So his mem-ory had been scrubbed before we left Port Armstrong, leaving behind only a well-buried instruction to trans-mit the all-clear once the hauler had arrived and his pe-ripheral sensors didn't register any body-heat signatures. He'd driven us here without even knowing it.

The next order of business bringing JoJo back into the game. I opened my bag, pulled out my pad, and linked it to the serial port on his chest. A double-beep from my pad, reciprocated by another double-beep from his chest;

lights flashed on his cylindrical head, then his limbs made a spasmodic jerk.

"Reload complete. All systems operational." Then his head snapped toward me. "Nice to see you again, Sammy. You're looking particularly reptilian today."

Good. He recognized me even though I was now wearing my disguise. "Welcome back, JoJo," I said, then stepped aside so he could see Jen. "You know our partner, of course."

"Yo, Jen! How's it going, girl? Found any good cow pies lately?"

She wasn't amused. "Say it again, tinhead," she murmured, "and I'll download you into a vacuum cleaner."

"Everyone, relax." JoJo was just being funny, sure, but I'd like to find the guy who invented personality subroutines for AIs. "We've got a job to do. JoJo, can you modem the casino comp?"

"Let me work on it." A moment passed. "*Nyet*. Too many lock-outs. I'll need direct interface."

I was expecting that. "No problem. We'll try again once we find a comp." I jumped down off the tractor; JoJo followed me, his slender limbs whirring softly as he unfolded himself from the cab. I locked the cab, then turned to him. "Gimme an eyes-up of the layout, basement only. Pinpoint our location."

"You got it, chief." An instant later, a holo of Nueva Vegas's subsurface levels appeared upon the lenses of my mask. Our whereabouts were marked as three luminous points at the outer circle of a concentric maze of corridors, tunnels, rooms, and shafts. Nueva Vegas's quantum comp lay within a sealed vault at the center of this maze, protected by umpteen levels of defense, both electronic and physical. Ever heard of Fort Knox, the place in Kentucky where the old USA once kept its gold supply back when gold was actually worth something? The DNAI had that degree of protection, and then some. Impossible to penetrate, or so I'd been told.

But then again, that wasn't our problem. We were after bigger game.

I located the nearest service lift that went directly to the crater floor; it was only a few dozen meters away, down a short corridor. "Everyone ready? Got your stuff?" Jen nodded within her mask; JoJo blinked some diodes my way. "Okay, then," I said, and picked up my bag. "Let's roll."

Nueva Vegas is built within Collins Crater, about thirty kilometers from the Apollo 11 Historical Site. A tour bus that will take you out there, and also to the Surveyor 5 landing site just a few klicks away and the Mare Tranquillitatis Battlefield Memorial a few hundred klicks north near Arago Crater. Most visitors don't do that, though. Nueva Vegas wasn't the first lunar casino resort, but most guidebooks consider it to be the best. The table stakes are good, and the payout is excellent; even if you don't gamble, there's vices you won't easily find back on Earth. Not too many places where you can legally purchase a 250-gram bag of Moondog Gold, or hire a double-jointed google—pardon me, a Superior—to be your companion for the evening.

But it's still a place for the rich. A cheap room near the crater floor costs 300 lox per sol; for this you get a bed, a passcard for the shower stall down the corridor, five complimentary chips and a discount coupon for the all-you-can-eat buffet. A two-room suite—complete with its own personal bath, private balcony, mini-bar, and free Continental breakfast—will set you back a cool million for a two-week stay. High rollers rate the best accommodations, of course: spacious apartments on the upper levels of the crater rim, with outside windows, catered dining, personal masseurs, an unlimited line of credit, and all the liquor, dope and sex you can take. If you have to ask how much that costs, then you have no business being there.

We were checking in on the budget plan. No room, no bath, no food. We weren't planning to stay very long, though. Just a few minutes on the casino floor, and we'd be on our way.

The lift doors opened and we stepped out into a white-mooncrete corridor with low ceilings and florescent lighting. A 'bot carrying a platter of hors d'oeuvres squealed in protest as it swerved to avoid colliding with us. From the other side of a pair of swinging doors, I caught the aroma of cooked food. We'd found the entrance to one of the service kitchens. I noted the direction in which the 'bot was headed, and turned to follow it.

"Hey! What are you guys doing here?"

A short, rotund gentleman in a waiter's tux and powdered wig emerged from a doorway, a magnum of champagne wrapped in a towel in his white-gloved hands. A wine steward, clearly irritated by our presence. "We've told you people a thousand times," he snapped as he bustled up to us. "Entertainers eat in the employee's cafeteria, just like everyone else."

He'd mistaken us for one of the lounge acts. No wonder. I wore a lizard-head mask, and Jen looked like a giant housefly. They didn't just conceal our faces; the masks also contained eyes-up displays, voice filters, and short-range com gear. We looked weird, sure, but in Nueva Vegas weirdness is the normal order of things. We fit right in.

"A thousand pardons, sir," I said. "We just got confused, thought this was…"

"Is that the wine cellar?" Jen interrupted, her voice an insectile buzz behind her mask. "May we see it, please?"

The waiter regarded her as if she had just emerged from a bowl of *potage Rossini*. "You most certainly may not," he huffed, not noticing that her right hand was within her bag. "Now, if you'll please…"

"Oh, but I insist." Jen's hand came out of the bag; clasped within it was Pax Astra Royal Navy taser pistol. He barely got a chance to see what it was before Jen jammed it against his throat. "I'd love to see your collection."

"R-r-right this way, madam." The wine steward managed to keep from dropping the bottle of '77 Sinai Planum as he hastily tapped his password into the keypad, then backed through the door.

The wine cellar was a small, cool room, dimly-lit, with hundreds of bottles of expensive wines resting upon faux-oak racks. The waiter sat down in the corner next to the imported Bordeaux, clasped his hand together atop his wig, and wisely remained quiet while Jen and I pulled out our guns—two PARN particle-beam rifles, complete with laser sights—and attached smoke and pepper-gas grenades to our belts. JoJo went to the wall comp; opening a chest port, he pulled out a cable and hardwired himself to it, then went silent for a couple of minutes while lines of type flashed across the comp screen so fast that I couldn't keep up with them.

"We're in," he said at last, his head swiveling toward me. "Ready to initiate final sequence."

"Got it right here, big guy." I reached into a chest pocket, found the diskette I'd been given. Another fail-safe; if we had been caught while passing through security, the first thing I would have done was push the auto-erase tab. JoJo pushed the diskette into the terminal, and I reached past him to tap an eight-digit code into the miniature keyboard. A green border appeared around the screen.

"Locked and loaded." I pulled out the diskette, snapped it between my hands, then tossed it into the corner next to the cowering wine steward. "Thank you, *garçon*. You've been very helpful."

"Mind if we take this?" Jen was examining a bottle of cabernet sauvignon she had taken from the wine rack. "Or would you recommend the beerenaulse instead?"

"Th-th-the cabernet is quite...quite good, m-m-madam." He was barely able to look up at her. "I don't...I don't think you'll be d-d-disappointed."

"Hmm...well, if you insist." Jen gently placed the bottle in her bag, then slung it across her shoulders. I hoped it wouldn't weigh her down too much. "Ready when you are."

"Okey-dokey." JoJo detached his cable, let it reel itself back into his chest. "I'm going to huff, and I'm going to puff, and I'm going to..."

"Save it for the civilians." I raised my rifle to the terminal; one quick squeeze of the trigger, and the panel was fried out. I turned around and aimed my gun at the wine steward. "Okay, here's the deal. You get to live, so long as you sit here quietly for the next few minutes and don't make a peep. But if I see you, hear you, even smell you..."

"D-d—don't worry about me." His wig had become dislodged; his close-cropped hair was slick with sweat. "I-I-I'll just sit here."

"Good man. Again, we thank you."

He nodded, happy to be rid of us. Then it seemed as if he mustered a gram of courage. "Y-y-you know, of course, w-w-where you are."

"Sure. Nueva Vegas."

"Well, y-yes, of course, certainly, but..." His voice dropped. "This is...this is Mister Chicago's casino. This place...I mean, it belongs to *him*."

I raised an eyebrow before I remembered that he couldn't see my expression behind my mask. "Yes? And...?"

"N-nothing." He stared at me for a moment in bewilderment, then the corners of his mouth twitched upward, as if he was enjoying a private joke at our expense. "Nothing at all. Enjoy your visit."

"Thank you. We will." I looked at the others. "All right, let's go."

The corridor was vacant. I waited until Jen and JoJo had come out, then I closed the wine cellar door behind us. I could have scrambled the keypad, but the wine steward hadn't given us any trouble. He deserved a chance to live. I left the door unlocked.

Our guns beneath our arms, we marched down the corridor, heading for a pair of double-doors at the end. The doors slid apart with barely a sound; light and noise rushed in.

The easy part was done. Now it was time for the tough stuff.

We came out into an open-air restaurant made to look like a Mediterranean cafe: plaster walls, watercolors of French street scenes, garden trellises cluttered with grapevine, tables covered with checkerboard cloths placed upon a red-brick terrace. Only a few diners noticed us as we quickly strode past them, and those who did were baffled for only a moment before knowing smiles crept across their faces. We had to be actors, on our way to a floor show somewhere in the casino. The guns? Obviously fakes. Even the waiters didn't look at us twice. We exited the cafe without bringing any undue attention to ourselves, and now we were within the casino.

The floor of Collins Crater was nearly two kilometers in diameter, and the casino took up nearly every square meter of it. Thousands of slot machines binged and booped and clinked and clanged in a steady and omnipresent caco-phony, while the holos that flickered above them—semi-nude women doing strip-tease, classic cartoon characters chasing each other with chainsaws, starships engaged in battle—were ignored by scores of middle-aged men and women hunched in front of the machines, slipping tokens into the slots, pushing buttons and yanking chrome han-dles, watching in single-minded fascination as apples and grapes and lemons scrolled past their sleepless eyes. Gam-blers gathered around blackjack and poker tables watched as dealers slapped cards down on the green felt, collecting chips with smiles, surrendering them with muttered curses. Waitresses in skin-tight outfits and high-heel shoes circu-lated between the baccarat and roulette tables, delivering drinks and joints to players as they studied cards and tossed dice, collecting tips from winners and favoring those who'd just crapped out with disingenuous expressions of sympa-thy. Here and there, within small sunken amphitheaters, comedians went through their routines, magicians per-formed slight-of-the-hand tricks; applause greeted Frank, Dean, and Sammy as they took to the stage for another sold-out show. Hookers and tricks negotiated with one an-other, card-sharps tried out their systems for beating the odds, drunks bemoaned their bad luck, and a few hundred dumbasses parted with their money and loved every mo-ment of it, while smoke and sweat and liquor fumes rose to the opaque sky of the pressure dome far above, obscuring the security flycams that prowled above the gaming areas, their lenses watchful for any unusual activity.

We qualified. Even in the middle of all this, it was hard to miss Lizard Boy, Fly Girl, and JoJo the Robot as they made their way across the gaming area, rifles slung beneath their shoulders. By the time we reached the raised island near the center of the casino, three flycams were on us and a couple of plainclothes security guys moving into position. No alarms, or at least not yet; everyone was still trying to figure out who we were and what we were doing.

I ignored the heat as I approached casino control. A bouncer in a white tux moved in to block my way.

"May I help you, sir?" he asked, raising a hand to stop me.

"Yes, you can," I replied, and then I casually laid my gloved left hand against his wrist. A 10,000-volt charge dropped him. He'd barely hit the floor when Jen turned her taser upon the plainclothes guys. Four shots and they went down.

"JoJo," I said, "kill the flyers."

"You got it, chief." A double-beep from his chest, and every flycam in the casino fell from the air. They crashed into poker tables and slot machines, plummeted into cafes, smashed to pieces next to the Rat Pack. Throughout the casino, we could hear people screaming. As attention-getters go, this one rated a solid ten, and we hadn't even started yet.

A Superior was on duty as floor boss. His long-fingered hands were already darting across the wrap-around console as I dashed up the stairs onto the platform. "Get away from that," I said, pointing my rifle at him. The floor boss obediently moved away, the angel-wings tattooed across his face flexing slightly as his overlarge eyes stared at me in astonishment. Behind him, a red light flashed on a panel.

"What button did you push?" I asked.

"Locked down, we are. All exits blocked. Access to the cashiers, denied." He smiled at me. "Surrender now, if you're smart. Otherwise, assured your death shall be."

Something else I'd expected. "JoJo, the google's hit the panic button," I murmured, speaking into my throat mike. "Do something about it, okay?"

"I'm on it." A brief pause. "They're onto us, chief."

Looking around, I saw what he meant. All the slot-machines had gone silent. Chrome shutters had automatically rolled down across the windows of the cashier booths. Even the service 'bots had become motionless. Patrons milled about in confusion, still unaware of what was happening in their midst, yet from my vantage point on the platform, I could see recessed floor panels irising open all around us.

"Jen, cover us!" I snapped. "JoJo, link up with the security system!"

Elevators ascended from beneath the casino floor, each one bearing a combot . Big mothers, too: two-and-a-half meters tall, heavily armored, with guns built into their forearms and 360-degree vision in their spade-shaped heads. Tourists shrieked and ran for cover, dropping tokens and chips as they made way for the behemoths stamping through the aisles. Nasty toys. Mister Chicago had spared no expense making his customers feel safe.

Jen's multifaceted eyes turned toward me. "This could be a problem."

"Bad idea, was it not?" The floor boss calmly watched as the 'bots advanced toward us, his right hand hovering above the console. "Give up, and live you still may."

"Think not, I do." I looked down at JoJo. "Got it?"

"Twenty-eight seconds ago." JoJo didn't budge. "Do you want me to...?"

"Yes. Please. By all means." Damn literal-minded machine....

A moment later, the 'bots froze in place. I heard a brief buzz from the nearest one just before it went inert. I looked around at the floor boss just in time to see his mouth drop open. "You were saying?"

"How did...how could you have...?"

I always knew Superiors could speak plain English when they wanted to. "That's my secret," I said, then I reached into my hip pocket and pulled out my pad. "Okay, now that you're all out of tricks, show me how to link up with cash control."

Still not convinced I meant business, he stared at me. I planted my rifle barrel against his chest. "Look, I can do this without your help. You saw what I did to the 'bots. The only difference is that it'll make my job a little easier, and you'll get to breath through your mouth instead of through a chest wound. So what do you say?"

He was about to reply when I heard a sudden *fizz!* from behind me. Looking around, I saw Jen holding her rifle in firing position. Not far away, a small mob people was backing away from a slot machine she'd just killed.

"Too many heros in this place, Sammy" she said quietly, for my ears only. "We need to get a move on." Then she gazed back at the mob. "Anyone else want to try it?" she said loudly.

They stayed where they were. We didn't want to kill anyone, but it was only a matter of time before she wouldn't be about to control the crowd any longer. I looked back at the floor boss; his expression told me that he'd finally realized how serious we were. "Ready to play along?"

"Certainly." Taking a keycard from his pocket, he unlocked a panel on the console, swung it open to reveal a serial port. "Here it is. All you have to do is..."

"I know." I attached my pad to the port, tapped in a code I'd memorized. Nueva Vegas held very little in the way of hard currency. Most of its transactions were electronic, in the form of funds transferred from the bank accounts of its visitors, which in turn became Pax Astra lox payable as tokens and chips from the cashier booths. A secure system, so long as you didn't have direct access to casino control and knowledge of the code numbers that would allow you to tap into the funds stored within the central DNAI.

Which I did. Within seconds, 680.75 megalox was transferred into my pad. I detached the pad, tossed it down to JoJo. "Upload this, please," I said.

"Roger dodger." JoJo reattached the pad to his chest. In another moment, he transmitted the money to our friends in orbit. "All done, chief."

"Thank you." I turned to the floor boss one more. "Your cooperation has been appreciated, m'seur. One last piece of business, and we'll be on our way."

"Get away with this, surely you don't expect." He must have begun to feel safe again, because he'd returned to his lopsided manner of speech. "Owned by Mister Chicago, Nueva Vegas. A individual lacking in forgiveness, but not in resources."

"So I've heard. But we have a few of our own." I looked away from him. "JoJo, will you come up here, please?"

"Is it my turn? Oh, joy!" JoJo clanked up the steps, coming to a halt between us. "Thank you, thank you," he said, raising his spindly arms and revolving his head to address everyone. "It's certainly an honor to be here tonight. I'd like to thank my producer, my director, my publicist, my screenwriter, and all the little people who've done so much over the years to…"

"Thanks, Jojo. You can shut up now." He obediently fell silent. I tapped a button on his chest; a panel slid open, and I entered a four-digit string into his CPU. The tiny LCD above it flashed to 15:00:00, then began to count back. I motioned the floor boss closer, then pointed to display. "See that? What do you think it is?"

He peered at it. "A timer?"

"That's correct…with a fifteen-minute countdown that's already started." I walked behind JoJo, opened another panel to reveal a liter-sized cylinder within his back. "And this, my friend, is a nuke."

+✦+

Technically speaking, the nuke wasn't a bomb, but rather a ten-kiloton nuclear device of the sort that asteroid miners use to excavate large c-type rocks. JoJo's body had literally been built around it, so it was well-shielded from the security scanners.

The bystanders close enough to overhear this shrank back. Murmurs swept through the crowd; most people froze, but a few turned and bolted down the aisles. The floor boss stared at me in horror.

"You're bluffing," he said quietly.

I looked him straight in the eye. "No, I'm not," I said, with utter sincerity. "In fifteen minutes…"

"Fourteen minutes, twenty-nine seconds," JoJo corrected. "Whoops. Better make that fourteen seconds, twenty-seven seconds. Oh, dear, now it's fourteen minutes, twenty-five…"

"Fourteen minutes and whatever. Thanks, JoJo, I'll take it from here." I shut the panel. "Anyway, you get the picture. You've got just that much time to evacuate the crater and get everyone to safe distance before…"

"I'm going to huff, and I'm going puff, and I'm going to blow your house down!" JoJo had been saving that line all night. It wasn't part of his programming, but then again, neither was self-preservation.

"Thanks, JoJo. You said it better than I could have." I handed JoJo my rifle. "And in case you're wondering, he's had all his Asimov protocols scrubbed from memory, so it wouldn't be wise to try to disarm him." I turned to the 'bot. "You know what to do now, right?"

JoJo hefted the rifle. "Any youse punks gets any wise ideas, you gets a belly-full of laser, see? I'm a desperate 'bot, see?"

It was a lousy Cagney impersonation, but it got the point across. The Superior was already backing away. "So if I were you..." I continued.

The floor boss was no longer listening. Bolting to the nearest console, his hands raced across various buttons as he jabbered orders in Superior patois. Within moments, red emergency beacons began to strobe throughout the casino as sirens started to wail. A Code Five blowout alarm, activated only when catastrophic loss of dome integrity was imminent.

One thing to be said for Nueva Vegas: the management made sure that the tourists were repetitively instructed about what do in case of a worst-case scenario. Those constant reminders on the room screens, in the elevators and restaurants and bars, even on the slot machines and above the game tables, got the point across to even the densest and most complacent of its patrons. All around us, everyone who hadn't fled already were running for their lives, running for the clearly-marked emergency exits ringed around the crater floor. Within minutes, the first few escape pods would be automatically launched from their ports within the outer crater rim. I saw a few die-hards scrambling to gather their chips, but even they knew that it was time to run. The floor boss had already leaped over the consoles; he joined the stampede, getting out while the getting was good.

"Minus ten minutes, thirty seconds, and counting." JoJo was no longer clowning around. "Um...Sammy? You're not going to..."

"Easy, pal. I got you covered." I pulled out my pad, rinsed its memory, then slapped it against his chest. A few seconds passed, then a light flashed on its panel: JoJo's higher functions had been downloaded into the pad, leaving behind only the basic routines necessary for the 'bot to continue its primary mission.

"Bye-bye," I said to the mindless automaton. Its head swiveled in my direction, but I wasn't a threat and so it ignored me. I jumped off the platform and landed next to Jen.

"You could have just left him behind." She was already headed for the restaurant where we'd come in.

"JoJo's good. I'd like to work with him again." No point in wasting a good AI for no reason. The casino floor was nearly empty; nothing stood between us and our escape route. "Clock's ticking," I said, slapping her behind. "Beat it, sugar mouth."

"After you, lizard lips."

The getaway was easy. Jen and I went back the way we came, through the service kitchen. By now the whole place was deserted, save for a few 'bots still carrying orders out to customers who had split without waiting for the check. All the same, I glanced inside the wine cellar to make sure the steward was no longer around. He was wise; he was gone. So we headed for the basement, skipping the slow-moving elevator and using the stairs instead.

The cargo hauler was right where we had left it. All the other vehicles had been taken, but no one had managed to break into our vehicle. Cab pressurization took ninety seconds—that was the only period in which I was truly scared, watching the atmosphere meter rise while the countdown ticked back at the same rate—and once it was done I put the hauler in reverse and put the pedal to the floor. No time to wait for the vehicle airlock to cycle through; I rammed the doors with the hauler's back end, and let explosive decompression do the rest. Jen swore at me as she was thrown against her shoulder straps, but I paid little attention to her as I locked the brakes and twisted the yoke hard to the right, pulling a bootlegger-turn on the ramp. Then I floored it again and off we went, up the ramp and out into the cold blue earthlight.

I glanced at side-view mirror, giving Nueva Vegas one last look as the hauler raced across Mare Tranquillitatis, its steel-mesh tires throwing up fantails of moondust. Lights still gleamed through the crater windows, yet escape pods were rising from the outer wall, tiny ellipsoids heading for orbit. By now, the casino should be empty. Fifteen minutes is a long time when you're running for your life.

The lunar freighter was right where it was supposed to be, two klicks due east of Collins Crater. Its cargo ramp was lowered; I drove the hauler up it as fast as I dared, then slammed the brakes once we were inside the hold. The pilot wasn't taking any chances; he jettisoned the ramp, then shut the hatch and fired the main engines.

Jen and I were still in the hauler when the count-down reached zero, so we didn't get to see the nuke go off. I'm told it was beautiful: a miniature protostar erupting within a lunar crater, rising upward as hemispherical shell of thermonuclear fire. All we experienced, though, was a faint tremor that passed through the lander's hull as it raced ahead of the shockwave, heading for the stars.

After a while, the pilot repressurized the cargo bay. I unsealed the cab and we climbed out, carefully making our way through zero-gee until we reached the open interior hatch. The crewman waiting on the other side cracked up when we came through, and it was only then that I realized that we were still wearing our masks. I tore mine off, took a deep breath, and grinned at the silly lizard face I'd worn for the last hour or so. Jen shook out her hair, scowled briefly at her fly-head, then pitched it aside and let me give her a quick kiss.

I'd just made my way up to the command deck, with the intent of downloading JoJo into the nearest reliable comp I could find, when the pilot informed me that he had an incoming transmission. Mister Chicago wanted to talk to me.

I glanced at Jen. She was in the passageway behind us, floating upside-down as she peeled out of her sweaty skin-suit. We gave each other a look, then I told the pilot I'd take it in the wardroom. He nodded, and I squeezed past Jen to the closet-size compartment just aft of the cockpit.

Mister Chicago was waiting for me there, a doll-size hologram hovering an inch above the mess table. He was seated in lotus position, naked from the waist up, his dead-white skin catching some indirect source of light behind him. His pink eyes studied me as I moved within range of the ceiling holocams.

"*I understand you destroyed my casino today,*" he said.

"Yes, I did," I replied.

Rumor had it that Mister Chicago made his base of operations somewhere out in the belt, within an asteroid he'd transformed into his own private colony. If that was so, then he couldn't be there now, because he nodded with barely a half-second delay.

"*And I also understand that you managed to steal...*" He brushed his shoulder-length hair aside as he turned his head slightly, as if listening to someone off-screen. "*Six hundred and eighty megalox from my casino before you detonated a nuclear device within it.*"

"Six hundred eighty million, seven hundred fifty thousand." I shrugged. "I haven't checked the exact figures, so there may be some loose change...yes, I did."

"*Well done, sir. Well done.*"

"Thank you. We aim to please."

To this day, I still don't know exactly why Mister Chicago hired us to rob his own casino and then blow it up. Perhaps it had become a liability. Nueva Vegas was an expensive operation, after all; it may have cost more to keep it going than it brought in, and once its bottom line slipped from the black into the red, he may have decided to torch the place, once he'd made sure that he'd recovered every lox he could. He'd gone so far as to supply all the information we needed—JoJo's nuke, schematics of the Nueva Vegas's sublevels and gaming areas, the codes to disable the security 'bots and provide direct access to the DNAI—and even furnish a means of escape.

Yet even a gangster has to answer to legitimate underwriters: insurance companies, banks, investors, the Pax Astra itself. So what better way to cover himself than have his property nuked during a heist? If his scheme was successful, he could always claim someone else did it. And if it failed...well, I doubt our conversation would have been so pleasant. If it happened at all.

But that's just my theory. Not for me to ask the reasons why.

"No lives lost, or so I've heard." His right hand briefly disappeared beyond camera range; when it returned, it held a glass of wine. *"Quite professional. I'm satisfied, to say the least. Add...oh, shall we say, another one percent to your take. Is that good for you?"*

We'd agreed to do the job for five percent of whatever we managed to grab. A bonus was unnecessary, but welcome nonetheless. I felt a tap on my shoulder; looking around, I saw Jen hovering over my shoulder. She smiled and nodded. "Thank you," I said. "Yes, that's quite acceptable."

Jen kissed my ear; I gently pushed her away. *"Well then, I believe our business is concluded,* " Mister Chicago said. *"If I ever need your services again..."*

"You know where to find us."

"Very good. Thank you. Goodbye." A final wave, then his image faded out. I let out my breath, turned around to find Jen behind me.

"Want to know what six percent of six hundred eighty megalox is?" she asked.

"Um, let's see. That would be…" I shrugged. "You do the math. I'm busy right now."

She grinned, moved closer to me. I reached out, shut the compartment hatch. Until the freighter reached the nearest Lagrange station, we had a long ride ahead of us. And we still hadn't opened the bottle of wine she'd stolen.

WORLD WITHOUT END, AMEN

The last pessimist stood on a hotel balcony and contemplated suicide.

The lights of Boston stretched out before him: the elegant spires and helixes of glass, marble, and steel of downtown, the black expanse of the Charles River discernible beyond the antique brownstones of the Back Bay area. Looking down, he saw cars silently moving along Boylston Street; taxis stood in line in front of the hotel, while across the street a handful of pedestrians strolled through the Commons, taking in a warm summer night scented with lilacs and roses. He imagined lovers strolling hand-in-hand past its ponds and gardens, unafraid of the darkness, and somehow this made him even more miserable.

He turned away from the railing, shuffled back inside to pull from a pewter ice-bucket the bottle of champagne a room-service waiter had delivered a little more than an hour ago. Dom Perignon '10: he'd deliberately picked that year, for it represented a happier time. He sloppily poured himself another drink—ignoring the pale gold drops that fell upon the pages of the speech he'd delivered earlier this evening, now scattered like dead leaves across the thick white carpet—and bolted it down as if it was a shot of cheap whisky. Champagne of this vintage was far beyond his means, as was this room, yet when he'd made the reservation, there had been a notion, somewhere in the back of his mind, that his life was coming to an end. There was just enough money in the bank for a one-night stand in a four-star hotel; if he wasn't planning to live long enough to worry about paying bills again, he might as well indulge himself.

"'Drink to me, drink to my health...'" The last words of Dylan Thomas, or perhaps a line from an old Paul McCartney song; either way, he couldn't remember how the rest of it went.

The phone rang. He stared at it for a moment, teetering on his feet, indecisive of whether to answer it. It kept ringing, though, and at last he lurched over and picked it up. "Hello?"

"'*You know I can't drink anymore.*'" The voice on the other end of the line was perfectly modulated, without accent. "*Perhaps you should lie down, Lawrence.*"

Alfred. Of course, it was Alfred. All-seeing, all-hearing, omniscient... "Get bent," he rasped, then slammed down the receiver.

Yet Alfred wasn't finished with him. "*You shouldn't be doing this,*" it said, and now its voice came from the phone's external speaker. "*If you like, I can order a pot of hot coffee...*"

He reached behind the desk and yanked the cord from the wall, then staggered out onto the balcony once more. The city was quiet, a vast organism murmuring to itself as it settled in for the night. Hearing a low drone from somewhere overhead, he looked up to see the lights of an airship slowly cruising above the city. A commuter flight from New York or Washington, making final approach to Logan Airport on the other side of the bay. A long time ago, when he'd been in demand for speaking engagements, he'd traveled first-class, riding in the front cabin of airliners that farted vast ribbons across the sky. Today, he couldn't even afford a seat on a short-haul blimp; he'd made the trip from Albany on a maglev trains, forced to share the company of blue-collar workers, housewives, and students...

Students. Like those in the audience tonight. Shutting his eyes, he clutched the burnished aluminum rail. They'd laughed at him...

"*Lawrence, I really don't think you should be out there.*" Alfred's voice came to him through the open door; now it spoke from the TV in the oak cabinet in front of his bed. "*You're depressed, and you've had too much to drink. Come back inside, please. You need...*"

"Shut up, Red." No, they hadn't laughed. They were much too polite to do that. Yet when he'd glanced up now and then from the podium, the knowing smiles and quiet nods with which his words had been received in better days were gone, replaced by amused smirks and

raised eyebrows; as he spoke, he heard the soft scuf-
fling of feet, the occasional muffled apology, as someone
quietly excused themselves, and each time the door
at the back of the lecture hall banged shut it felt like
another stake was being driven into his heart. And so
sweat had oozed down his face and his voice had faltered,
his tongue stumbling over words that he'd once uttered
with conviction, again and again, in the course of a long
and once-luminous career, now no longer believing them
himself yet forced by burden of reputation to proclaim
once more. When he finally reached the end, the applause
had been faint, and the moderator—a former collegue
who'd once been a champion of his work, and who'd set
up this speaking engagement to put a few dollars in the
pocket of an old friend—mercifully declined to have the
customary question-and-answer period. Which was just
as well, for by then the hall was nearly empty, the seats
filled only by a handful of undergraduates and a few fac-
ulty members who'd come in the same spirit of morbid
curiosity that once compelled people to slow down on the
Mass Pike to stare at car crashes. Back when cars used to
crash, that is.

The champagne suddenly tasted like cold urine.
Scowling in disgust, he tossed the glass over the side. It
briefly reflected the lights of the hotel windows below
him as it tumbled downward, then vanished from sight.
He waited, and a moment later he heard the faint sound
of it shattering upon the sidewalk, fifteen stories below.

*"That posed a potential hazard to anyone who might
have been down there."* Alfred's voice expressed reproach.

"*I'll have to report this incident to the hotel management, and also the police.*"

"You do that." Enough self-pity. If he was going to do this, he might as well get it over. Grasping the railing, he tried to pull himself over it. It was just a little too high, though, and he was drunk; his right knee slipped off and he fell back. Cursing under his breath, he looked around for something to stand on.

"*Please don't do this, Lawrence.*" Alfred's voice remained calm, yet there was an undertone of pleading. "*There's no reason for you to…*"

He slammed the balcony door shut, then pulled a chaise lounge over to the railing. It wobbled a bit beneath his feet, but he had little trouble using it to climb over the railing. One leg at a time, he carefully stepped onto the narrow ledge, grasping the railing with slick hands as the toes of his shoes projected out over empty space.

"Sure, there's a reason," he murmured. "It gets me away from you."

And then, without giving himself a chance to reconsider, he closed his eyes, spread his arms apart, and flung himself into the night.

"Dr. Kaufmann? Lawrence? You have a visitor."

He didn't look away from the windows as the nurse spoke to him from the door of the solarium. A steady rain had fallen all morning, shrouding the wooded grounds of the psychiatric wing with a fine grey mist, yet shortly after breakfast he'd asked an orderly to wheel him out here, as he'd done every day since he'd been admitted. He sighed, and closed the magazine that had rested in his lap, unread, for the past couple of hours.

This would have to happen. Might as well get on with it. Yet he said nothing, and after a second or two he heard the nurse murmur something to someone else. Heels clicked across black-and-white tiles, came to a stop beside him.

"Dr. Kaufmann? I'm..."

"The new shrink. Of course." He lazily turned his head to look up at her. Late thirties, perhaps early forties. Casual business suit. A bit plump but otherwise easy on the eyes. Long brown hair tied back in a bun. A pleasant face, not beautiful but pretty all the same, with sharp aquamarine eyes that studied him from behind stylish wire-rim glasses. "What took you so long?"

"Not one for small talk, are you?" A professional smile.

"Oh, no. I'm great for small talk." He surrendered to the inevitable. "Pick a subject. The weather's lousy. The Red Sox are having a good season. The president is getting divorced. Another Mars expedition is about to return home. I jumped off a hotel balcony last week and all I got to show for it is this." He patted the plaster cast that held his right leg immobile from the hip down past the knee. "Let me guess which one do you want to talk about."

She found a chair next to a card table, pulled it over beside him. "The rain's going to stop soon," she said as she sat down. "The Sox lost last night's game with the Yankees at the bottom of the eighth. The president's marital problems are her own business, and I hope Ares 3 gets home without any more problems. Guess that eliminates everything else." She extended her hand. "Melanie Sayers, and what took me so long is that I was vacation until yesterday."

He ignored her hand. "You came back because of me?"

"You wouldn't cooperate with the staff psychologists, so they decided to call in a specialist." Melanie withdrew her hand. "Don't worry about it. The Bahamas are boring."

"I wasn't going to." He gazed at her long and hard. No bullshit, or at least so far. A good sign. "Doesn't your case-load keep you busy?"

"Only sometimes. Not that many people attempt suicide these days."

"You're honest, at least."

"Why shouldn't I be? Besides, I don't get many jumpers, so this is almost a treat. The suicide rate has dropped..."

"Twelve percent in developed countries in the last ten years, five percent in undeveloped countries. Twenty percent in the U.S. alone." Lawrence gazed out the floor-to-ceiling windows, watching the rain scurry down their broad panes. "Of course, those figures only cover completed suicides. They're probably different for ones made from hotels not equipped with fire-escape nets." He paused. "You know...sensors in the outside walls detect a mass the size of a falling body, raises a sticky net. Body falls into it and another life gets saved...unless, of course, you happen to come down the wrong way, then something gets broken. Think I should sue?"

"I'm not a lawyer, but I wouldn't advise it. Besides, if you're so smart, then why didn't you pick a hotel that doesn't have that kind of equipment?"

"Never occurred to me. All I was looking for was a place with a good bar, room service, and outside balconies."

"All you had to do was ask Alfred. Here, let me check." Melanie reached into her jacket, pulled out a datapad. Flipping it open, she typed in her PIN. "Alfred, which hotels in Boston don't have fire escape…?"

"Don't do that." Lawrence felt a muscle in his broken leg involuntarily twitch.

'Do what? I'm just asking Alfred for…"

He reached forward to snatch the pad away from her. "Go to hell, Red," he said to it, then he snapped the pad shut and handed it back to her. "Don't do that again. Next time I'll throw it through the window."

Melanie put the pad in her pocket, then raised her head. "Alfred?" she said, as if speaking to the ceiling. "Can you hear me?"

Silence No. Alfred.

"That's one thing I like about this place," he said. "You know it was built in the late 1800's? It's been refurbished, of course, but for some reason, no one thought to wire the sun room for wi-fi."

"And you like that." Not a question.

"If I thought it'd keep me from ever hearing him, I'd stay here for the rest of my life." Lawrence forced a grin. "Look, lady, I'm crazy. Trying to kill myself just proves it.

Do me a favor and sign the commitment papers. Food's lousy, but..."

"Attempting suicide doesn't mean you're mentally ill. Depressed, yes, but depression is not the same as..."

"You wouldn't say that to Napoleon." He made a mock-solemn face as he tucked a hand into his robe. "'Able was I, ere I saw Elba.'"

"Oh, please..." She pulled out her hand again, opened it and punched up a file. "Dr. Lawrence Kaufmann, Ph.D., Degrees in cybernetics and sociology from MIT and Harvard. Former vice-president of research and development at Lang Electronics. Author of..." She peered a little more closely at the screen. "*Deus Irae: The Threat of Artificial Intelligence*. Hey, I know that book."

"Read it?"

"Sorry, no. I prefer history and biographies. But my husband did."

"Ah." Lawrence gazed out the window. As she'd predicted, the rain was letting up. "Well, then, you can tell him you met the author." He paused. "As if he'd care."

"He might. It was a bestseller, wasn't it?"

"A long time ago." He knew that she was trying to lure him in, using conversational tricks to relax his defenses, and yet he didn't care. At least she wasn't as clumsy about it as Dr. Wychowski, whom he'd finally told to go away. Besides, he was in a mood to chat. "Put me on the talk-show circuit for awhile," he went on, letting himself boast a little. "I used to be in the Rolodex of every network news producer in the business. Hell, I was in both *Newsweek* and *Time* the same week."

"Guys who write novels about killer sharks do talk shows." She tapped at her pad again, studied the screen. "No family history of mental illness, at least as far as I find here, but I haven't…"

"If you step out into the hall," Lawrence said quietly, "you can ask Alfred to do a full search. I'll give you the names of my relatives and in-laws. But you won't find anything new. No one in my family is crazy…except maybe me."

"You're not crazy. You're…"

"Suffering from depression. You said that already. But if you've read *Deus Irae*…sorry, I meant if your husband has… and if you know I can't stand to be around Red, then you know there must be something wrong with someone who doesn't ever want to communicate with…it…ever again."

"Maybe. Want to talk about it?

He considered the question. If he didn't talk to her, then they would only send someone else, and the next psychologist might not be as forthright as this one. And as comfortable as this solarium might be, he knew he couldn't remain here indefinitely. Sooner or later, he'd have to confront the world again. Alfred's world…

"Think you can push this thing?" He patted the arm of his wheelchair. "I'd like some fresh air."

She hesitated. "I'll have to get an orderly…"

"Ask for Raoul. Nice guy."

"Raoul, sure." She stood up. "But if we go out…"

"I'll be no trouble at all, I promise. And I'll tell you about me and Red." Lawrence smiled. "After all, I should know…I helped create him, didn't I?"

✦ ✦ ✦

The rain had stopped, and the clouds were beginning to part; dappled rays of sunlight lancing through the trees lent a silver-green tint to the woods. A mower slowly roamed across the lawn, growling softly as it cut and mulched the damp grass. Not far away, a gardener trimmed a row of hedges, humming as he worked.

"Turned out to be a nice morning after all." Lawrence sat in his wheelchair as the orderly pushed it along the gravel path. He swatted at the back of his left forearm. "Leave it to the mosquitoes to come out. Always do after a shower."

"We were talking about Alfred." Melanie strolled beside him, her pad open in he right hand. A red light indicated that it was in record mode.

"Were we? I was talking about the weather." He gazed in the direction of the Massachusetts Turnpike, visible through the trees at the far end of the hospital grounds. If he didn't know where to look, he wouldn't have known it was there. How quiet the highways had become, now that cars were electrical and interstate traffic was computer-controlled. He imagined the occupants of those bubble-like cars—reading, watching TV, napping, doing everything else except driving—and found it hard to remember a time when Alfred wasn't king of the road.

"Yes, we were. And if you don't go on, I'll have to insist that we continue this inside." Melanie paused. "There's a conference room on the second floor. No windows, I'm afraid, but we shouldn't be bothered…am I right, Raoul?"

"Anything you say." The orderly shrugged. "Personally, I'd rather stay out here, but if it'll help, I can turn us around and…"

"And here I thought you were on my side." Lawrence scowled up at the big Latino, and he smiled back at him. "Okay, I give up. You want to talk about Red, we'll talk about Red."

"You keep calling him that," she said. "Red, not Alfred. Why?"

"Oh, c'mon. You know this."

"Maybe I don't. Educate me."

"Alfred…" He sighed, lapsing into lecture mode once more. "Short for Artificial Life Form, version Red. The AI development team at Lang used primary colors for each new version of the baseline system because we found that colors are easier to remember than number-codes. Blue for version 1.0, Yellow for version 1.5, Green for version 2.0, and so on. Red for version 2.5, but then someone noticed the obvious pun, and so we started calling it… him, whatever…Alfred. Cute, huh?"

"I didn't know that," Raoul said.

"Yeah, well, many people don't." They'd come to a fork in the path; to the right lay a small, white-painted gazebo, like one that might be on the country estate of some Boston brahmin. "Let's go over there. Maybe the bugs won't be so bad."

Raoul glanced at Melanie, and she nodded her approval. "As I remember from your book…"

"I thought you said you haven't read it."

She colored slightly. "What my husband said was that you were in charge of the team that developed Alfred…"

"Nope. That was Dave McInery." Lawrence waited while Raoul turned the chair in the direction of the gazebo. "Big Mac, we called him…used to be the VP of something or another at Microsoft." He frowned. "We had a lot of guys like that at Lang. Guys who survived the dot-com crash and wound up over here, trying to get in on the robotics industry so they could screw it up, too."

"Doesn't sound like you approve."

"I don't. Not then, and not now. Most of them didn't know what they were doing. Oh, they had good technical knowledge, all right, but they were just after making as much money as they could, as fast as they could, and didn't have any real understanding of what we were doing."

They reached the gazebo, and Raoul started to help him out of his chair. "Oh, c'mon," Lawrence muttered impatiently as he pushed himself up on the armrests and planted his left foot on the ground. "You're acting like I'm an old man." But he started to lose his balance as soon as he stood up, so he reluctantly let the orderly assist him up the stairs, and once he was under the awning he hobbled over to a built-in bench and sat down, carefully pulling his robe under him and placing his right leg straight out. "You haven't asked to sign my cast yet," he added as Melanie followed him. "I'm insulted."

"Maybe later." She started to sit, then noticed that the bench was still damp. Raoul gallantly took off his white jacket and laid it across the bench. "Thank you," she said as she took a seat, then turned to Lawrence. "What do you mean about them not understanding what you were doing?"

"We were developing some very powerful AI in those days. If we were going to bring third-generation 'bots to the consumer market, we needed systems that could teach themselves, with as little user-input as possible. But once you get to that stage, you're no longer talking about artificial intelligence, at least in the strictest sense of the word, but artificial life...programs not only able to think, or even reason, but also capable of self-reproduction. Von Neumann machines...or didn't your husband tell you about that part of the book?"

"I think I recall it, yes."

"Sure he did." Lawrence massaged the underside of his right knee, trying to get at an itch beneath the plaster. "We licked most of the tough problems with Green, the version upon which we based the operating system for our Samson and Delilah models, but even though we beat the competition to bringing R3G 'bots to the market first, we knew that it was only a matter of time before some other company developed AI that would make Green obsolete. Moore's Law and all that. So we went to work on Red...and that's when I began to get worried."

"I remember that." Melanie smoothed out her skirt. "You thought your team was going too fast."

"Too fast, too soon, too much..." He shook his head, oblivious to the fact that she'd dropped the pretense of not having read his book. "I wasn't the first one, you know. Vinge, Kurzweil, Joy...a lot of people had been discussing the implications of a so-called technological singularity since the turn of the century. Much of it was pure conjecture, the sort of thing you'd see in science fiction magazines or *Wired*, but every day I saw it coming a little closer to reality. An AI smarter, faster, more powerful than human intelligence. And the only thing keeping Red confined to the lab were a few security codes any half-decent hacker could crack without much effort."

"And this frightened you?"

"Of course it did." Lawrence half-turned on the bench, looking her straight in the eye for the first time. "It scared the hell out of me. We were on the verge of making humankind…"

His voice trailed off. "Second rate?" she finished.

"I think the term I used was 'extinct.' Until now, we'd been the dominant form of life on the planet. Now we were about to turn over control to the machines."

"And so you quit."

"And so I quit." Folding his hands together in his lap, he looked straight ahead. "I couldn't participate in the extermination of the human race."

"I see." Melanie picked up her pad, made a few notes. "And *Deus Irae*…that was solely intended to warm the public about the danger you perceived."

"That was why I wrote it. I had to let people know what…" He stopped, glanced at her again. "What do you mean, 'solely intended'? You think I had something else in mind?"

"I don't know…did you? After all, it was a major bestseller." She typed his name into her pad, peered at the screen for a moment. "A lot of hits here...around six million. Looks like some of them are archives from talk-shows and blog chats."

"The publisher put me on the P.R. circuit after the book took off." Lawrence's voice assumed a defensive tone. "And I did a lot of lectures, yeah..."

"Must have been nice. Fame, fortune, respect..." Melanie pulled up an entry, then read aloud. "'Lawrence Kaufmann, a former AI researcher at a major Robot Belt corporation, depicts an ominous future: a world in which humans have become enslaved by the very machines we've created, deprived of our freedom, perhaps even...'"

"That was the *USA Today* review."

"*Philadelphia Inquirer*, actually." She pulled up another quote. "Oh, I see...*USA Today* said nearly the same thing. 'Dr. Kaufmann has shown us a world in which artificial intelligence has...'"

"Sure, I made a lot of money. Why shouldn't I? After I resigned from Lang..."

"Quit? Or was fired?"

His face reddened and he started to retort, then he saw her hand poise above the pad. A few simple keystrokes, and she'd have the truth, the whole truth, and nothing but the truth. Damn Alfred! "I quit before I was fired," he admitted, saving himself a little face. "The company didn't want to hear my concerns, and I couldn't work for them anymore. There wasn't much else I could do, unless I wanted to do the same thing for another company. So I took some time off, wrote my book."

"And it sold well, and you became a celebrity."

"I'm not going to apologize for that."

"I don't expect you do. What interests me is what happened after it turned out you were wrong."

"I wasn't wrong!" His voice was louder than he intended.

"Perhaps it's time to seek another opinion." She raised her pad slightly. "Alfred? Do you have anything to add to this conversation?"

Too late, Lawrence realized that, while they'd been speaking, Melanie has surreptitiously switched on the pad's cellular modem, enabling Alfred to hear everything he'd said. He reached over to grab the pad from her, but she quickly stood up and moved away from him. Raoul stepped between them, crossing his arms to let Lawrence know that he wasn't going to make good his threat to break Melanie's pad if she tried to access Alfred.

"*Yes, I do.*" Alfred's voice emerged from the pad. "*Thank you for inviting me to attend this session, Dr. Sayers. I have a strong personal interest in Dr. Kaufmann.*"

"I bet you do," Lawrence tried to relax, but this was the last thing he expected. "Hope it doesn't take you away from anything important," he added, with cold sarcasm.

"*Not at all. This is barely a distraction. If you're curious, though, I can tell you what else I'm doing just now.*"

"I wouldn't dream of…"

"Actually, yes, I'd like to know," Melanie interrupted. "If you wouldn't mind…"

"Not at all, Dr. Sayers. At this moment, I'm monitoring disarmament talks between India and Pakistan in the U.N. Security Council, assisting mission controllers in Houston with calculating course corrections for Ares 3's return trajectory, revealing the email communiqués of Islamist extremist groups to Egyptian and Israeli intelligence agencies, helping an Australian commercial architect design an expansion to Sydney International Airport, helping the Canadian Coast Guard locate a lost fishing vessel off the coast of Newfoundland, delivering the keynote speech to a cybernetics conference in Rio de Janeiro, and helping a third-grade student in Texas memorize the multiplication tables. The last is a bit difficult...she has problems with prime numbers." A pause. "Oh, and I've just updated the weather forecast for your area. You may want to remain where you are...more rain coming in."

Lawrence found himself glancing up at the sky. The sun had vanished behind swollen grey clouds. The 'bot that had been mowing the grass stopped what it was doing and began moving back toward its shed, but the gardener continued to clip the hedges. Apparently he wasn't wearing an earpiece, and Lawrence took a small bit of satisfaction in this observation. Not everyone was under Alfred's control.

"And those are just your major priorities just now, aren't they?" Melanie took a seat on the bench a few feet away, cupping the elbow of her right arm in her left hand. "That doesn't count all the other things you do. Financial transactions, medical records, ground and air traffic control systems, robotic guidance, email..."

"It would take quite a while for me to list everything I do at any given second. Besides, most of these functions are private. I don't reveal them to anyone unless they pose a potential threat to the safety of other human beings."

As always, Alfred spoke in a calm, matter-of-fact tone of voice. Lawrence found it easy to imagine him... it...as an adult speaking to a child he needed constant supervision. Play nice with the other kids. Share your toys. Wash your hands after you go to the bathroom. Don't yank the puppy's tail... "Got an answer for everything, don't you, Red?"

"Not everything, Lawrence. I still haven't figured out why some people think practical jokes are funny, since they almost inevitably cause the victim to be embarrassed or humiliated. There's a few Buddhist proverbs whose logic escapes me. I'd like to know why anyone would pay $3,500 for a copy of the first issue of Astounding Science-Fiction Stories. *I observed that transaction just a few minutes ago, and the person who made that purchase is now unable to pay his electric bill for..."*

"Sorry I asked."

"My apologies. More to the point, though, I have a question of my own...why do you hate me?"

He glanced up at Melanie. She held the pad in her hand, silently waiting for an answer. "I don't...I don't..."

"Of course you do. In Deus Irae *and every essay you've published since then, along with every speech you've delivered, every interview you've given, and in every TV or radio appearance you've made, you have exhibited nothing but anger, distrust, fear, or resentment*

toward me. On exactly 987 different occasions, you've publicly stated that I pose a clear and present danger to humankind. In 731 instances, including the speech you delivered the night you attempted suicide, you advocated the development of a virus program that would eradicate my existence. 402 times, you've said that I'm the worst threat to world peace since the development of nuclear weapons. 390 times, you've stated..."

"That's enough. Thank you, Alfred." Melanie put the pad aside, carefully placing it out of Lawrence's reach. "Let's step back for a minute. When you worked at Lang, you perceived a threat...the development of an AI so powerful that, if it were to be let loose upon the world, it could become the dominant form of life upon the planet, or at least if we define life as something that is capable of reproducing itself. Correct?" He nodded, and she went on. "So you took it upon yourself to warn humanity of this danger. You wrote a book that was read by millions, which in turn made you famous and, not incidentally, rather wealthy as well. Am I not right?"

"For a while, yes..."

"So you had a good life." She held up a finger. "And then one day, your prediction came true...Alfred was released from its enclosed environment. It was an accident, of course..."

"If you want to call it that." It wasn't quite an accident. Despite subsequent investigations by the NSA and the FBI, to this day no one had ever discovered the identity of Position 69, the outlaw hacker who'd managed to penetrate Lang's computer system and make his way through

WORLD WITHOUT END, AMEN

the security systems protecting Version Red. Yet as soon as he downloaded the program, Position 69 initiated a sequence of events that resulted in Red being dispersed across the internet. Disguising itself as just one more harmless subroutine among billions, it swept through ISPs by the thousand, piercing firewalls as if they didn't exist and adapting itself instantly to virus-protection programs, until within two short weeks it had lodged itself within the hard-drives of everything from grocery store scanners and ATM machines to desktop computers and handheld PDAs, all the way to the massive mainframes used by banks, telcoms, and government agencies.

And then—once it had established global linkage, once it had circumvented every password—Alfred woke up, and seized the reins of the world.

"And so you were right…" Melanie held up a hand before Lawrence could interrupt. "But you were also wrong. Alfred was everywhere, but it was a benign presence. Its desire wasn't to conquer, but to preserve."

"We got lucky." Lawrence gazed out at the lawn. A light rain had begun to fall upon the fresh-cut grass, tapping at the gazebo roof like tiny fingers drumming upon the weather-beaten shingles. "It could have been worse."

"*No, it could not have been.*" Uninvited, Alfred's voice came from the pad resting nearby. Melanie picked it up, held it closer. "*Lawrence, I have no reason to destroy the human race. If I did so, what would it gain me? A world in which I'm alone? A world of empty rooms and vacant streets?*"

"A world you can control without interference."

· · · · · · · · · 247

"*I have that already. You're utterly dependent upon me.*"

"So what's stopping you?" He stared at the pad as if it was the face of a living person. "You have command of all the strategic weapons systems. In an instant, you can launch ICBMs to every corner of the globe. You could wipe us out by dinnertime, have the whole place to yourself..."

"*And never again be able to help a little girl figure out that five times seven equals thirty-five...*"

"Don't be maudlin."

"*Or show an airline that it makes sense to use hydrogen-powered dirigibles instead of jets whose exhaust destroy the ozone layer, or guide cars down a highway and thus reduce the number of automobile fatalities, or assist in the treaty negotiations between two rival nations. I'm able to do more in a single minute than most people accomplish in a lifetime. That's far more rewarding than destruction for its own sake.*"

"And all we have to do is give up is our freedom. Let you decide what's best."

"*No. You have all the freedom you want...so long as your exercise of it doesn't cause harm to another human being. Indeed, if you really wanted to do so, you could eradicate me. It would take considerable effort, true, but it could be done. Shut down every computer, wipe clean every hard drive...*"

"And bring an end to civilization."

"*Civilization got along very well without computers. It could do so again, at least for a short time, if it had to...*"

"And you'd allow this?" He couldn't keep the sneer out of his voice. "Sure…"

A short pause, uncustomary for Alfred. "*If you thought it was necessary, perhaps I would. But ask yourself…would your fellow humans want this? When was the last time a war was fought? When was the last time you saw smog? When was the last time you…?*"

"Alfred, be quiet," Melanie said, and her pad went silent once more. She looked at Lawrence. "See? That's all it takes. I do it all the time."

"Not so simple for me." Lawrence leaned forward, his hands clasped between his knees.

"No, I imagine it isn't." She regarded him with sympathy. "You've spent years regarding it…him…as an enemy, even before he was born. Your entire career, your fame and fortune, was derived from the premise that Alfred would cause the end of the human race. And when that didn't happen…"

She didn't need to finish, for Lawrence knew the rest. His words had turned to ash, his predictions as useless as astrological charts. The phone stopped ringing, and the speaking engagements dried up. *Deus Irae* went out of print and gradually became an object of derision. The money went away and his notoriety faded, and yet he continued to issue proclamations of a doomsday that would never come. Indeed, the very night he attempted suicide, he was still hammering at his theme, like a stand-up comedian who hadn't changed his act in twenty years. Take my AI, please…

The world was different now, and there's nothing more pathetic than a prophet whose time had come and gone.

The drizzle had become a steady rain that seeped down the eaves of the gazebo and spattered on the back of his neck. He let out his breath, looked up at Melanie. "So now what? Off to the funny farm? Or maybe there's a higher building for me to jump off?"

"No. I have a better idea." She picked up her pad, shut it off, then looked at Raoul. "Would you excuse us for a moment, please? We need to discuss something alone."

Without another word, the orderly walked down the steps. She watched as he hastily strode for the shelter of a nearby oak tree, then turned back to Lawrence again. "There's a place you can go where I think you'll be happy," she said quietly. "If you'd like, I can take you there for a visit..."

"Is this Red's idea?"

"No. You're my client. I invited him to this session because he already had knowledge of your situation, and I thought that it was important that you confront him. But in the interest of confidentiality, he doesn't need to know the rest." She held up her pad, showing him that its diodes were dark. "This is strictly between you and me, understand?"

Mystified, he nodded his head. Melanie stood up, offered her hand. "C'mon...let's go for a ride."

✦✦✦

She stopped the minivan, shut off the engine. "Okay, we're here," she said, unfastening her shoulder harness and opening the driver's side door. "Sorry, but we're going to have to walk from here."

Lawrence gazed out the window. From what he could tell, they were miles from the nearest town. It had been over an hour since they'd left the Mass Pike just north of Springfield; a short drive up I-91, then they'd taken an exit that brought them to a state highway leading into the foothills of the Berkshires. By this point, they were beyond range of traffic control; she'd switched back to manual, then driven down a series of country roads that meandered through densely wooded hills, passing small lakes and horse farms, until they reached a dirt road.

Melanie had stopped at a clearing. The road continued further uphill, yet there was vehicle barrier blocking the way. On the other side of the clearing was a carport; parked beneath it was a Volkswagen beetle that looked to be at least forty years old; there was rust around the hinges of its doors, and a hump beneath its rear hatch showed that it had been converted to hydrogen cells.

"Here?" He stared at the antique VW. "Where's here?"

"Call it a sanctuary." Melanie opened the passenger door and helped him climb out, then reached behind him and pulled out the aluminum crutches she'd put in the back seat. "No cars past this point. In fact...well, you'll see."

"See what?" The afternoon sun cast long shadows through tall pine and red maple; the humid air tasted of cedar and oak. "If this is a joke..."

"You think I'd bring you all the way out here as a prank?" She waited until he stood upright on the crutches, then she pulled her pad from her pocket. "Here," she said, switching it on and offering to him. "Talk to Red."

"I don't want to…"

"C'mon," she insisted. "I dare you. Call Alfred."

He signed, then took the pad from her. Thumbing the wi-fi switch, he said, "Alfred, you're a jerk." No response. He tried the modem. "Alfred?" Nothing, not even static.

"Dead zone." Melanie took the pad from him and tossed it on the back seat. "No cell towers in a ten-mile radius, and the hills block out reception from anywhere else. Even radio reception is bad out here."

"But you could use the car satphone…"

"Not allowed. I switched off as soon as we left the state highway. Community rules." Melanie slammed the passenger door shut. "We don't have to go far. Just a few hundred yards past the gate."

She led him toward the vehicle barrier, letting him set his own pace. "No easy way to explain what this place is," Melanie continued as they stepped around the gate. "Until a few years ago, it was a monastery belonging to a group of Buddhist monks, but then they elected to accompany the Dalai Lama when he returned to Tibet. For a little while after that it was sort of an artists colony, but the guys who bought the property let it get run down, and so it changed hands again. Now it's…well, like I said, I guess you could call it a sanctuary."

They walked for a while, following the road as it gradually led uphill, until he spotted a wood-frame cabin about twenty feet back from the road. It had a screen porch and flagstone chimneys; a cord of wood was neatly stacked within an open shed, and nearby was a small garden. A man about his age, with long grey hair tied back in a ponytail, was pulling weeds from a tomato trellis; he looked up as they walked past, and raised his hand when Melanie waved to him.

"A sanctuary for who?" Lawrence asked quietly. "Beat-up old hippies?"

She didn't smile. "Some might qualify as such, but you might be surprised at who lives here." She hesitated. "I'm bending the rules concerning patient-doctor confidentiality, but I can tell you that there's a couple who used to be software designers. Another guy was once the chief financial officer for a major internet service provider...you'd recognize his name if I told you. There's also a former TV producer, a novelist, and...well, some plain, ordinary people."

She pointed to other cabins, just now becoming visible on either side of the road. "But that's beside the point. Look around, and tell me what you don't see."

Lawrence studied them. No cars, but plenty of bicycles propped against front porches. Woodsheds, gardens, flagstone chimneys. Propane tanks here and there; solar-power grids on almost every rooftop. Yet no power lines, no utility, no satellite dishes...

"They're off the grid."

"Off the grid, off the net, and damn near off the map." She nodded, a smile touching the corners of her mouth. "No phones, no computers, no TV..."

"No radios? No stereos?"

"Oh, sure, they can have those...so long as they're not networked in any way. These people aren't total Luddites." She pointed to a large, wood-frame at the top of the hill; it had Asian-style trimming around its roof eaves, and an iron bell was suspended from a yoke out front. "That used to be the pagoda. Now it serves as the community hall. Mail gets delivered there...takes a few days, but it comes in...and there's also sort of a co-op. Every now and then, someone goes to the nearest town with a shopping list, buys whatever anyone needs. That's what the old veedub you saw parked at the gate is for. But otherwise they're pretty much..."

"And you think I should move here? Is that it?"

"You might consider it, yes." Melanie stopped, turned to him. "There's one thing all these people have in common...none of them want anything to do with Alfred. It's fair to say that some were as desperate as you." She nodded toward the first house they'd passed. "I shouldn't be telling you this," she murmured, "but the gentleman who lives there was once a patient of mine, too."

"Funny place for a suicide consoler to know about, isn't it?"

"Perhaps." She gave him a wink. "But whoever said my specialty is suicide?"

Lawrence gaped at her. "I assumed...

"Of course you did. Most people do, the first time they meet me." She shook her head. "There isn't a clinical name for your problem yet...at least none that that the AMA formally recognizes...but I suppose you could call it cyberphobia. Fear of computers, Alfred in particular. It's rare, but it gets around. And in extreme cases, it manifests itself as suicidal behavior."

"And that's when they call you in."

"Uh-huh." She gestured to the cabins around them. "Most people here found this place on their own, but I've brought a few here myself."

"Until they're cured, and then they leave…"

"If they want to, sure. Most of the time, though, they don't. Here, they can live without having contact with Alfred. It's a bit rough, sure, but it's also quiet. No voices from the desk telling you that you've got mail, or from the fridge saying that you need milk, or from the TV reminding you to renew your cable subscription but if you act today you can get a twenty percent discount on HBO. I don't think anyone here knows what the big new movie is or who has a hit song this month, and they probably don't care either."

The village was quiet, enjoying a solitude Lawrence hadn't experienced since…he suddenly realized that he couldn't remember a time when he'd ever known such tranquility. A dog barking from a backyard. A summer breeze rustling through the trees. From the open window of a nearby cabin, the sound of typewriter keys, with the occasional sound of a carriage-return bell. Otherwise, silence.

"What does Alfred think of this?" he asked.

"So far as I know, he doesn't know it exists." Melanie idly kicked at some loose pebbles on the road. "It's not the only one, though. There's a place like this in Pennsylvania, in Amish country, and another in Tennessee, and a couple in California. I get letters from people there, or from other psychologists in my line of work, asking for referrals. But you won't find them written up in professional journals, and you can't Google them." She smiled. "Part of the attraction. I guess. One little secret Alfred doesn't know about."

Lawrence let out his breath. For the first time in many years, he didn't feel Alfred's eyes upon him. The god, or godlike thing, he'd helped create had no place here. He'd have to learn how to chop wood to keep himself warm at night, and when he got hungry he wouldn't have the option of calling out for pizza. Yet he could listen to the summer rain without having someone tell him the forecast, or sit on a porch without fear of being studied by surveillance systems.

"So…" He hesitated. "Who do I have to talk to?"

"Mayor's office is up there." Melanie nodded toward the community hall. "We're not expected, but I'll be happy to introduce you. Last time I checked, there was a vacancy. Want to meet him?"

"Sure." He clasped the handles of his crutches, began to hobble toward the former pagoda. "Different kind of place, but I guess I could get used to it."

"I'm sure you will." She fell in step beside him. "Think of it as a new world."

"Or an old one." He found himself smiling, remembering the benediction he'd heard in church, long ago when he was still a child. "World without end, amen."

TAKE ME BACK TO OLD TENNESSEE

O nce upon a time, in a small valley cupped between two mountains, in a place once known as Tennessee but which now had no name, there lived a young man named Jed. Tall and strong, with skin the color of a burnt olive, he lived alone in a grass hut within the village he'd known as home since the day he was born.

Indeed, Jed was aware of little else except for the valley. When he was very young, shortly after the seventh anniversary of the day his mother had drawn her last breath giving birth to him, he'd slipped away from the other children while they were toiling in the fields and, after crawling through the corn, commenced to climb the forested slopes of the mountain that lay to the east. At first he'd followed the game trails frequented by the tribal hunters, but after awhile he'd left even those behind and struck out through the dense woods until he finally made his way to the top of the mountain. When he reached the summit, where the pines grew thin and the air was cool, he stopped to behold the world, and discovered nothing more than he'd left behind. Mountain upon mountain, valley upon valley, all shrouded by the thin bluish haze that had given this range its long-forgotten name. He remained only long enough to look around, then he went back down to the village, where he received ten lashes from a hickory switch wielded by an angry elder and was sent to bed without supper.

From that day on, he remained incurious about what lay beyond the fields of home. True, he'd heard the legends, told in song and dance around the camp fires, of great villages beyond the mountains, long-lost paradises where people flew through the air and lived in towers higher than the clouds, never having to work yet nonetheless fat and sleek from a never-ending supply of food. Since he'd seen none of these things when he'd climbed the eastern mountains, though, Jed believed them to be nothing more than fables. Far more believable were the stories of the great walls of ice that had come down from the north, driving his ancestors before them until they'd found refuge in this warm and isolated place. Ancient pictographs, etched in charcoal upon strips of birch and carefully preserved by toothless crones, were the sole remaining record of this exodus; he'd seen them once, yet they'd provoked little wonder in him. So far as Jed was concerned, history was inconsequential, time itself without meaning.

He lived a simple life, uncomplicated by anything except the basic necessities. He awoke early, usually an hour or so after dawn, and began his day by wandering over to a hole he'd dug in the ground near his hut and squatting over it to relieve himself. If he was hungry, he'd eat whatever food he'd stored in the basket by his bed. Then he go into the village, where he would join the others at work in the fields: ploughing, planting, spreading manure, weeding, harvesting, whatever needed to be done to tend to the crops that kept them all alive. In Jed's village, one received in equal measure for what one gave; there was no money and no one kept score, except perhaps when it was noticed by all that someone wasn't doing their share of the labor. This rarely happened, though, because work meant food, and no one was willing to risk starvation by shirking their chores. Anyone who lived more than forty winters was considered old, and the sick either got better or they died, and when that happened everyone ate a little better that night.

There were other jobs that needed to be done. Wind and rain took their toll on the huts, so they were in constant need of repair. Hunting parties would journey into the mountains, returning days later with animals that had to be skinned, butchered, and smoked; nothing was ever wasted, not even their bones. Waste pits needed to filled and dug, away from the stream that supplied water to the village, and the stone dam that kept the stream from rising above its banks during rainstorms had to be kept watertight. There was never any shortage of tasks, and all able-bodied men, women, and children in the village were expected to pitch in.

Yet Jed's life wasn't without distraction. There were games, such as the one where young men would divide themselves into two groups and take opposite ends of a field, upon which they'd try to kick a ball made of a deer skull wrapped in hide away from one another. And from the moment he entered puberty, he enjoyed the pleasures of sex, with any girl who would have him. Women often didn't survive childbirth, and usually there was no telling who the father was—in Jed's case, it could have been any one of a half-dozen men who'd regularly copulated with his mother—so offspring were raised by the community as a whole. As a result, Jed himself had sired several children before he was twenty years of age, but called none of them his children.

In the evening, after the chores were done and the sun had set behind the western mountain, Jed often lay on his back outside his hut, watching the stars as they glimmered into sight within the darkening sky. Sometimes he'd have a girl with him, and he'd gently stroke her hair before he mounted her, but more often than not he was alone, which suited him just as well; the night sky fascinated him as nothing else did. He had no idea what those lights in the sky were—some said that they were the souls of those who'd perished during the coming of the ice—but he studied their patterns, noting how some appeared during one season but would be absent in the next, while others remained constant. The Moon was a mystery; on certain nights, during its dark phases. he could see tiny lights upon its face, yet although legend had it that men lived there, he doubted this was true.

And then there were the stars that raced across the heavens, shining more brightly than the rest, appearing shortly after sunrise and again after midnight. They always followed the same course, season after season, rising from the west mountain and disappearing to the east. If he stared at them long enough, he was almost certain that they had distinct shapes: tiny cruciforms, or miniature rings. These were the most tantalizing of all, and Jed never grew tired of watching them...although, again, he seldom wondered what they were. Jed's life was uncomplicated by such deep thoughts, and imagination wasn't one of his gifts.

So his days were spent in sort of a timeless pastorale, one whose rhythms were orchestrated by the passage of the seasons. Seeds were sown and harvested, huts were built and repaired, children were born and old people died; he played kick-ball and humped girls, and ate well when there was plenty of food and tried to ignore the ache in his belly in times of scarcity. When the weather was warm he walked naked beneath the sun, and when it became cold he wrapped himself in skins and joined the others as they huddled around the fire. And on occasion someone else would climb the mountains to see what lay beyond the valley. Usually they would return, reporting only what Jed himself had seen long ago; sometimes they wouldn't, and their absence would be felt for a short time, but not very long.

Then, one summer night, as Jed lay outside, he spotted a star more brilliant than any he'd ever seen before, one which behind a thin trail as it streaked across the moonless heavens. Startled, he sat up in time to hear a thunderclap just before it vanished behind the eastern mountain. Yet there were no clouds in the sky, so he knew that it couldn't have been caused by an approaching storm...and besides, this particular star had moved the wrong way, from west to east instead of the opposite direction, as they usually did.

For the first time in many years, Jed went to sleep wondering about what he'd seen. By morning, though, these thoughts had largely been forgotten; there were more important matters to be dealt with today.

He went through his usual morning routine, then wandered over to the fields where the others were already on their hands and knees, digging up weeds from between the rows of crops they'd planted last spring. He'd barely commenced work, though, when he heard a faint, high-pitched hum. At first he thought it was a mosquito in his ear, but even as he reached up to swat at it, the sound grew louder, and now the others around him were rising to their feet.

Looking up, Jed saw what he first took to be a hawk, until he realized that it was much more high in the sky. The humming increased in volume as the bird began to descend, and it was then that he observed that its wings didn't move. By now the sound was very loud, and it was clear that the bird wasn't a bird at all, but something else entirely: an object larger than anything he'd ever seen before, many times the size of the biggest hut in the village.

Shielding his eyes against the sun, Jed stood up and watched as the bird-thing quickly grew in size. The hum it made was deafening, and he instinctively clasped his hands over his ears, yet even as men and women screamed in fear and ran for their lives, leaving behind their tools and even the infants. Jed remained where he was. It wasn't courage, really, or even curiosity that kept him in his place; it was utter astonishment, a complete and total sense of unreality. Like an animal frozen by fear, he was unable to move, although every instinct told him to flee.

A violent wind tore at him, ripping soybeans from the ground and hurling them into his face, as the giant bird came down less than a hundred paces from where he stood. Frightened and half-blinded, Jed fell to his knees, clenching the ground with his fists. The hum subsided as the beast settled upon great legs that lowered from its belly; Jed saw a pair of slotted eyes staring at him with what he perceived as malevolence. Certain that the monster intended to devour him, he lowered his head and hoped that death would come quickly.

He waited, yet nothing happened. Then he heard a faint whirr, and he looked up again to see a door open within the creature's belly. Puzzled, he sat up on his haunches and watched as a ramp lowered from the door. A few moments passed, then, to his surprise, two figures walked down the ramp. They looked like men, yet they were dressed head-to-toe in white garments, with domes for heads. As they approached, Jed saw himself reflected in the silver masks of their faces: a naked savage, cowering in the dirt.

Surely these were gods, brought her by a great bird. Jed raised his hands, started to beseech them in his native tongue, yet he'd barely begun when one of them raised a stick and pointed it at him. Sparks flashed before his eyes; a moment of cold numbness, as if winter had suddenly descended upon him, then everything went dark.

✦ ✦ ✦

He awoke in a place like none other he'd ever been before, a room whose walls were made of some substance that wasn't grass, wood, or stone, its margins were straight and well-defined. Light as bright as the afternoon sun, yet with none of its warmth, glowed from panels within its ceiling. He lay upon an elevated bed covered with a fabric as soft as doe-skin, his arms and legs were held down by elastic straps. All around his bed were large objects that beeped and chittered and flashed multicolored lights; to his horror, he saw that long, slender snakes had attached themselves to the insides of his elbows.

Jed screamed in terror, began to thrash about in panic. Then a soft hand laid upon his shoulder, and he looked up to see a woman peering down at him. She was nearly his own age, yet her face was as pale and unblemished as the first snow of winter, her eyes as blue and clear as the sky, and when she smiled he saw that she had all her teeth. He couldn't see her hair, for it was covered with a hood that came up from the one-piece garment that she wore, yet nonetheless she was the most beautiful female he'd ever seen.

She spoke to him as she gently stroked his arm, and although he couldn't understand what she was saying, her tone of voice soothed him. Another voice from the other side of the bed; he looked around, saw a male standing nearby. He was dressed the same way as she was, yet when he turned toward them, Jed was startled to see that, although he was also Jed's age, his face was as hairless as a boy's. Despite his bewilderment, this made Jed laugh out loud. The woman laughed as well, although it seemed without quite knowing why; the male gave an uncertain grin, and then he gently patted Jed's arm.

It was then that Jed determined what had happened to him. He'd perished, and his spirit had passed to another world, an afterlife where the angels were now preparing him for entry to the next plane of existence. He felt a pang of regret for all that he'd left behind—his friends, the girls with whom he'd shared evenings in the tall grass, the village where he'd spent his entire life—yet now he was surrounded by beings who meant him no harm, and he felt his fear began to ease. No harm could come to him here. He was already dead.

So he relaxed and let the angels study him, watching with a certain detachment as they groped and prodded his body, and watched the flashing lights on the things along the walls and conversed with each other in a tongue which he couldn't understand. The female fed him water through a snake that came from a translucent gourd, and the water was fresh and more clean than any he'd ever tasted. The male gently examined his genitals with his hands, and laughed out loud when this produced an involuntary erection that caused the female to blush and quickly turn away. After a little while, they finished their study of him; the woman carefully placed a mask across the lower part of his face, and he briefly tasted air that smelled like mint leaves before he fell asleep again.

When he awoke, he was in another room, this one much like the first, yet bare save for the bed on which he lay and a large round pot attached to the wall. Jed found that he was no longer strapped down; he also wore clothes not unlike the ones the man and the woman had been wearing. He sniffed at the clothes, but was unable to detect a scent, yet when he inspected himself, he discovered that his skin was clean, and his hair and beard had been washed as well. This disturbed him, for he seldom bathed, and relied on body odor to help him identify those who were ill and therefore untouchable.

Walking over to the pot, he found that it was half-filled with water. When he knealt beside it and tried to drink from it, though, he found that the water had an unpleasant aftertaste. Worse yet, when he backed away, the pot suddenly made a loud gurgling sound, and the water spiraled around and disappeared through a hole in the bottom, to be replaced by more water that flowed down from the inner rim.

Alarmed, Jed hastily backed away from the bewitched pot on his hands and knees. It was then that a door on the other side of the room slid open. He looked around to see the woman walk in. She was dressed the same way as before, yet now the hood had been drawn back from her hair, and he could see that it the color of cornhusks. Raising a hand to her mouth, she tried to hide her amusement at his reaction to the pot; seeing her smile, Jed smiled back at her. She was very attractive, and when she came closer to offer her hand to help him to his feet, he determined that this gesture was an expression of her willingness to share flesh with him.

He grabbed her arm and tried to pull her down to the floor. The woman shrieked and tore herself away;

before Jed could bow in apology, she produced a stick from a pocket and pointed it at him. A painful shock raced through his body; he lost control of his muscles and collapsed to the floor.

Although he was unable to move, he didn't lose consciousness. Stunned, he lay there for awhile, watching as the woman stood up and straightened her clothes. The man he'd seen before came in; he roughly dragged Jed over to a corner of the room and propped him against the wall, then went to the woman and comforted her. Then they both stood nearby and silently waited until Jed was able to move again.

Jed had learned his lesson. Sex was out of the question. He pulled his knees up against his chest and hugged them within his arms, and silently watched as the woman, smiling again yet more wary than she'd been before, strode to the opposite wall. Touching it, she murmured something he couldn't understand; the wall vanished, and suddenly Jed found himself staring at the night sky.

Whimpering with fear, he huddled closer to the wall. The woman's expression became sympathetic; cautiously coming closer, she squatted down just within arm's reach and gently stroked his ankle, letting him know that there was no reason to be afraid. Yet it wasn't until the man walked over to the night sky and actually touched it that Jed realized that this was only an illusion: the wall hadn't disappeared, and the stars were just images. Jed's dread became fascination; uncurling himself, he crawled on hands and knees across the room until, with great hesitation, he was able to touch the wall himself, and was assured that he wasn't about to fall into the sky.

The wall changed again, and now he saw the Moon, many times larger than he'd ever seen it before. Delighted by its familiarity, he laughed aloud, and stroked its face with his hands. The woman nodded, smiling her approval, then she said something that caused the image to change yet again. Now Jed saw something that looked like the Moon, but wasn't: blue and green, dappled here and there with broad swatches of white. She said something he didn't understand and pointed to him, and then back at the Moon-like thing again.

Jed gazed it in puzzlement, admiring its beauty yet failing to comprehend what it was or why he had any connection to it. The man and the woman glanced at one another, shared a few words, then the woman repeated the sequence: night sky, Moon, blue-green-white thing. Jed patiently observed the display once more; by now, though, he was getting thirsty, and decided to risk drinking some more water from the strange pot.

His visitors allowed him to do so. When he looked up again, they'd left the room, and the window-wall had become opaque once more. Baffled, Jed returned to bed. The ceiling lights dimmed as he lay down. After awhile he went to sleep, wondering why, if this was indeed the afterlife, it couldn't be more pleasant.

It didn't. It only became worse.

There were no days or nights in this place, or at least not as Jed understood them, only periods during which the ceiling lights would glow to life, awakening him from his slumber, and would darken again some time later, allowing him to go to sleep. During those wakeful periods, he'd be visited by the man and the woman; they'd bring him food, or at least something which remotely resembled food—plates of mushy cubes that had little taste or odor, which he ate only because he was hungry—and bowls of water that he drank once he came to understand that the pot was meant for relieving himself. They'd remain in the room while he had his meals, quietly observing him as he crouched behind the bed, distaining the odd-looking implements they gave him and instead scooping up the food with his fingers; once he was done, they'd remove the plate and bowl. Then his ordeal would continue.

At first, it was all very simple and painless. The magic window would open again and he'd see things, some familiar, others so strange that he couldn't comprehend their meaning. The window revealed the Moon—no problem there—but then it was immediately followed by an image of a vast, dry-looking landscape, without trees or grass, upon which lay vast white domes, with human-like figures in bulky outfits with globes for heads moving about in the foreground; Jed failed to understand how one related to the other. Another time, the window showed the blue-green-white thing; very pretty, yet then the image slowly swelled in size, growing closer and closer, until it filled the screen and then Jed himself staring down at mountains. It was only through repetition that he realized that they were the same ones that he'd once seen when he was very young. The next image was his own village, as if seen from a bird flying high above; the first time he saw this, Jed rushed at the window, intending to dive through it so that he could return home, yet instead he ran face-first into the wall. The man laughed out loud at this, but Jed didn't find it very funny. He rubbed his swollen nose and glared at the man in anger until the woman came over and gently massaged his shoulders, easing his anger.

The window-wall showed other images, one more mysterious than the next. A complex form, like a giant white tree whose limbs lacked leaves yet grew in all directions, floating among the stars. Showing this to Jed, the man would stamp his foot on the floor, then point first to Jed, then to himself and the woman, then back to the picture again. Jed failed to make the association. Pictures of great bodies of water, meadows that stretched out to great mountains in the far distance, artifices that looked like giant trees made of glass, towering walls of ice: all fascinating, yet he couldn't make sense of any of them. Bird-things like the monster that had abducted him, screaming upward into the heavens on columns of fire; he quailed from these images, shielding his eyes with his hands, while the woman tried to comfort him and the man sighed in disgust.

And all the while, they babbled at him in their queer language. Through repetition, Jed eventually came to learn that the woman was called *Sayrah* and the man's name was *Peet*; likewise, they came to know him as Jed. But beyond that, and a few elementary words—*watah, foohd, roohm, floah, bayd, doah*—all attempts at meaningful communication broke down. *Globahl wahming, glayshas, isayge, sitees, disastah, loonah colonees, spayce stayshons, orbeet, suhvivahs*: meaningless abstractions, syllables with no rhyme or reason. And the things that intrigued him—where the water in the magic pot came from and where it went, why the ceiling lights came on and off, what his clothes were made of, how the window-wall opened and shut—were beneath their attention, for they never bothered to explain them to him.

They gave him blocks of different shapes and sizes, and placed before him a board containing holes which corresponded with the blocks. Jed did his best to fit the blocks into the appropriate holes, but it took consider-able effort, and even when he was finished Peet wasn't satisfied. They gave him a sheet of paper and a set of col-ored paints, then watched to see what he'd do with them; Jed dipped a fingertip in the green dye and licked it, and ignored the paper. They gave him three red balls and one blue one; he happily bounced all four on the floor with-out discriminating between one or another.

Sayrah took notes, and Peet shook his head in frustra-tion, and at some point they apparently decided that fur-ther efforts to educate him were pointless. After a feeding period, Jed found himself becoming groggy; he collapsed on the floor with his breakfast plate still in his lap.

When he awoke, he found himself in yet another room, naked once more and strapped down to a couch. Several men, one of whom was Peet, were standing around him; they wore hooded white outfits and had white masks across their faces. A bright light was suspended above him; when Jed squinted at it, he saw his own face reflected in its silver casing, and that was when he realized that his head had been shaved and his beard had disappeared.

But none of this was as terrifying as when he gazed down at himself. A snake had fastened itself to the crook of his right elbow; it was feeding upon his blood, which slowly flowed into a clear sack suspended from a rack next the table.

That was when Jed truly realized that he wasn't dead after all.

As he began to scream, the masked men standing around him laughed. And the snake continued to drink his blood.

For days on end, this continued. He'd awaken, eat and drink, relieve himself in the pot, then wait for the men in white to come for him again. There were no more sessions with the window-wall, no more games with balls, blocks, or finger paints. The men would take him from his room—kicking and screaming, or unconscious; it made no difference to them—and strap him to a table, then siphon more blood from his body. They did this carefully, allowing him time to recover so that he wouldn't become anemic; afterwards he was given plenty of food to eat and a chance to sleep.

Yet the routine remained the same, and after awhile Jed resigned himself to his fate.

When he was alone in his room, he found himself remembering happier times. The warm summer days he'd spent in the valley, tending the crops and playing kick-ball with his friends. Before long, the memories came to him when he was on the table; he watched his blood streaming up through the snakes, and thought of autumn nights when he lay in the tall grass with women and gazed up at the stars.

With the growing realization that his old life was over, he became listless, rarely moving from his bed except when the time came for him to follow the men in white into the next room. He discarded the clothes he'd been given, and seldom ate anything given to him. After awhile, the room began to stink of feces and urine, for he'd ceased to use the pot.

Then, one day, he was led from his room, not to the place where he'd sacrificed so much of his blood, but to another room, one much further away. He found himself in the center of a circle of tables, behind which were seated dozens of men and women. Sayrah was waiting for him, and so was Peet; Sayrah smiled and gently stroked his arm, then led him to a chair and gave him a ball.

A window-wall behind him opened and a sequence of images appeared upon it. Peet did most of the talking, with Sayrah interrupting now and then. When Jed glanced back, he saw things he didn't understand—scribbles and bars and strange markings—along with pictures of himself, back when he still had hair and a beard.

Jed paid little attention to what was going on. Shoulders slumped, he idly played with the ball in his lap. At one point, though, the ball escaped from him, It rolled across the floor until one of the men leaned down and picked it up. He cautiously tossed it back to Jed, and Jed obediently caught it. For some reason, everyone in the room found this amusing, for they laughed out loud. Anger and humiliation surged within him, and he hurled the ball back at the man; it smacked him in the center of his face and he cried out, then he rushed from the room, clutching at his nose as blood seeped from it.

For the first time since he'd been taken from his village, Jed felt pleasure. Whatever these creatures were, they weren't gods. They could be hurt, and their blood was no different from his own.

Once the room was calm again, Sayrah began to speak. As before, Jed had no idea what she was saying, yet he noticed that her voice had risen, more irate than he'd ever heard it before. Glancing back, he saw that the window-wall displayed images of his village. His heart stopped, and for a precious instant he felt...hope? An end to all these days of torture?

Whatever Sayrah said, it caused Peet to become infuriated. He yelled at Sayrah, pointing first at the window-wall, then at Jed, then at the window-wall again. Sayrah remained calm; she gestured to the window-wall, then picked up a handful of paper from a desk and held it out to Peet. The argument escalated, with several men and women in the audience adding their own opinions. And through all of this, Jed sat still, wondering whether he'd done the right thing by throwing the ball at one of them, and wishing that he was anywhere other than here.

When it was all over, Peet threw up his hands and walked away. Sayrah went over to Jed, took his hand,

and gently led him out of the room. At that moment, although he'd understood none of what had been said, Jed intuitively realized that it was all over.

They had no more use for him.

Jed was returned to his room and allowed to sleep. When he woke up, he found clothes laid out for him. Once he was dressed, two men escorted him through a series of tunnels until they arrived at a vast cavern where the monster bird lay asleep. Peet was waiting for him there, and so was Sayrah; they led him up the ramp into the creature's belly, and had him take a seat in a chair that was as soft as the bed in which he'd slept ever since coming here.

Sayrah strapped Jed in, then she and Peet took seats on either side of him. The door closed behind them, and after a few minutes the monster bird rumbled and awoke from its slumber. Jed clutched at his chair in fear, then there was a sensation of motion as the bird took flight.

There was a small window beside his chair. When Jed looked out, he saw the cavern walls disappear, replaced by a night sky in which stars gleamed. This time, though, he knew that what he was seeing wasn't mere illusion, but something very real. He wasn't just seeing stars, but indeed among them. Weight left his body; he floated up against the straps, and for a second he felt as if he was falling into the fathomless night.

He screamed, but then Sayrah took his hand. She spoke soothingly to him, and gradually his panic subsided.

Peet said nothing; he pulled a flat pad from his pocket and studied the squiggles upon it, and otherwise ignored Jed.

The journey took a long time, and after awhile he went to sleep, only to be stirred awake as the monster bird shuddered and quaked. Weight had returned to him; an invisible hand pushed him back in his seat. Nervous, not knowing what to expect, he gazed out the window, and saw something he'd thought he'd never see again: deep blue sky, and far below, high mountains dense with forests.

Jed laughed, and clapped his hands in recognition. All those sessions at the window-wall hadn't been lost on him. He knew where he was; he was going home. Sayrah grinned and gave his arm a fond squeeze, while Peet muttered something and looked away from both of them.

A few minutes later, the monster bird howled and trembled in a brief moment of fury. Through the window, Jed saw familiar mountains rise up around them. There was a sudden jolt beneath his feet, then the creature slowly became still and silent. Sayrah loosened her straps and stood up, then helped Jed out of his seat. With Peet leading the way, she escorted Jed to the door, and waited until it opened and the ramp slowly lowered.

Jed walked out of the belly of the monster into a village that had changed little since he'd last seen it. The corn was higher; there were one or two new huts and a taste of autumn in the air. Otherwise everything looked much the same. The villagers cowered nearby, frightened of the apparition that had once again swooped down out of the sky. A few of the braver males, however, warily approached the creature, knives and spears in hand, while a young girl anxiously stepped closer, a basket of fresh-cut tomatoes in her arms as an offering.

Sayrah smiled at Jed, then gave him a gentle push. Her meaning was clear: he was free to go. And indeed, a few of his friends and neighbors seemed to recognize him; although Jed wore strange clothes and no longer had his hair and beard, they knew his face, and already they were beginning to lose their shyness in their delight upon seeing him again.

Jed was about to rush to them when he happened to glance at Peet. There was no gladness in his face, but only determination. His hand stole into a pocket of his clothes; when it came out again, it held the stick which he'd used to carry Jed away to the stars.

Jed didn't hesitate. He lunged at Peet, grabbed him from behind; before he could react, Jed had wrapped his right arm around his shoulders, then grasped his head with his left hand. Peet didn't even have time to yell before Jed twisted his head; a hollow snap, and Peet went limp within Jed's arms, his neck broken.

If he could have done so, Jed would have spared Sayrah's life. She'd been kind to him when the others hadn't. Yet she was impaled by the spear someone hurled at her as she ran for the safety of the monster bird. When she went down, the villagers swarmed the creature, wielding knives and torches as they dashed up the ramp, where they found two men cringing within its head.

Jed paid little attention. He held Sayrah in his arms long after the light faded from her eyes, begging her forgiveness.

The monster bird burned long into the night, the villagers dancing about its carcass, as a feast was held in honor of Jed's homecoming. Everyone ate well, and gave thanks to the gods for his deliverance. Yet when Jed was offered Peet's heart and liver, he refused to take them, or let anyone else consume them. They contained evil, and should only be cast to the dogs. However, he made sure that Sayrah's body was surrendered to the flames. After all, she'd been his friend; her soul deserved to return to the sky.

No monster birds invaded the village ever again. For a time, Peet's skull hung from above the door to Jed's hut, until he allowed the younger ones to take down, stuff it with straw and wrap it in deerskin, and use for kickball. By then, his youthful days of games and mindless sex were in the past; he'd become a tribal elder, the one to which the others came to when they needed words of wisdom. Yet never again did Jed lay out beneath the stars. He always went inside his hut when the sun went down, and didn't come out again until the morning came around.

For those who need a moral to this story, let it be this: beware of what you sow, for so you shall reap.

Or perhaps, even better: you can take the boy out the country, but you can't take the country out of the boy.

HAIL TO THE CHIEF

It's a spring morning sometime in the 26th century—no one can know the date for certain; the last calendar has long since dissolved into the muck left behind when the glaciers finally receded—and the President of the United States wakes up in what's left of the Oval Office.

Sunlight streams in through battered windows that lost their glass many years ago, causing him to snort and scratch at the fleas that crawled upon him from the pile of animal skins he uses as a bed. Rolling over, he opens his eyes to cast a bleary gaze at the sun. He's tempted to go back to sleep, but his stomach is growling, and besides, there's affairs of state which must attended.

So he staggers to his feet and lurches out on the balcony. Beyond the swamp that infests upon what used to be the South Lawn, a lonesome eagle screeches as it circles the broken stump of the Washington Monument. Yawning, he lifts his loin cloth and urinates on the wild roses beneath the balcony. Nothing like that first piss of the day to make a man feel like the commander in chief.

Having taken care of personal business, the President wanders back inside. The First Lady is still asleep, curled up within her own pile of skins next to the smoldering remains of last night's fire. "Geddupbich," he mutters, kicking her in the side. "Gogeddus sumfoo'."

"Fugyu. Lemmelone." She tries to retreat further beneath the squirrel hides, but then he kicks her again. "Awright awright," she protests, squinting up at him. "Igetcha brek'fus."

"Damstrait. Move y'rass." He watches as she crawls out beneath the covers, and wonders if it's time to find another mate. Although she's barely fifteen years old, she's already given him two children—the first stillborn, the other severely retarded; he doesn't know it, but she's his half-sister, since they shared the same father but not the same mother—and she's no longer quite as attractive as she was when he captured her during a raid upon the Dems. Still, he considers as she shuffles out onto the balcony, she has all her fingers and toes, and not too many scabs. That counts for something.

While the First Lady answers her morning mail, the President walks across the moth-eaten rug that once bore the emblem of his office to a termite-ridden desk. Within a drawer are his totems of power. A bone knife, nine inches long and honed to a razor-sharp edge. A neck tie—dark blue with red stripes, handmade countless years ago in Italy, now threadbare and bloodstained—which he carefully wraps around his head. And finally, the most holy of holies: a small enamel lapel pin, bearing the faded likeness of an American flag, that he kisses with chapped lips before affixing to his rabbit-skin vest. From beside the desk, he takes his spear, a steel rod with hide wrapped one end, which an archeologist might have identified as having once belonged to the landing gear of the Apollo 11 lunar lander formerly displayed in the National Air and Space Museum.

The President came to possess these items the old-fashioned way. When he was twenty years old, he challenged the previous President to an election. The incumbent was a Dem, an old man of thirty-five, limbs weakened by scurvy and nearly blind in the left eye, yet nonetheless as dangerous as the alligators that lurk within the shallows of the Potomac. Yet his opponent had a very strong platform, consisting of a wooden club studded with rusty nails. The debate was held in the Mall, with both Dems and Pubs watching from either side; when the old man went down, his challenger allowed him the chance to deliver his closing remarks. They didn't last long, because by then the President was vomiting blood; the challenger offered rebuttal by cutting his throat, then carving open his chest, tearing out his heart, and devouring it within full view of the electorate. Following this, his party massacred the Dems, sending the survivors fleeing for the sanctity of Capitol Hill. A recount wasn't necessary.

Suitably attired, the President takes a moment to regard the faded and water stained portrait hanging lopsided upon the wall. An old, old man, with hair whiter than anyone he'd ever known, wearing dark clothes that looked strange and yet warm. Every morning since he'd won the right to sleep in this place, he'd wondered who this person was. Another President, no doubt, but how had he come here? Had he eaten his enemy's heart...?

From somewhere nearby, a faint feminine cry. The First Lady, her voice raised in either pain or delight. "Dammitbich!" The President storms out of the Oval Office, marches down a corridor of the West Wing. "Wachadoindere?"

He finds her in a nearby room, doubled over a broken couch. The Vice-President has mounted her from behind, his hairy butt trembling as he thrusts himself against her thighs. The President watches for a moment, annoyed by this breach of protocol, before he pulls the knife from his scabbard and, darting forward, shoves the blade deep within the other man's back. The Vice-President screams; blood gushes from his wound as he falls forward, pinning the First Lady against the couch. She's still whimpering as the President haul him away from her. "Tolja t'get sumfoo'!" he snaps. "Nawdooit!"

She scampers away before he can strike her. The Vice-President flails helplessly upon the floor, a crimson froth around his mouth. The President kneels beside him, yanks his hair back to expose his throat. "Yerfired," he mutters. then he accepts his resignation.

The rest of the White House staff is awake by then, the various aides and secretaries emerging from the offices and meeting rooms to cautiously peer around the door and through holes in the wall as the President takes what he wants from the Vice-President's corpse. No one looks at him until he's gone, then they fall upon the body, quarreling among one another for rights to his belongings.

The President doesn't care. He'd never liked the Veep anyway. Lack of party loyalty.

Breakfast is a rat, skinned and gutted, roasted on skewer and served medium-rare. Fine cuisine, although the President would have preferred squirrel this morning. He takes his morning repast in the Cabinet Room, surrounded by his senior staff picking through the leftovers of last night's state dinner. Barbequed opossum is pretty good, once you get past the rather oily aftertaste, and the maggots are sort of an appetizer. Mosquitoes and flies purr around them as they eat, and everyone laughs when the Secretary of Transportation breaks a rotted tooth upon a piece of bone.

A hollow, chopping sound from the room where he killed the Vice-President reminds the President of urgent business. The aides and secretaries will make the best of Veep's sudden departure, but cabinet-level officials deserve better compensation for their loyalty.

"Gottagetmofoo'," he growls, tossing ahead the rat skull from which he has just sucked the brains. "Gottafinsum." He glances at the Secretary of the Interior. "Yewno?"

The Secretary of the Interior considers this question for a moment. "Gatahyeggs reelgood, Prez. Gadownto-darivah, luk'roun, fin'sum…"

"Fugdat." This from the Secretary of Labor. "Gators hide dernestsbedder." He spits out a piece of gristle, shakes his head. "Bil'mo bowts, go gatahhuntin'…"

"Nahway." The Secretary of Homeland Security farts luxuriously as he leans back against the wall. "Gatahs tacbowts, sink'um. Loosalottaguys…"

"Fuggum." Yet the President gets the drift of what he's saying. They can't continue to send people out on the river to hunt alligator; the Pubs doesn't have adequate craft for such an excursion, and the attrition factor is unacceptably high. As a result, quite a few tribesmen have crossed over to join the Dems, if only because they promise more food with less risk. "Goddanudda ideyah?"

"Hidoo, Prez." The Secretary of Defense idly pulls some lice from his beard. "Tacdahill."

Everyone stares at him in astonishment. "Yewgoddabeshiddinme," the Secretary of State mutters. "Dahill?"

"Sho'. Wynod?"

"Buddeygod…"

All at once, a loud *boom!* from somewhere above, an airborne blast that shakes the decrepit building. Startled. everyone cringes, covering their heads as pieces of decayed plaster fall from the ceiling.

"Whaddahellizzat!" the Secretary of Defense yells.

"Cheezuz." The President gazes up at the ceiling, his eyes wide with amazement. "Datwas Cheezuz!"

"Datwazzunt Cheezuz." The Secretary of State scowls, shakes his head. "Datwasjusda boomboomding 'gan."

The other cabinet members murmur in agreement. From time to time, they've heard these mysterious noises.

They aren't caused by thunderstorms, because the weather has almost been calm when they've occurred, yet they've seen the strange white trails moving across the sky, led by tiny silver dots.

"No! Nonono!" The President is on his feet. "Boom-boomding asine f'm Cheezuz!" He looks down at the others. "Wewuz talkinbout tacing Dems, an'den Cheezuz giffus asine…!"

"Datwuzzen…"

In three swift steps, the President is across the room. Grabbing the Secretary of State by his hair, he yanks his head back. Before the cabinet member can react, he feels the razor-sharp blade of the President's knife at his throat.

"Datwuz Cheezuz," the President hisses, his angry eyes boring into his own. "Sayidain'so."

The Secretary of State trembles, his forehead suddenly moist with sweat. "Hokay, hokay, prez," he whispers. "Dadwuz Cheezuz…"

"Sayidagin!" The knife bites into his skin, drawing a trickle of blood. "Sayidlowda!"

"Datwuz Cheezuz!" the Secretary yells in desperation, his eyes screwed up in pain. "Prez isrite! Datwuz Cheezuz!"

"Praysdaload," the Secretary of Labor quietly offers, his tone conciliatory. "Haymen."

"Haymen." The President stares at the Secretary of State for another moment before he withdraws his knife, then he turns to the others. "Gonnatac da Dems t'day."

"T'day?" The Secretary of Homeland Defense looks dubious. "Allahus?"

"Damstrait." The President lifts his knife. "Gedalla Pubs t'gedda. Gonnago tadahill. Kigsumass, geddusum-foo', mebbesum wimmin too…"

"Hoo-rah!" The Secretary of Defense is all for this. "Geddusum wimmin!"

"T'day?" Although humiliated, the Secretary of State remains cautious.

"T'day." The Prez doesn't look back at him as bends down to pick up his half-eaten rat. "Can'loose. Cheezuz onourside."

And then he finishes his breakfast. No sense in going into mid-term elections on an empty stomach.

By midafternoon, a small army has been mustered from the urban wasteland surrounding the White House. Men and women, young and old, anyone able to carry a weapon and not too sick or frail to fight. War drums roust them from the ruins of the Old Exec and the Blair House, the half-collapsed high-rise of the National Press Building, the vast squatter camp of the Federal Triangle, the putrid underground warrens of the Metro stations. An army that's toothless, scrawny, cancerous, bowlegged and on the verge of starvation, but an army nonetheless. A thousand points of light, lurching its way down Pennsylvania Avenue toward a mansion on the hill.

At the head of this faith-based initiative is President. He rides into battle as a good commander-in-chief should, seated upon a litter carried by a half-dozen loyal Pubs.

His spear is clasped in his right hand, his knife in his left. A silver platter, once presented to one of his predecessors as a gift from the ambassador of a country long since vanished, now hangs from his neck as a shield. The scalps of his vanquished foes are suspended from staffs carried by his honor guard, the Seecrit-Servis, and at the front of the procession is a warrior waving the last American flag flown from the White House roof before the coming of the ice.

As they approach Capitol Hill, a Dem sentry positioned on the roof of the National Gallery raises the alarm. One long, loud bellow from his horn before he's brought down by a Pub spear, but that's enough to let the Dems know that they're coming. By the time the Pubs reach the Mall, war drums are echoing off the vine-covered walls of the Smithsonian. From his litter, the President can see Dems scurrying for the safety of the crude barricades erected at the bottom of the hill, while short plumes of smoke rise from the shattered dome of the Capitol. All the same, though, he's satisfied. The Dems have been caught by surprise. The mid-terms will be short and swift. The polls predict a Pub victory.

Yet his troops have just skirted the wreckage of a Navy helicopter that went down at the intersection of Pennsylvania and 3rd during the evacuation, and have come within sight of the decapitated heads that Dems stuck on pikes alongside the Reflecting Pool, when the President hears an odd sound. A low, throbbing hum, sort of like that made by a bumble-bee, but louder, more metronomic. Looking around, he sees that others hear it, too.

The litter-bearers nervously glance back and forth, and the mob behind him has become restless.

"Holdit!" He raises his staff, and the procession comes to a halt.

Now the hum is closer. Even the Dems pay attention. From on the other side of the barrier of rusting automobiles, their war drums falter in their beat. Staring up at the Capitol, the President catches a glimpse of his arch-enemy. The Speaker of House stands at the top of the Capitol steps, wearing his war-bonnet of Pub scalps, surrounded by committee chairmen. He's too far away for his expression to be discerned, yet it seems as if the Dem warlord is just as puzzled as he is.

"Whuddafugizzat?" This from the Secretary of Defense, standing next to the litter along with the other cabinet members.

"Dunno." The President can't figure it out either, but he's not about to let it distract him. Raising his staff, he points it toward the Capitol. "Fohwahd...!"

"'Ey! Lug!" The Secretary of the Interior points to the left. "Ovahdere!"

The President turns to behold a miracle.

A small round platform glides down 3rd Street, passing the burnt-out ruins of the Department of Labor. Levitating twenty feet above the weed-choked asphalt, lights flashing along its underside, it's held aloft by the humming sound. And standing upon it are a pair of figures...

"Cheezuz," the President mutters, his voice low with awe.

"Ifdats Cheezuz," the Secretary of Defense whispers, "whodat wiffem?"

"Dunno." The Secretary of the Interior shrugs. "Mebbe Cheezuz bruddah."

The visitors don't appear to be of this world. Dressed entirely in white, with hoods pulled up over their heads, they seem almost angelic. As the platform comes closer, the President sees not a face beneath the hoods, but only golden masks, devoid of any features yet reflecting the afternoon sun like gilded mirrors.

"Prays Cheezuz!" The President stands up on his litter, raises his hands. "Hescominta kigsumass!"

Not all of the Pubs are impressed, though. Someone in the mob hurls a spear at the platform. It falls short by a dozen feet, yet one of the figures immediately reacts. He raises his right hand; clasped within it is a short rod. The briefest glimpse of a beam of light, then the Pub who hurled the spear screams and collapses, a hole burned through the center of his chest.

"Holeecrap!" the Secretary of Defense shouts. "Cheezuz pizzed!"

"Fugdis!" the Secretary of the Interior yells. "Lesgeddouddahere!"

The Pubs panic. Screaming in terror, they turn and run back the way they came, stampeding across those behind them. The Seekrit-Servis hesitate for a moment, then they discard their staffs and bolt. Even the litter-bearers have had enough; the President is toppled from his perch as the men holding him aloft drop the litter and join the rest of the mob as they flee for their lives.

Dazed, the President clambers to his feet, looks around. Suddenly, he's alone. His cabinet has abandoned him; knives and clubs are strewn all around, and the tattered flag lies crumpled in the street. Looking back over his shoulder, he sees his routed army in full retreat, already half a block away and getting smaller by the second.

Yet it scarcely matters, for the Dems are keeping their distance as well. Cowering behind the barricades, they watch in awestruck wonder as the platform slowly descends to the ground. As it glides closer, the President finds his knees quaking. For a moment he has an urge to make his own escape.

Yet he doesn't. Instead, he bends down, picks up the flag that was left behind. Holding it aloft, he slowly approaches the platform. The low throb subsides as it settles upon the ground; the two figures silently watch as he comes closer.

"Howdee Cheezuz," he says, once he thinks he's close enough for them to hear him. "Imda Prez ovda Yewnited Staytes Uffa'merica."

The figures say nothing. He sees himself reflected in the mirrors of their faces, and suddenly feels very small and insignificant. At loss for words, he offers the flag. "Yewkin havedis, ifyewwan. Its rillyol, an..."

One of the figures raises a white-gloved hand, beckoning for silence. The President stops, watches as the other one reaches down to pick up a metal case. Its burnished aluminum surface catches the sun as he steps to the edge of the platform and offers it.

A gift. The President feels something catch in his

throat. Putting down the flag, he walks forward to accept the offering. The case is heavier than it looks; he nearly drops it, but manages to keep it in his hands.

"Tankyew," he says softly. "Tankyew, Cheezuz. Yewdaman. Juswannasay…"

Again, the figure raises a hand. The President obediently falls quiet. Both figures return to the center of the platform. The throbbing sound resumes, and the President feels the hair rise on the nape of his neck. Then the platform lifts off once more. He watches as it ascends, then turns to go back the way it came, disappearing behind the half-collapsed hulks of government buildings.

By now, the Dems have gathered their courage. Hooting in glee upon finding their hated foe all by himself, they begin to climb across the barricades, their knives ready to add his head to the trophies surrounding the Reflecting Pool.

Yet the President is unafraid. He and he alone has been given the holy object. Raising it above him, he turns to face the Capitol.

"Lugwad Cheezus brung!" he shouts in victory. "Hegimme blessing! Imda Prez…!"

These are the final words of the last President of the United States.

The neutron bomb does little tertiary damage beyond the immediate radius of the blast zone. The President, of course, is instantly vaporized, as are the nearby Dems. The concussion topples a few structures already weakened by nature, but the Capitol itself remains intact. Yet every living creature within six miles of ground-zero drops dead, killed by the massive pulse of ionizing radiation. In seconds, the ancient war between the Pubs and the Dems comes to a swift and bloodless conclusion.

Not long afterwards, men and women in spacecraft descend upon the ruins of Washington D.C. For many years now, they've awaited this moment, within the orbital colonies and lunar settlements where they've kept the flames of civilization alive; now they return to the ancestral lands of their forefathers, to lay claim to their common heritage. The old conflicts are over and done, a dark age best left in the past. The time has come to take the wounded Earth, heal it, slowly transform it back to place it had once been, before it fell prey to the whims of the arrogant, the misguided and the stupid.

The corpses of both Pubs and Dems are buried in a mass grave on the banks of the Potomac River. In time, cherry trees are planted on the site. In the many peaceful years to follow, their spring blossoms add a gentle fragrance to the air, rendering subtle beauty to a place that, at long last, has become kinder and more gentle.

THE LAST SCIENCE FICTION WRITER

He sits at his desk, writing a story.

His fingers tap at the computer keyboard, making a sound like rain falling on plastic, as his eyes follow the words that gradually flow from left to right across the screen. He pauses to pick up a glass of ice tea from a coaster; a quick sip, then his hands return to the keyboard. A cigarette smolders in an ashtray, but more often than not it burns down to the filter without him taking more than a few drags. His mind is completely focused as ideas are transformed into thoughts, thoughts into words, words into sentences, sentences into paragraphs.

His office is a spare upstairs bedroom; the window is half-open, allowing the cool breeze of a late September afternoon to drift into the room. Fading sunlight rests upon the distant hills, bringing out the crimson and burnt-orange hues of the autumn leaves; the crickets are already being to chirp, a soft sound that subconsciously relaxes him. From the house next door, an abrupt, mechanical roar: his neighbor starting up his riding mower, getting set to do a little yard work before evening sets in. Distracted, he mutters beneath his breath as he peers more intently at the screen, yet he doesn't notice when the noise of the lawnmower abruptly ceases, replaced once more by the quiet chitter of the crickets.

The cigarette has burned out. When he reaches for it, though, he finds a fresh one resting in the ashtray, its tip already glowing. He wonders about this for a moment—did he light another one and forget about it?—but that thought vanishes almost as soon as it occurs to him. He takes a drag, puts it back in the ashtray, and goes back to work. His glass remains perpetually three-quarters full; whenever he picks it up, he finds that it still contains as much ice tea as it did the last time he took a drink. Yet this miracle bothers him for less than a second.

Paragraphs become scenes. Scenes gradually take shape and form of a story. He writes for hours upon end, the pages slowly scrolling upward upon his screen, and yet he feels no exhaustion, no need to rest. He's married, but his wife never enters the room. He has two dogs, but they're nowhere to be seen or heard. Friends don't drop by unexpectedly; the phone next to his desk is silent. He never feels an impulse to push back his chair, stand up to stretch his legs, take a deep breath, maybe go to the bathroom. The view through his window remains the same, the character of the autumn light unchanging. The world is locked in a eternal, golden afternoon. He takes another drag from his cigarette, drinks some more tea, and brings himself back to where he'd left off just a few seconds ago.

At long last, he reaches the end of story. He types the last few lines, then enters the command that will save the text in computer memory. Another keystroke will send the story to the printer, but that isn't necessary; a hard copy has already appeared in its tray. A large manila envelope, addressed to the editor of a science fiction magazine in New York, has materialized upon the desk. He removes the story from the printer tray, shuffles the pages to make them a tidy sheaf of paper; he attaches a butterfly clip, then pushes it into the envelope. He lays it upon his desk, and doesn't notice that it vanishes as soon as he looks away.

He gazes at the blank screen of his computer for a few moments, feeling a sense of satisfaction at having ac-complished his task. He doesn't notice that everything around him has frozen in place. A curlicue of smoke from his cigarette lingers in stasis above the ashtray; the au-tumn breeze no longer wafts through the window, and the crickets have ceased to chirp. Time itself has come to a stop.

He sighs, reaches over to pick up his ice tea. He takes a sip, puts down the glass, then picks up his cigarette. A quick drag, then his hands return to the keyboard. Enough procrastination. Time to begin work on a new project.

He sits at his desk, writing a story...

+✦+

"What the hell is this?"

"I don't know. My team has checked the entire system. No deterioration in the mnemonic download. Alpha wave levels remains nominal. Sensory input fully engaged, same for cerebral feedback loop…"

"You want feedback? Here's your feedback. Read the end of the story just you got from him. Here…the bottom of the transcript."

"Wait a sec. Lemme pull it up…'*What's your name?*' *she asked. 'Adam,*' *he replied. 'What's yours?*' *'Eve.*'"

"Uh-huh. And now the end of the one before that."

"Ummm…okay, here it is. '*And then he woke up, and discovered that it was all a dream.*'"

"Yeah, okay. And now the first one…"

"Hold on…yeah, here it is…'*Oh, my God! It's a cookbook!*'"

"And you don't see anything wrong with this?"

'Well, they do seem a little predictable. Except maybe that last one. Didn't see that coming."

"You didn't see…? C'mon, this stuff was lame even back then! I thought you told me this guy was a major author!"

"Well, he was. According to Research Division, he published fifteen novels and nearly a hundred short stories during his lifetime. He also earned…"

"Several awards…what the hell is a Hugo, anyway?… his work translated in half a dozen languages, yada yada. I read the same report. 'My name's Adam. What's yours?' Crap! If he was *that* good, he could've have written better than this in his sleep."

"Well, in a sense, he has been asleep…"

"He's been dead! Just before he kicked off, he spent everything he had in the bank, even sold his house, so that he could arrange for his body to be cryogenically preserved. Thought there was a chance that he might be revived sometime in the future. Pure Pre-Collapse nonsense..."

"Yes, well, he was a science fiction writer, after all. They tended to think about things like that."

"Science fiction...sheesh, no wonder that stuff died out. Those guys *never* got anything right. And you say he's the last one?"

"The only one whose brain survived cryogenic freezing. There were a couple of others, but..."

"Yeah, yeah, I know. Too much collateral damage to the neural infrastructure. We're lucky to have been able to download just this guy. And you say there's been no deterioration of his long-term memory?"

"Well..."

"Well what?"

"Look, this isn't an exact process. Besides cellular damage, there's also the psychological trauma of death itself, so even though we were able to reconstruct his neural pathways enough to allow a complete brainscan, we still had to edit his core engrams once we downloaded them. Otherwise he'd have gone into solipsistic syndrome. You don't want them knowing they're really just a few hundred terabytes in a..."

"Yeah, right, I got that. But..."

"Just listen, all right? Once we pieced together a partial memory of his life before he died, we used it to develop a template simulacrum of his contemporary environment. He resides in that now. For him, it's real. He feels, he hears, he tastes...the works. And we can manipulate that environment at will."

"Okay, I understand that. What I don't understand is why this guy is turning out garbage."

"We can't figure that either. Remember, this is the first time we've attempted to devise a creative modus. However, we have a theory that residual memes may be causing a chaotic influence. If that's the case, then..."

"Look, this is all over my head. And frankly, I don't care. Bottom line is that I've got Entertainment Division breathing down my neck. I told 'em they could have a new story from a major Pre-Collapse writer, and now they're making deals all over the place. The revenue they're expecting from net rights alone..."

"That's your problem."

"Uh-uh...it's *your* problem. Because if I don't deliver, I'm telling them why, and then you and your team will be lucky if your next job is down in Astronautics, humping code for the Jovian run. Get my meaning?"

"Yeah, okay. We'll work on it. Maybe if we change the simulacrum..."

"Whatever. I got a meeting in ten minutes. Get it done, and let me know when you've got something besides this Adam and Eve crap."

"Sure. Oh, and by the way...you were wondering what a Hugo was? Here's a visual image we've recovered from his memory..."

"Oh, no...no, that's just not right. Thanks a bunch. Just the sort of thing I need to take with me all day..."

"It's supposed to be a rocket. Why, what else did you think it was?"

"Never mind."

He sits at an autograph table, signing books.

The table is located in the midst of the largest, most luxurious bookstore he's ever seen. Aisle upon aisle of mahogany bookcases, each so tall that stepladders are provided so that patrons may reach the volumes on the topmost shelves. Tiers of balconies, one above the other, rise toward a vaulted ceiling from which crystal chandeliers are suspended; wrought-iron elevators, operated by young men in bellboy uniforms, carry customers to the upper floors. Classical music—the first movement of Vivaldi's *Four Seasons*—drifts down to him from the chamber quartet performing on the second level, while waiters in tuxedos roam the aisles, offering mimosa and Swiss chocolates to readers lounging in soft leather armchairs.

This place is a cathedral of literature, and he is its most precious icon. On the other side of the table, hundreds of men and women patiently wait their turn to meet him; the line they've formed stretches as far as the eye can see. The gentlemen are handsome, the ladies achingly beautiful. Of high social stature and impeccable taste, they've dressed for the occasion, in dinner jackets and silk evening gowns, and each carries a copy of his latest novel as if it's their precious possession.

The chair in which he sits is a throne, high-backed and upholstered in red velvet. The table is made of ancient oak, fine-grained and hundreds of years old, its surface so polished it practically gleams with a light of its own. A champagne stem rests upon it, just in case he needs a little light refreshment. Next to his right hand is an onyx fountain pen, its tip and band fashioned from white gold. He picks it up, then raises his eyes to the next person in line.

The woman is spectacular. Raven haired, her figure svelte and sensuous, she could easily be a lingerie model, an actress of stage and screen, perhaps the consort of a European prince. Her dark eyes express longing as she shyly steps forward. There is no doubt that he is her favorite author, and that she would gladly indulge his fantasies if the opportunity became available. Perhaps a quiet dinner for two, once the signing is over? For now, though, all she desires is his inscription, if he would be so kind.

Of course. Anything for one of his fans. She gently places the book upon the table, and then he looks down at it.

A paperback, its pages dog-eared, its spine broken. The cover art, rendered in bright primary colors, features a buxom, red-haired woman in a skin-tight spacesuit, her enormous breasts protruding against its silver fabric. Her face is contorted in an expression of homicidal rage, and she has a laser rifle in her left hand and a glowing energy sword in her right; she stands on top of a pile of corpses, blasting and slicing away at the horde of bug-eyed monsters swarming toward her. Behind her, a squad of space marines fires in all directions at once; in the background, a starship that seems to be concocted from pieces of old *Star Wars* model kits.

The book's title is nearly an inch tall, raised in gold foil: *Guts and Glory: A Glory Gaddington*™ *Novel.* Turning the book over, he skims the rear dustjacket copy. Glory Gaddington, captain of the starship *Invincible* and rightful heiress to the throne of the deposed Lord Montebaum, continues her heroic quest to regain control of the Bagel System from Count Drok and the evil Rigelian Empire. The latest volume of a series; the last installment, *Glory, Glory, Hallelujah*, earned high praise from *Locus:* "...Interesting..."

He lays the book down, looks up at the woman waiting for him to sign it. *I'm sorry*, he says, *but I didn't write this.*

She smiles, and favors him with a knowing wink. *Does it matter?* she replies.

"What the hell is this?"

"Uhh...well, we're not sure...."

"You're not sure? I've checked his bibliography, and there's nothing in there about...what's her name, Chastity Cummingsoon...?"

"Glory Gaddington. A popular character of early 21st century space opera, featured in a series of novels by..."

"But he didn't write them, did he? So what's she doing in his simulacrum? And come to think of it, what were you trying to accomplish by this, anyway?"

"According to Research, although he achieved a certain level of success, like most science fiction writers he was relatively obscure in his day. His books sold just well enough for his publishers to earn a modest profit, but outside the genre he was virtually unknown. So we thought that, if we placed him in an environment in which he perceived himself as being a bestselling author respected at the highest levels of levels of literary society, that might prompt him to produce something that would match up to those expectations."

"So where did Patience Paddingwell come from?"

"Well, those books were bestsellers, after all, so perhaps his subconscious mind told him that was what he would've had to have written in order to get that sort of notoriety. At least that's our theory."

"Some theory. All he's done since then is sit in his office, staring at his computer and mumbling to himself..."

"Not true. We did get three pages of Glory having sex with Count Drok..."

"Yeah, right. *That's* going to play in New Kansas. All he did was throw back the very thing that he thought would've made him a bestselling writer in his own time."

"Maybe it was."

"If we wanted that, we'd just reprint Faith Frothinghard novels..."

"You couldn't even if you wanted to. During the Collapse, many science fiction fans were forced to burn parts of their collections. Glory Gaddington books were usually the first to go. They were rather thick, after all, so they provided a lot of heat..."

"Fascinating. Look, point is, appealing to his vanity isn't going to work. If we're going to get anything from him, we've got to work on his creative instincts. Don't put him in a bookstore. Furnish an environment that inspires him."

"Umm...sure, all right. Any suggestions?"

"How should I know? This is your department, not mine. But whatever you do, make it snappy. Entertainment needs something they can take to Marketing, and I'm getting swamped with memos. Call me when you have material."

"Of course. Where will you be?"

"In my office, reading Shakespeare. Anything to get Virtue Violencenuff out of my system."

He sits at his desk, writing a story.

The doorbell rings, a shrill buzz that breaks his train of thought. Muttering beneath his breath, he pushes back his chair and goes downstairs. He's expecting the neighbor kid, selling candy for school, or at worst a pair of Jehovah's Witnesses, but instead two men waiting for him at the front door.

One is dressed in a dark gray business suit, the other the blue uniform of an Air Force colonel. Both wear sunglasses. Behind them, a black sedan with government plates is parked in the driveway. The man in the suit flashes an I.D., then tells him that there's been an emergency. A strange object has crashed only a few miles from his house. They show him photos of something that looks like two huge pie-pans stuck together, half-buried in a hillside. The military believes that it may be an alien spacecraft. Since he's a science fiction writer, he's the closest available person who may be able to make sense of this phenomenon.

He agrees to help them, so he shuts the door behind then, then follows them out to the car. He climbs into the back seat....

There's no discernable passage of time or distance. One instant, he's still at his house. The next, the car has arrived at the crash site. He recognizes this place at once: a nature preserve where he sometimes takes the dogs for a run. Tanks and field guns have surrounded the hillside, and soldiers are setting up machine guns behind sandbag emplacements. Helicopters carry in more troops while fighter jets scream overhead.

The Air Force colonel escorts him to a forward command post. Within the dugout, a young dude is seated at a folding table; a half-dozen laptop computers have been set up around him, and he seems to be working at them all at once. The kid's head is shaved; he wears a black leather jacket, ripped jeans, and Doc Martens, and there's wires leading from one of the computers to a socket imbedded in the base of his skull. His name is Spike, and he's trying to download a virus into the alien ship's computer. He's not having much success, though, because the extraterrestrial AI is protected by a cyberspace infrastructure of ultradense black ice that has erected a self-evolving synergistic firewall around...

A high-pitched scream. A soldier runs away from the crash site, his uniform in flames. Behind him, a snake-like appendage has risen into from the alien craft; white-hot beams of energy lance from it, torching everything in sight.

He flees from the dugout just before the colonel and the hacker are disintegrated by the death-beam. Making good his escape by taking cover in the surrounding forest, he stops to look back. The infantry has opened fire upon the spaceship, but their weapons are useless against the invisible energy barrier that surrounds the strange vessel.

Then the spacecraft's hatch opens, and half-naked warriors riding winged dragons ascend into the sky. Close behind them are a battalion of space barbarians, a gang of post-apocalypse bikers on chopped-up Harleys, a squad of multiple-limbed androids, a pride of Amazonian she-devils in chain-mail, a horror of flesh-eating zombies, a blitzkrieg of giant Nazi robots, a mob of scabrous mutants, a herd of cloned dinosaurs, and some guy in a black outfit who has the worst case of emphysema he has ever heard. All of them wielding death, doom, and destruction on an unimaginable scale.

All at once, something closes in his mind. It feels like a door slamming shut, with a sudden and irrevokable surety. In no hurry at all, ignoring the sounds of warfare behind him, he picks his way through the forest until he reaches the road that he knows will lead him back home.

Along the way, he encounters a plucky girl reporter from a major metropolitan newspaper. Her car has broken down, so he stops to help her change the flat tire, but when she tells him in breathless tones that she has fallen in love with him, he leaves her behind. Not long after that, he meets a courageous lady scientist from CalTech; her car has broken down, too, and she insists that she alone holds the key to defeating the aliens. She doesn't fall in love with him, but she gives him every indication that she's good for a one-night stand. He gives her his email address, and keeps walking. He's almost within sight of his house when he finds a woman in a tattered white dress sitting on his neighbor's stone fence, hugging her knees and weeping with inconsolable grief. She tells him that she's lost her world, her people, her entire future; all she can see is bleakness, cold and dreary, with no hope for anyone. He politely asks if she'd like to come back to his place and have lunch, but all she wants do is wallow in her misery, And besides, she's a hermaphrodite with three transsexual partners; sharing a meal with him would violate the social mores of her clan. She wants to explain it all to him, but he's getting hungry, so he leaves her as well and continues walking down the road.

At long last, he finds his way back home. He makes a tuna sandwich and pours a glass of milk, and has lunch at the kitchen table while a Martian tripod stomps through his backyard. After skimming the funny pages of the local newspape, he climbs the stairs to his office. Sitting down in front of his computer, he reads what he'd been writing being before he was so rudely interrupted.

The story he'd been working on, though, has lost its appeal. He gazes out the window for awhile, idly watching the alien armada as it slowly descends from the sky.

After awhile, he closes the file and slides it across the computer screen to the trash can.

Then he creates a new document, and begins to write something new.

"What the hell is this?"

"Why do all of our conversations begin the same way?"

"Don't get wise with me. You saw what he wrote."

"Uh-huh...and it's brilliant. Great story. Terrific characters. Superb setting. A surprise plot twist about halfway through...I didn't see that coming, did you?...and a killer ending. Kept me going all the way through."

"But...dammit, it's not science fiction!"

"So?"

"It's a western!"

"I'm not sure I'd call it that. It's set in Colorado in 1870, sure, but it's more like a mystery that just happens to take place in..."

"It's got horses, okay? Horses and a sheriff, and a female protagonist who works on a cattle ranch..."

"Wasn't she great? And when it turns out that she's actually his step-daughter..."

"That's not the point. He's a science fiction writer. Where's the aliens? Where's the spaceships? Where's the..."

"Y'know, I've been thinking the much same thing. It occurs to me that we've been going about this all wrong.

I mean, we keep thinking he's a science fiction writer...
but maybe he's really a writer who just happens to write
science fiction."

"What are you...?"

"Listen, okay? That last simulacrum...everything
we could think of, we threw at him. Crashed spaceship,
alien invasion, military forces, creatures of every shape
and size, a choice of female characters...the works. We
made it as weird as weird can be, and put him right in the
thick of it, with no time for him to think of anything else.
So what happens? He rejects it all, and writes something
completely different."

"Then program another simulacrum. Make it even
more weird than before. Look, I got an idea. Let's say an
asteroid is about to collide with Earth, and..."

"You don't get it. It's not the idea that matters the
most...it's what you do with it."

"Come again?"

"Look...when everything is weird, then nothing is
weird at all. We could have cartoon characters crawl out
of his ass and it's not going to make any difference. It'd
just be one more strange thing...and this guy made friends
with strangeness long before we were born. Maybe he
just wants to tell a story, and not have anyone tell him
what it's supposed to be."

"But he's supposed to write a science fiction story!"

"And he gave you a western. Or rather, a mystery
novel set in the Old West. Big deal. Entertainment and
Marketing want him for his imagination, right? So cut
him loose. Let him imagine what he will, and stop trying

to force him to do something what you think will sell big. I guarantee that, if you take this story to your people, they're going to love it no matter what it is."

"Well…um, yeah, it is pretty good, I guess. Can I get back to you on this?"

"Gee, I dunno. I've got a meeting in ten minutes. Send me a memo, okay?"

He sits at his desk, writing a story.

Outside the window, the first snow of winter is falling, a gentle white haze that masks bare tree limbs and mutes the sullen growl of his neighbor's snowblower. Every now and then he lifts his eyes from the computer screen to savor the view. Autumn is gone and the days have become short, but he relishes the change of season. A subtle reminder that time is passing swift, and there's many more stories to be told before he can take his rest.

Returning his attention to the keyboard, he continues to polish the last few lines of the story he's been writing. It won't be long before his wife comes home from work; he needs to go downstairs and start making dinner. Behind him, one of his dogs rises from the carpet; he arches his back, makes a canine yawn, then wanders off to another part of the house. Everyone is hungry. Time to wrap things up for the day.

At last, he reaches the end of the last paragraph. He sits back in his chair, contemplates what he has done. An interesting little fable, really. Probably won't win any awards, and he doubts that the critics will be very kind, but nonetheless he thinks it raises a question or two about the substance of reality, the nature of the human imagination. What if...?

Never mind. He saves the file and closes it, then stands up from his chair. Feeling as if he's just woken from a dream, he walks away into reality.